Losing Herself

LYLA FAIRCLOTH ELLZEY

DocUmeant *Publishing*
244 5th Avenue
Suite G-200
NY, NY 10001
646-233-4366
www.DocUmeantPublishing.com

LOSING HERSELF

Published by
DocUmeant Publishing
244 5th Ave, Suite G-200
NY, NY 10001

646-233-4366

Edited by Philip S. Marks

Cover by Roslyn N. McFarland

Formatted by DocUmeant Designs, www.DocUmeantDesigns.com

Library of Congress Control Number: 2019938475

ISBN: 978-1-950075-01-0

DEDICATION

This book is dedicated to a very special person who, as a young adult, was diagnosed with DID after a childhood of sexual abuse. On a number of occasions I witnessed the changes occurring in my friend as other alternative personalities came forth. Years of therapy helped integrate all of them into just one. I am pleased to say my friend is no longer fragmented but now leads a fulfilling life free from confusion about what is happening, what has happened, and what is likely to happen in the future. She is now finally herself again.

FOREWORD

Dissociative Identity Disorder (DID) is a very real mental health issue that affects thousands of people. It is understandable that, unless it is observed in person, there are those who doubt its existence. As with most mental health disorders, it affects not only the patient but can have far-reaching effects on family and friends as one struggles to find resolution.

This book is based upon a very real, very brave woman I had the good fortune to work with as she brought her secrets to light in her desperate desire to regain her true self.

My wish is that this book brings hope to anyone who may be struggling with this or any other mental health issue. There is light at the end of the tunnel, but you must have the courage to let others in on your situation. Don't try to go it alone. There is help from professionals, family, and friends—if you let them in.

Lyla Ellzey was one of those people who stood by her friend through years of confusion and heartache. She used her experience and her love to write this book. I feel privileged to be able to play a small role in introducing her to you.

Susan Lannak, LCSW (Licensed Clinical Social Worker)

ACKNOWLEDGMENTS

I would like to thank those directly involved with this book about the devastating illness, Dissociative Identity Disorder (DID), better known as Multiple Personalities. From the person I know and love who suffered the consequences of "others" living within who dictated much of the actions in which my friend participated, to the therapist who helped return this broken person to the original through integration of all the parts, I say "Bravo!" You have my gratitude.

I thank my publisher, Ginger Marks, owner of DocUmeant Publishing for a job well-done by ensuring this book conveyed what the author intended. I also thank my artistic designer, Roslyn McFarland, for the creative, eye-catching artwork that produced a cover perfect for this book.

To those who offered advice along the way and to those who read and provided feedback in its many stages of creation, I say "I would never have succeeded in this undertaking without your help. I owe you a huge debt of gratitude." You are legion and too many to name lest I omit someone and suffer remorse and have to self-flagellate. You know who you are.

My husband, Frank Ellzey, supported me through intense writing periods as well as occasional dry spells. To say "Thank you" is an understatement, but I'll try anyway. "Thank you, Frank. I love you."

PART I:
CHAPTER ONE

Hell no!" The shout reverberated in the quiet classroom.

The students all turned to look at Emma Montford. Her body rigid, she sat three seats back in the second row glaring at her teacher. A buzz of confusion rose and soared around the classroom. The teacher rapped hard on the corner of her desk with a ruler and the room quieted again.

Emma glanced at the papers she held. Scowling at Sister Magdalene, she jumped up from her desk and shook them, waving and ready to spill from her clutch.

In an uncharacteristically deep voice, she bellowed: "A one-thousand-word research paper, my ass! You can't make me do anything I don't want to do, and I sure as hell am *not* doing this crap." She slammed the papers onto her desk. Two pages drifted to the floor, one almost obscuring the other. Leaning down, she spat on them before again directing a malevolent glare at her teacher.

"I don't even want to listen to this shit, much less do research on it." Her voice dripped venom as she finished,

"It's ridiculous for anybody to think this fucking stuff really happened."

Sister Magdalene put her hands on her hips, huffing quick shallow breaths while her right black-shod foot tapped ever faster.

"Emma Montford, just who do you think you are? You can't talk to me that way!" Red blotches marred the sister's face and a vein pulsed in her left temple.

"Oh, yeah?" Emma growled, her voice deepening further. "Well, listen to this you old *bitch*! *You* can't tell *me* what to do! I'll do what I damned well please," she smirked. With a quick jut of her lower lip she flung herself back into her seat.

"Emma! What's wrong with you? What's happening?" Sister Magdalene covered her mouth with her hand, her eyes huge behind the lens of her glasses. "You don't sound like yourself at all!"

Emma's body seemed to soften, losing its tautness and molding into her seat, and she shook her head as if confused. She raised her eyes to look at her teacher.

"What?" She blinked and glanced around the classroom. "I'm sorry, Sister. What did you say?"

The teacher stared hard at her and exclaimed, "I've had enough of this, Emma. We're going to the principal's office. She can deal with you."

"But I didn't do anything," Emma protested, uneven lines wrinkling her forehead.

"That's enough!" Sister Magdalene shrieked. She stomped to Emma's desk and grabbed her arm, pulling her from the seat. Tugging her toward the door, she yanked it open and thrust Emma through it and into the hall. Without so much as an admonition to the rest of the class, she hustled her to the principal's office, what the kids called The Devil's Den, with Emma cringing and stumbling along behind her.

Earlier that morning Susie Montford climbed out of her mother's Lincoln Town Car wishing it was the weekend. It was Friday, so she and her sister Emma had only one long day of classes at St. Michael's Catholic School before them.

"Later, Emma," she threw over her shoulder to her sister sliding across the seat behind her.

"See you when school's out, Javier," she called to her mother's driver as he eased the Limo into the lanes of BMWs, Mercedes, and Volvos, each lined up to disgorge its cargo. While Emma hurried off to her homeroom, Susie's attention was on the group of girlfriends, her crew, waiting for her by the school's entry steps.

Laughing and acting like mischievous seventh-graders, poking each other and grabbing books out of arms, they climbed the steps and entered the hallway.

"Whoa!" Susie wrinkled her nose as the odors of the Catholic school assaulted her. Chalk and incense battled for first place in the almost overpowering smells that clung to the ubiquitous beige walls. Brussel sprouts and broccoli from the cafeteria just down the hall added to the aromatic greeting.

"Yuck. That stuff smells like throw-up! I hope we don't get that for lunch!"

Bored with her classwork, Susie feigned the need to use the bathroom. In the stall, she pulled up her uniform skirt, wadded it around her waist, and sat down on the toilet at the far end. *I can't take a chance on getting my skirt tail wet should it fall into the toilet.* She lifted her right foot and kicked the door shut, leaned forward, and slid the lock in place. In less than five minutes her legs were going numb from the pressure against the split toilet seat. *They*

should have toilet seats that are all one piece like we have at home flitted through her thoughts as she killed time looking through the pictures in her smart phone gallery. She stopped and cocked her head, listening. The hall door opened and what sounded to her like several girls came in. Their voices rose and fell, chatting about some other girl. *They're skipping class, just like me.*

Rising from the toilet, she reached for the door latch and eased it out of its slot. It slid back with a squeak. Susie opened the door a slit, allowing her to see the girls. She opened her eyes wide and her mouth became an "O."

"This is so totally bogus," one said, applying stark black mascara to her already clumpy eyelashes.

"Like, Emma's soooo in for it now," a plump blonde said as she rolled bright pink lipstick onto her cupid bow mouth.

"She's going to wish she'd never called Sister Magdalene a bitch," a third girl said as she searched in her purse and glanced at the other two primping. She came up with a pink wide-toothed comb.

Susie's mouth made a happy face smile. *Huh! Putting on makeup seems to be the only thing eighth grade girls do. Besides gossip, that is.* Suddenly, her smile vanished. *Wait! Did she say Emma?*

"Right, she was salty," a fourth girl said with a giggle. "I totally can't believe she had the nerve to do that." She drew a comb through her hair and worked at untangling a snarled knot with the fingers of her left hand. "Like, I'll bet you Sister Mary Agnes is throwing a fit right now."

Susie widened the slit.

"What was that scene when Emma sounded just like a boy?" The first girl's voice ended on a high note. She put her mascara back into her purse decorated with smiling lips made of red sequins.

"That was filthy! I can't imagine, like, how she did that. It was all low and crackly." The third girl tried to mimic the voice Emma had used. She failed, judging by the rolled eyes she received. She was good, though, at affecting the valley girl talk.

"You know what? She sounded just like Joey Bigelow," the plump blonde said. "And we know his voice is *finally* changing . . ."

Her rendition of a teen boy's voice was cut off by the loud laughter of the other three. Their laughter faded away as the door closed behind them.

Susie plopped back down on the toilet and tried to put together what she knew of Emma's strange behavior with what must have just happened. She stood up, brushed down the blue and yellow plaid skirt that was the school's seventh grade girls' uniform, and opened the stall door. She peered around. Silence, almost palpable, seemed to reverberate off the pea-green tiled walls. There was no one in the bathroom but her.

Finding out what was happening with Emma was more important than getting in trouble for skipping class. Pumping several squirts of hand soap into her palm, she washed her hands, taking her time while she made a plan. The medicinal smell of antibacterial soap rose like vapor around her. *I hate that smell. Why can't we have something minty? Lemony would be even better. This stuff stinks!*

Susie's thoughts returned to Emma. *Oh, boy, Mom and Dad will have fits. Especially if Dad has to come home from wherever it is he's gone this time. And, naturally, Mom will be mad as heck if word of this leaks out to her adoring public.*

She dried her hands on several paper towels she yanked from the dispenser and threw them in the direction of the waste basket, not looking to see if they hit their target.

Who cares? I hate always having to do things to suit the rules. Just because Emma and I are forced to be in Catholic parochial school because the Los Angeles County school system sucks doesn't mean I have to like it. It's as bad as if we were in the TV show "Orange is the New Black."

She opened the bathroom door a crack and peeked to see if anyone was outside. The halls were empty, so she slipped through the door and endeavored to meld with the gray lockers lining the tan-colored hallway. She kept her head down and walked so close to the lockers she bumped her elbow.

"Ow!" she said aloud without thinking. She looked to make sure no one was around to hear her and ask what she was doing. All clear.

"Thank God," she muttered. Cringing and holding her smarting right elbow with her left hand, she set out for the Devil's Den.

Pacing, she hung around the staircase at the end of the hall near the principal's office and edged ever closer to try to hear what was happening. The bell rang and Susie mixed in with the kids changing classes, waving gaily to a few of her friends. She returned and bent down under the staircase. *I hope I don't get caught. I'll probably be in as much trouble as Emma.*

Looking back up the hallway from her hiding spot, she saw Sister Mary Martha, teacher of the class she was supposed to be attending now, look up and down the deserted hallway. She went back into the classroom and Susie let out the breath she was holding. Her heart stopped knocking against her chest wall.

Still under the staircase, Susie heard shoes clacking down the hall. *That's Mom!* She could tell by the force of her step that she was pissed. "Whoa! Get a load of her face!" was out of her mouth before she realized it.

"Crap!" she whispered. "I've got to think before I say things. I've really got to work on thinking it but not saying it aloud!" *Wow! Mom is always lovely, but now her jaw is set, and her eyebrows are hanging like batwings over her eyes.*

Susie watched her mom twist the door handle and throw open the door to the Devil's Den. She watched as her mom's whole attitude seemed to change. Anita Montford, the actress, spread a smile across her face and became charm itself as she entered.

Figuring they'd be talking about Emma and they shouldn't notice her, Susie crept up to the door and dared a quick peek through the lightly frosted glass at the top half. She captured a fuzzy glimpse of a figure that could've been her mom standing before Sister Mary Agnes' desk. Since she couldn't determine who the shadowy figures were, she squatted down to listen. She heard Emma say, "I don't know what you're talking about."

Susie pressed her ear close to the wooden door, not daring to rise and take another peek. She heard the teacher say Emma had called her a bitch. She sounded angry.

To herself, Susie whispered, "That's bound to get Mom's attention real quick!"

In an icy voice that could've won her an academy award, Anita Montford informed them *she* was Emma's mother and *she'd* handle this. She ended with, "Emma and I will be going now."

Sister Mary Agnes said, "Yes, you will. I'm expelling Emma until such time it is proved she has received counseling and a significant change in her behavior is documented. I suggest the entire family receive counseling. I must tell you there have been similar incidents of Emma acting up before and we've chosen to not get the family involved. However, none was as disruptive as this. This was one time too many and we can no longer overlook it."

Susie could imagine her mom gritting her teeth as she ground out, "Fine. We'll see to it. Until Emma is welcomed back, Susie will no longer be a student here either. Thank you for your time."

Stretching her leg muscles and then leaning down low, Susie beat it for the stairs as fast as she could. She turned around just in time to see her mother hurry Emma out of the office and toward the front door of the school. By the look on her mother's face, Susie was glad it was Emma in trouble and not her.

"Emma's probably gonna be grounded for a million years. Shit! Did I hear right? Mom's taking me out of this bogus place too?"

After pondering the best answer to her predicament, Susie decided she'd better go to her last class of the day since she'd already skipped two others. Hoping Sister Fabiana wouldn't make a big deal about her coming in late, she opened the door and headed to her seat without looking at her teacher.

"Wait a minute, Miss Montford," Sister Fabiana ordered, looking her up and down. "Why are you late to this class?"

"Oh," Susie said with eyes wide and earnest. "My mom had something to talk about with Sister Mary Agnes, and my sister and I needed to be there. Mom just left but she wanted me to stay for the rest of the day."

"Right. Do you have a note?" She swept her narrowed eyes over Susie as if expecting the note to pop out from somewhere. It didn't. "Take your seat."

Sitting at her desk, Susie paid little attention to her teacher droning on. Her thoughts turned to the paparazzi.

I sure hope they won't hear of today's business with Emma. They don't leave anyone alone. She knew the paparazzi were everywhere, even in the schools that famous people's kids go to. She shook her head and a smile appeared as she remembered the time Jeremy Fender and Maddie Langley were making out in the janitor's closet. When they came out with her hair all mussed and stringy and his sticking up in all directions and with lipstick smeared all over his face, the photographer was snapping away. Since the guy caught them still kissing when they opened the door — stupid idiots — his photo was the real 'tell all' deal and the next day it hit the entertainment papers. The school was embarrassed and the kids' parents were furious.

But how in the world did he get into the school with cameras hanging around his neck? Hello? Wouldn't you think someone would've seen him and asked him what he was doing there? Like, "Hey Dude. What's up?"

The parents sued the newspaper and were thinking about suing the school. *But, that's the kind of stuff that happens to us kids who are just trying to be normal in this land of fruits and nuts. Our family is going to be the subject of gossip. I can tell you that things at home tonight will not be sunny and bright. Nor anytime soon.*

CHAPTER TWO

It *is* a crazy world Susie lives in. It has not always been this way. In fact, Susie believes she was meant to live a normal life and for a long time she did so, considering her mother is a well-known movie star and her father travels most of the time on secret missions out of the country. She is the younger of two sisters, Emma being older by two years and practically perfect. But things are changing.

Susie's parents' jobs provide everything they need. The family lives in the Hollywood Hills above Los Feliz Boulevard in an older but trendy section of Los Angeles near Griffith Park. The life they live now has a damaged cog causing the engine to sputter. It has the potential to blow the family's once smoothly-running world completely off the track.

SUSIE

Being normal, to me, means doing the usual things my friends do. My sister Emma and I and 'our crew' delight in doing stuff kids enjoy. We swim in our parents' expensive designer pools, which have all kinds of weird shapes and are hidden in the back yards among the flowering trees and shrubs. All around us the gardeners deftly wield their pruning shears and rakes. We don't pay much attention to them because most of them don't speak English. We love to go to each other's homes and rummage in our mothers' closets and play dress-up, trying on glistening gowns — most of which have only been worn once. There's always some movie opening that Mom and Dad get invited to, or a charity benefit or award ceremony that requires getting all dressed up in fancy clothes. Some of the gowns have big billowing skirts and some are skin tight. Others are so low in front that you may as well not even have a top on. The fake fur coats look like the real thing. The real ones are in storage, so we can't get to those. There are gorgeous suits which are perfect for meetings with agents. I like the ones with pants, but Emma likes the ones with the skinny pencil skirts. I've even seen her slip into Mom's closet and try on those skirts when she doesn't know I'm looking.

We spend hours in our mothers' dressing rooms applying makeup including putting on their false eyelashes. I think they kind of look like spiders sitting on our eyes. On our mom, they're the bomb.

I remember one time when Emma and I were messing with Mom's makeup. When Emma put a ton of goop on her face she wound up looking like a hooker. Then she got all ditzy and went on and on, saying things like, "I am so beautiful!" or "I look fantastic!" about fifty times, drawling it out real southern-like. It sort of reminded me of Tallulah Bankhead, an old-timey movie star who talked so southern until you could hardly understand her. Mom has some really old movies that she loves and I've seen a lot of the old actors and actresses. I could watch them for hours, even though they are in black and white.

I said, "We look like real movie stars," and hoped she'd just shut up. But nope, she put on even more of the colors on the palette, and honestly, I fell out giggling when she wound up looking like a clown.

My mom needs the role of a lifetime to come her way. It seems she's usually cast second to the lead, like *any* actress in a movie with Meryl Streep. But, I have hope. She almost won an Oscar for Best Actress. At least she was nominated. Lots of actors never even achieve that.

Oh, back to our crew: When we get dropped off at the mall by one or the other of our parents' drivers we go in all the teen fashion shops, and boy, let me tell you, they are always glad to see us go. Another fun thing we love to do is play games in the mall arcades — even though they're a little old school now. We always yell and cut up when we win.

But, the absolute most fun of all is watching our moms or dads in movies. Every actor we know has a home theater. We sit in the comfy seats, usually in the front rows, of the small theaters and flick popcorn at the screen when a character comes on that we don't like. Then each of us runs up and kisses our mom or dad whenever they're in the picture.

Oh, this is a hoot! One time we'd been in Camille's mom's makeup and didn't take it off. I tell you what — Camille made a mess of that screen! Her mom was furious. She finally calmed down a little when the rest of us told her it was because Camille was so proud of her and couldn't resist kissing her on the screen. And, no doubt about it, each of us thinks our own mom is the prettiest.

"I think it's a shame that Mom hasn't truly been recognized for her talents," Emma told us one afternoon. Several girls were gathered with Emma and me in our home theatre and we were watching *The Yellow Moon*, starring you-know-who for maybe the tenth time. It's one of those Southern Gothic movies where Mom got to wear dresses like those in *Gone with the Wind*.

"Oh, man! That Vivien Leigh was gorgeous! Mom looks so much like her." I'd always say this when we saw Mom in her long, full-skirted costumes, looking a lot like Scarlet O'Hara—except for her hair. Mom's hair is blonde.

You'll love *The Yellow Moon's* story. It goes like this— Penelope, played by Mom, lives with these plantation owners who keep her locked up at night because she is so beautiful every man wants to marry her. But, the man and woman know she's an heiress and don't want her to get married so *they* can get her money. She falls in love with the most handsome man of all and sneaks out to meet him in the moonlight, but they come looking for her. You guessed it. In trying to take her away with him and fight off the bad guys, he shoots her by mistake and kills her. We're all crying by the time he kisses her in the moonlight because we know what's coming. She did get an Oscar nomination for that one, but she didn't win. Those idiots!

So, I said to Emma, "That's right. She deserves an Oscar for this role alone. Maybe this next year will be the year she wins." I mean it. Many of our friends' mothers or fathers have already won Oscars. You know, sometimes things just aren't fair.

Then there are our dads. Every girl knows that even though, all around the world, women and girls are swooning over him, he still belongs to her and her family. Our dad is not a movie star, but he's as handsome as the fathers who are. The other girls say so.

Yep, this goes to show you what a happy bunch of girls having a really good time we were. Our friends acted normal, and Emma and I did as well. That was after Emma and I grew from those cute little girls who wore pretty pinafores and Mary Janes with our blonde hair caught back in barrettes, to be pretty decent looking middle-school students.

Now, here I am twelve and Emma is fourteen. She must not have been ready for school because she flunked kindergarten the first time. I can't think of any other reason because she's pretty smart now. That's why she's only a year ahead of me in school instead of two. And now I've been noticing lately that Emma often, well—maybe not often, but sometimes—acts kind of weird. We're best buddies, but I tell you it's not all roses putting up with her. It's more like Guns N' Roses. Funny, come to think of it, Emma sings strange stuff and dances all over the place when a Guns N' Roses video comes on. She doesn't sing the words they're singing, as if anybody could! It's hard to understand the words in these rock bands sometimes. And it's definitely hard to try to figure Emma out. I think she's a bit of a fruitcake. You should just hear some of the words she says when she's singing those songs. If Dad ever hears her, Emma will be in trouble for the rest of her life!

Talking about my dad, I'll bet he's been just about everywhere on earth. When I grow up, I want to travel all over the world, too. That would be a-okay. I think it would be interesting to meet all those strange people and try to figure out what they're saying when I talk to them. I wonder how he ever gets anything sold. I guess he shows them what he has and demonstrates it, and then if they want it, they buy it. Or maybe they have interpreters who have learned all those foreign languages, and if they do, that would help big-time with the selling process. I know he's good at it because he makes like a gazillion dollars. Truth is he hasn't been around in a long while, so he hasn't seen Emma do any of her crazy stuff. I wonder if he'll believe it.

I also don't think Mom knows anything is going on with Emma because she's been really busy lately. She's working on a film shooting out in the desert and leaves early. Then, Javier has to go back and get her late in the evening. A couple of times we've long been in bed before she comes in. We can hear her high heels clacking on the marble floor of the foyer when she starts walking toward our bedrooms to check on us.

Oh, yeah! Mom's name really isn't Anita. She was born Mathilda, but the movie people didn't think that was a cool enough movie star's name, so she changed it. Mathilda Montford kind of has a ring to it, don't you think? Mom thinks Anita Montford sounds better. Emma and I are always calling her Anita when she can't hear us. It's great fun, but several times she's almost caught us and then we just hee-haw like the couple of hooligans Dad calls us. He loves that word. I think he learned it growing up in England.

EMMA

Sometimes Susie can be such a big brat. She gets upset with me for no reason. We've been close friends since she was born. I love being her big sister and showing her how to do things. Just because I wasn't paying attention the other day while Susie and one of her friends were nattering on a mile a minute is no reason for Susie to act like she did. I must have been thinking about something else, I don't remember what it was now, because when I did look at them, Susie and her friend were standing there with their mouths open and looking at me like I had a horn on my head. It must've been really boring, what they were talking about. Probably something about seventh grade boys. Oh, brother! I have *no* interest in seventh grade boys, so that's why my attention drifted away.

But, oh, the fun times we've had together! Even when she was a baby and just a lump who couldn't do anything, Mom tells me I'd stand by her crib and jabber away trying to get her to play with me. She also says I loved that baby so much! Of course, I still do. But it ticks me off that we get mad at each other over nothing! At least I think *Susie* gets mad at *me* over nothing.

Some of my friends tease me about always having Susie around so much. They think I'm catering to "the baby" and that we do baby things together. One of the baby things they talk about us doing is going to Griffith Park. It's only a few minutes from our home and Javier, Mom's driver, takes us. Sometimes he waits for us in the black limousine. Other times he just drops us off and comes back to get us later.

The very first thing we do at Griffith Park is ride the merry-go-round. It's been there a long time. There's a sign that tells about it, but we've seen it so many times until our eyes glaze over when we glance at it. We really have no idea what it says. Each of us has been on every one of the horses and the other rides. You should see it. It's colorful and the music is special. I think it is pretty neat. So, I really don't care if the girls tease us. If only Susie will stop accusing me of doing strange things when she doesn't even know what she's talking about, everything would be grand. Susie tells me I'm weird. I think Susie's the weird one.

CHAPTER THREE

ANITA

Anita gripped the steering wheel so tightly her knuckles stood up white and knobby. She was afraid to say anything to Emma because she knew she would erupt, saying horrible things that would make a very bad situation much worse. For the same reason, she wouldn't even attempt to look at her daughter as she drove them home after the meeting with the school's principal and Emma's subsequent expulsion. Anita drove the exact posted speed limit with her jaws clenched, staring straight ahead.

"Go to your room and think about the mess you've gotten the whole family into," she hissed to Emma as she unlocked the door. She stomped into her bedroom and kicked off the high heels, sending one bouncing against the bedroom's wall leaving a black mark from the spiked heel. Stripping off her clothes, she flung them to the floor and sat down at the dressing table, its top filled with cleansers and lotions. A large collection of makeup sat on the right side and she thought of sweeping it all off the dressing table onto the floor. *I feel small and of no consequence, and that makes me livid.*

She wasn't sure with whom she should be the angriest. *Ahhggh!* She picked up a jar of cleansing cream and began to massage it into the makeup on her face and neck. Plucking a cloth from a container she began to wipe away her makeup. *God, I'm mad all over again just thinking about it. I'm not used to being treated like that.*

"Get counseling, indeed! I'd like to give her some counseling with my foot!" she spat out, her voice quivering.

Gazing at herself in the mirror, Anita saw the bunched lines between her eyes and the ruts making parentheses around her mouth. "Ohh, I've got to calm down," she groaned.

Take a deep breath. Anita inhaled, lifting her substantial bosom, and followed it with a cleansing exhale ending in a long "Hmmmmmmm."

That feels better. Talk this through, Anita," she said to her reflection.

"I was upset to start with when I arrived at the school." She tapped her left forefinger with the right one. "That's one." She tapped her middle finger. "We were shooting in LA on the Tantamount Lot instead of in the desert where we filmed yesterday, so it didn't take as long to get to the school, and I didn't have a chance to really calm down after the school called. That's two." She tapped her ring finger. "And then I got furious with Sister Mary Agnes and left without trying to work out some kind of compromise. That's three." She sighed and wiped the remaining cleanser from her skin.

Alternating hands, she smoothed the skin from her collar bone to her chin. *Oh, I know I was short with Emma's teacher. But, imagine! My sweet girl, Emma, calling her teacher a bitch? That's truly unimaginable. If it had been*

Susie, I might have believed she was misbehaving. But—Emma? Never! Anita held up her left hand and tapped the pad of her pinkie finger. "And now I've got to talk with Emma. I can't just let it go. That's four."

She moved to her temples, her fingers soothing the throbbing pain. *But, if they're to be believed, she did do that—and more! What's puzzling me is the boy's voice they said she used.* Anita picked up the comb and laid it back down as she gazed into the mirror only to see the scene in the principal's office as it once more played out in her mind.

Selecting her hairbrush, she drew it through her long, dark blonde hair. *Now, that just doesn't make sense. If it were true, what they said about Emma, you'd think I would've seen evidence of her doing that here at home. I would've heard her somehow. This is a big house and yard, but the only days I don't see them is when I'm shooting out of town and it's past their bedtime when Javier drives me home. By then, they're sound asleep.*

Anita put her elbow on the table and leaned her aching head into her right palm, abandoning her hair brushing. *What on earth am I going to do? It's imperative that I find a doctor who can tell me if there is a medical problem with Emma. But counseling! As if counseling can cure what it is that causes the behavior they accused Emma of having!*

Taking her hand from her face, Anita placed both hands palm down on the dressing table, needing the added strength to stand. *I'd better start by talking with Emma to see what she has to say about all this. She denied all of it in the principal's office—but, something must be going on. And, of course, I must talk with Susie. Those two are as close as twins, so I should be able to get to the bottom of this soon.*

As she started out her bedroom door to talk with Emma, she had another thought. *Jenkins. My Monty. No one else dares call him that, but when I pout and wheedle and call him Monty, it works. I need him to come home and help me work through this.*

EMMA

Emma went to her bedroom and lay curled in the fetal position in her king size bed under the big windows, her school uniform wrinkling under her. She told herself she wouldn't cry, but now her sides hurt from heaving silently, and even though she squeezed her eyes shut, she can feel the tears escaping.

Oh, God, I am so humiliated! I wish I knew what's going on with me. I thought Susie was throwing shade when she said I do weird things. I'm not so sure now, since I had to go to the Principal's office because everyone said I was acting like somebody totally different. They said I sounded like a boy!

She abruptly looked toward the door, listening. On a quiet sob, she moaned, "Oh no, I hear somebody coming. I know that's Mom. She's going to want to talk about why she had to leave her movie shoot to come to school today because of me. I have no idea what I'm going to tell her. If I understood what's happening, I would tell her. But, I just simply don't have a clue. I truly don't know!"

They talked while the afternoon turned into evening, arriving with the setting sun. Its descent sent shards of orange and yellow through the trees visible outside Emma's windows.

Anita rose from the bed where she had lain so long with her daughter.

She said, "I'm going to call your father now, Emma. And, we also need to eat something. We're both exhausted and we need to keep our strength up." She slipped out the door and went to the kitchen to see what Madonna had prepared for their dinner.

Emma sat up, swung her legs over the side, and got up from her bed. She reached to turn on her bedside lamps. Sitting at her modern white desk in the corner of her room, she made notes. Deciding she'd write a list of all she knew about everyone's perspective on her behavior, she hoped it would help her sort through it. She turned on her computer and opened a new document.

Her thoughts flowed through her fingers and appeared on the screen.

Mom's gone now, and for a while before she came, I huddled in a ball on my bed. I feel like when I lie on my side and draw my knees up close to my chest that I can protect my heart. After all the crying Mom and I did together, my heart really needs protecting. I feel like somebody is holding it in huge hands, twisting and wringing it and all the blood is dripping out of it.

In the end, though, I think Mom was truly convinced that I don't remember anything about these incidents and that I didn't mean to do them. She told me what the teacher said, that I'd called her a bitch. I've never done anything like that in my life! She also said the principal won't let me go back to school until we've had counseling. Not just me, but all of our family, including Susie and Dad. He's really going to love that! I hate it when Dad disapproves of me or something I've done.

You know, I was right there when all of this was being talked about and I don't even remember that! It certainly is bizarre. There has to be something wrong with me, and I think something is really bad wrong with my head. Or my mind. Why can't I remember?

Mom says she's going to call Dad and ask him to come home. She's really angry and upset. I've never seen her cry like she did tonight, but at least she seemed to get past it. She probably cried because she was so angry. And then she held me while I cried. She held me! I felt like I was her little girl again and that she would protect me and make every-thing all right. Oh, God, make it so. I don't think I have any more tears left, so please God, make it be okay.

Scrolling to the top of the document, Emma reread what she'd written and then decided to make it an easy-to-read larger font. *That'll be good enough to help me remember.* Her gaze moved to her desktop and there she saw the cup. It was special to her because it had a picture on its side of Susie and her in their pajamas on Christmas morning. The right corner of her mouth rose as she thought about them, remembering that Christmas when they were seven and five. *What a great family day it had been. Everyone together and so happy.*

Remembering that wonderful day from the past made her sigh at her unhappiness now. Letting out her pent-up breath, she hit the PRINT icon and gathered the sheets of typing paper as they came out of the printer, tapped their ends on the desk so they'd be perfectly evened up, and placed them in the wide middle desk drawer. She pulled off her white shirt and red, green, and gold plaid skirt that the eighth graders wore and draped them over her desk chair. Then she lay down again on her bed.

JENKINS

Jenkins Montford sat in a mahogany colored leather chair in the hotel's lounge in Beijing, China. The chair was designed in a half-circle. Idly, he wondered, *Do they make them round and then cut them in half before upholstering them?* He crossed his knees, but his expensive designer suit trousers did not wrinkle. Taking a sip from his glass of 10-year-old Scotch, he swallowed it slowly, savoring its warmth in his mouth before it spread in his stomach.

A business associate, also from Los Angeles, and who often traveled with him, sat opposite him with the small, yet ornate jade table separating them. Jenkins sat his drink on the table. Uncrossing his legs, he sat erect in his chair and spoke to his companion. "I received a call from Anita this afternoon, Winston."

With his brown eyes wide and questioning, Winston remarked, "You did, huh? Is everything all right at home?"

"I hope so. Here I am in Beijing, in a meeting of great importance with the Chinese government, and I get a call from my wife. I assumed it must be an emergency and I pictured her and the two girls lying in hospital beds with their bodies swathed in bandages." He took a sip of his drink and cradled the glass in his hands. "As I found out, that is not the case."

Leaning forward in his seat, Winston asked, "Well, what was it? They are okay, aren't they?"

Montford drew back the sleeve of his suit coat and pristine white shirt cuff to expose the Versace watch on his left wrist. He checked the time and slipped the cuff back in place.

"It seems Emma has been talking like a boy," he began, and paused to acknowledge his associate's raised eyebrows with a nod. "She's using unladylike language and is being disruptive in class. Anita reported the school has closed its doors to Emma until it's proved that she has been to a doctor in order to determine the cause of her atrocious behavior. And that her family—Anita, Susie, and I—must all join her for counseling sessions to try to resolve her problems."

Standing, Winston's six feet seven inches loomed over Jenkins' six feet two. "That's too bad." His expression softened as he saw his friend's uncertainty, something he'd rarely seen. "I'm really sorry, Jenkins." He placed a hand on the seated man's shoulder. "What are you going to do now?"

Montford picked up his glass and sipped slowly as he looked over the rim at his long-time associate. He set his glass on the jade table and put his fingertips together in the shape of a steeple. "While, I dislike having my business dealings interrupted, I shall be certain to participate in getting the care Emma needs."

A low rumble indicating his sympathy prompted Jenkins to wave away his friend's concern, and uncharacteristically feeling the need to sound out his concerns, he continued talking. "My career is of utmost importance to me. I like the intriguing world of foreign governments and their intricate issues. We arrive already immersed in whatever problem there is, and then, through negotiation, much discussion, and our problem-solving skills, we resolve the situation. I tell everyone, including my family, even Anita, that I'm a salesman representing our government."

"Really? You tell them that, Jenkins?" He set his beer down, and frowning, he peered at his friend. "Why?"

Montford gave a sardonic laugh. "Of course I do. Because I suppose I am a salesman of sorts. Most of all, I'm a trouble-shooter. Don't we repair communications and offer solutions?"

Winston nodded, a puzzled frown between his eyes.

"I never leave until the broken is whole again." With the fingers of his right hand, he rubbed his platinum wedding band. He laid his hand on his thigh and again looked at Winston.

"Being called home is a first for me. For now, I have to leave, but I will return to China as soon as possible. I'll go home because Anita made it crystal clear that at this moment *she* is the one who needs me by her side the most. She and Emma."

With drink in hand again, Jenkins indicated an approaching figure. His secretary stopped before him and handed him an envelope. He opened it and slid out the new airline ticket. He took his time scanning it.

"Thank you for taking care of this for me, Georgia." He indicated the third chair that was drawn up to the little table, "Won't you sit and have a drink with us? I was just telling Winston what's going on at home that makes my early departure necessary."

Georgia sat and Winston signaled the bartender for another round. Jenkins continued his story while the bartender made the drinks and brought them to their table.

"When the girls were smaller, they were a noisy lot and it seemed I was always reprimanding them. Anita laughed at my frustration and told me they were behaving normally. My parenting problem is caused by being used to being with adults. I suppose I often make a dog's dinner of things."

"Don't we all?" Georgia remarked. "I sometimes think my kids forget who I am when I'm gone for more than a day or two. And I sometimes forget they are children and

I can only expect so much from them. I have to work on my mommy routine and forget the world of high-powered executives when I'm home."

"Do you mean you can forget Jenkins and me?" Winston joked.

Jenkins smiled, loosening up a bit.

"Even you two," Georgia admitted with a grin. "But do go on. You were saying . . . what?"

"Oh yes. I guess this is what makes me who I am today. I don't believe I've ever told either of you about my childhood." It was a question couched in a statement.

"No, I don't believe you have," Winston said.

"No, but do tell us, if you will," Georgia added.

"Actually, now's not the time. I must get ready for tomorrow's meetings and my flight home." He slid his sleeve back and again checked the time. "But I will tell all one day." He stood and the three said their goodbyes. Montford strode to the elevator and disappeared inside.

CHAPTER FOUR

enkins opened his front door and entered his home. He'd flown all night from Beijing and was exhausted. He tried sleeping on the plane but the scenes playing out in his head made it impossible. It was a twelve-hour direct flight from Beijing to Los Angeles International Airport. And this last-minute direct flight was enormously expensive. He'd shelled out seven-thousand dollars for his one-way flight. But it was worth it because he couldn't bear the thought of a three- or five-hour layover in Chicago or Dallas Fort Worth. It seemed he'd lived this day twice, as Beijing was sixteen hours ahead of Los Angeles and it was now eleven o'clock in the morning in the Pacific time zone.

Anita sat in one of two ivory-colored eighteenth century French Bergere chairs in the library to the left of the entry foyer. She swallowed the last of her fourth cup of morning coffee with a final bite of cinnamon rice cake. Nourishment without the calories. Hearing the door open, she flew to greet him. Wrapping her arms around his waist, she laid her head against his chest and hugged him close.

"Thank God, you're home, Monty! I missed you so much."

"I missed you also, my love."

Leaning back to look up at him, her arms still firmly held him in place against her body. With eyes big and luminous, she divulged in a husky voice, "I'm sorry to make you come home, but I've never needed you as badly as I need you now, Monty."

Holding her tightly, Jenkins rested his chin atop her soft cloud of upswept blonde curls. "I'm here now, Anita. What can I do to help?"

"There's so much to talk about." Anita released him. "I need you to help me with making decisions about Emma. I've made some calls; there are several doctors to choose from. I've made one appointment already with a doctor who had a cancellation and was able to fit us in."

"That's good. Perhaps this doctor may turn out to be the one we need." He paused and a line grew between his eyes. "The appointment is for all four of us?"

"Yes. All of us. And it's all I've been able to think about. Come put your baggage in the bedroom and we'll talk."

Jenkins caught her hand and drew her back to him. "Come here," he whispered. He dropped his mouth to hers and kissed her thoroughly. His eyes were warm as he gazed at the beautiful woman he knew was his. He swept his hand from her curls down her cheek with great tenderness. "We'll see this is taken care of, my love."

Lifting his gaze from Anita's face to look around, he asked, "Where are the girls? Where's Emma? Is she all right?"

"They're in their rooms. I told them I'd get them when you got in and we'd have some lunch and talk things over. Okay?"

"Okay. That's fine."

"Besides, I wanted a few minutes to talk with you alone."

Jenkins patted her on the bottom. "Let's do it. We'll have a good old chin-wag."

Susie stared at the computer screen. When she sat in her desk chair she intended to compose an email to Camille. She knew the word would be all over the school by now about why she and Emma were not attending classes. Camille was her friend and deserved to know the real deal about what was going on. She put her fingers on the keyboard and filled her screen with half-answers, afraid to say too much. Camille and Addie had already sent emails to her saying, "What's up with you, Susie? We miss you boo-coo." *They must have written it together* was her first thought. Then she laughed: "Boo-coo? They actually said boo-coo! Even I know it is beau coup."

She placed the hovering cursor on "send" and clicked twice. The email disappeared with a swish. She hit the "sent" icon and reread what she'd written, now a little fearful she'd divulged too much. Her dad wouldn't like her telling their family's business. She wrote:

> Hi, Camille and Addie,
>
> Thanks for emailing me. This is pretty much what's going on. Dad got home from China in super-quick time. We don't see much of him, but he comes through when we really need him. Boy, I wish you could have seen Mom. She was beside herself, just about counting the minutes until he got home. She'd already called a bunch of doctors and explained what was going on with Emma. She found somebody who would see Emma because she was doing that little hiccup crying

thing she does when she's really relieved about something. Plus, I heard her tell Dad practically the second he walked in the door that we had an appointment for all of us with Emma and a doctor. Then, as they were walking to their bedroom, Dad asked about me missing school, too, and Mom said I wasn't going back to that school until they were thrilled to welcome Emma back. Goody! I may be out of school for a long time because I sure don't see them welcoming Emma back any time soon. Yippee!

I'll let you know what I know when I know it. I really miss you guys. Tell everyone hello for me and I'll see them sometime— I just don't know when. Don't do anything I wouldn't do. Hah! That ain't happening!"

Jenkins Montford thought how best to go about getting the information he needed from both girls in order to know what he was dealing with.

"Should I perhaps talk with Susie first and see what she can tell me—or us? It might be better for them both, separately, and together afterward, to divulge what they know to both of us at the same time. And I'm hoping it's not a bunch of codswallop."

The corners of Anita's mouth drew down. After considering for several seconds, which likely seemed like hours to Jenkins with his growing impatience, she decided.

"Yes, I think we should have Susie talk with us first." She took Jenkins' clean underwear from his suitcase and laid them in his underwear drawer. "That way we have something to go on, some kind of idea, of what Emma is actually doing." She lifted out the dirty underwear and socks in the hotel bag Jenkins had placed them in and emptied the bag into the laundry basket in their closet.

Jenkins laid on the bed the ties he'd taken from their special carrier in his suitcase.

"All right. I'll get Susie and the three of us can go sit by the pool and talk privately."

"You should tell Emma what we're doing so she won't think we're hiding this from her," Anita cautioned.

"That's a good idea. I'll do just that." He opened the door and headed into the hall leading to the girls' bedrooms. Anita soon heard his voice as he knocked on Emma's bedroom door. "Emma," he called lightly. "May I come in? I'd like to speak with you."

Anita hurried along the deep piled wheat-colored carpet of her bedroom to the hall leading to the girls' bedrooms. There, in front of Emma's closed door, she met Susie, arriving from her room in the opposite direction. Susie abruptly stopped in mid tip-toe, one foot comically hovering above the shining dark oak floors. Anita put her finger to her lips in the classic shushing gesture and joined her daughter. Together, they listened to Jenkins' deep rumble and Emma's high, anguished voice.

"So, we're going to talk about this, Emma."

"But, I don't know what to tell you, Dad."

"It'll come to you. You'll be just fine. I'm home now, for a while, and your Mom and I will take care of this."

"Thanks, Dad."

"Certainly, Emma. First, we're going to talk with Susie so she can tell us what she has observed in your behavior. We'll call you when we're ready to talk with you. So be thinking about it and what you can tell us."

"That's all I think about," Emma said, as Jenkins turned the knob on the door.

In the hall, Anita and Susie each fled in a different direction. Jenkins departed Emma's room, calling out, "Okay, ladies, let's go out by the pool and talk about this."

"Lemonade! Cool," Susie said, as she lowered herself into a chaise lounge by the pool. She settled in on the yellow-and-blue-striped cushion, finding the most comfortable spot for her bottom. She accepted the tall, frosted glass from her mom. Lifting it to her lips, she took several long swallows and released a gratified "ahh" as she set the glass down beside her on the fiberglass surface.

"Boy, you must have been thirsty," Anita smiled at her daughter.

"I was."

"Susie?"

"Yes, Father?" Jenkins was "Dad" in a relaxed atmosphere. Susie deemed this one to be anything but relaxed, so she figured she needed to be more formal.

"Could you give your mother and me some instances of Emma's behavior when she was supposedly acting strangely? We need to understand why she's being accused of these various things that she denies." Jenkins sat in a strapped chair, body tense, and looked piercingly at his daughter.

Susie knew he needed answers. And right now. She looked at the pool, avoiding eye contact with her father. She took another swallow of lemonade and carefully set the glass down on the table by her chaise lounge.

"Uh . . . Emma got totally upset when I told her some of the things I've seen her do. Things that she couldn't remember doing." Shrugging her shoulders, she threw her hands up and blurted, "She was mad at me, like, forever!"

Both parents stared at her. "Well, she *asked* me to tell her!"

"Yes, she did, honey," her mom agreed. "You did the right thing."

"So," Susie went on, "I did it, but I really didn't want to tell her what I'd seen. It didn't make any sense then and it doesn't make any more sense now." Picking at a loose thread in the hem of her shorts, she twisted it into a tight little ball, then tugged on it to loosen it into one long strand. With her attention still on the thread, she began to talk of what Emma did.

"She said Jessica and I were staring at her with our mouths hanging open the other day and she wanted to know what the heck she'd said. Or done."

Susie squeezed her eyes shut for a few seconds and then relaxed them. Her forehead was still creased, as if she was envisioning something she wished she wasn't. She opened her eyes and looked at her mom. Next, she turned her beseeching look on Jenkins.

Both parents remained silent, waiting.

"Okay, this is what I told her . . ." She looked into the distance, eyes unfocused, concentrating on what she was going to spill about her adored big sister and best friend. Halting at first, she began.

"Jessica and I were, um, talking about what the gardeners were doing one day. That they were trimming all the bushes along one side of the pool and that they, um, sure were taking their time about it." Her voice picked up speed. "Then Emma said to us in this real mad adult sounding voice, 'Leave those damned gardeners alone. Stay away from them or you're going to wish you had.'" Susie ducked her head and gave a small shrug. "No wonder our mouths were hanging open!"

"Good, honey," Anita said. "Go on and tell us the rest."

"I can still hardly believe Emma said that. The weird thing is she didn't have the slightest memory of any of it only a minute later. So, either she's going crazy or there truly is a problem that I sure hope can be fixed. I don't know if it's something counseling . . ." Susie paused a moment and sneered, "Yeah, right," and then resumed, ". . . *can* cure or if it's a problem that medicine can handle."

"We'll have to see which is the better course of action . . ." her father began. He was interrupted by Susie's enthusiasm.

"I'm pulling for medicine to cure it because even though it's gonna be cool to miss school, I think those counseling sessions will be a pain in the patoot! I don't even want to think about what it might be like in there with you guys, Dad."

For the first time, Susie looked her father right in the eyes. "Do you think for one minute that Emma is gonna spill her guts in front of you and Mom?" She looked from one parent to the other. They looked at each other.

Susie answered for them. "No way, Jose! If it could only be just me and Emma, we could probably get somewhere."

"That's a thought," Jenkins allowed.

"Do you have any other incidents that you can share, sweetie?" her mother asked. "We really do need to know all we can learn about how Emma has acted. I mean those times when she didn't realize what she'd said." Anita paused for a moment. Speaking low and softly, she added, "Or done."

Susie drained her glass of lemonade, savoring its cold, tart sweetness as she again gazed past the pool, seeing nothing, and pulling things from her memory.

"Some more lemonade, Susie?"

"Please, Mom."

"How about you, Monty?"

"No, thank you. I'm good."

Anita picked up their glasses and started into the house through the large sliding glass doors. "Think about it while

I'm getting our lemonade, Susie. I'll be right back." She slipped through the opening and the door swished shut.

"There was this one time," Susie slowly began.

"No, please wait for your mother to return, Susie."

"Oh, okay," Susie replied. "I wasn't thinking, because I remembered a time that is so weird. Emma was really carrying on like crazy that day."

Anita returned and set the cold, beaded glass by Susie's lounge. "Here we are," she said, setting her glass down and then settling in her chair.

Jenkins turned to Anita. "She says she remembers another time, a time when Emma was really acting strange."

"I'm ready. Let's hear it, Susie." Anita leaned forward encouragingly in her chair.

"Well, it was one afternoon after school when you came home early, Mom, and Javier took us to Griffith Park." She looked at Anita for confirmation.

"Right. And?"

"Naturally, we hurried over to the merry-go-round so we could ride it first thing. Everything was normal and going fine." She stopped, looked down at the poolside pavement, and took a minute to get the happenings of that day in order. She raised her chin and continued to talk.

"After riding the merry-go-round, we decided we wanted something to drink. So we went over to the snack bar. This is where it gets weird."

Jenkins sat up straight. "In what way?"

Anita put her hand on his arm. "Shhh, Monty. Let her tell it at her own speed."

"All right. Sorry." He looked at Susie and nodded. "Go ahead, Susie."

Susie glanced from one parent to the other. "Well, Emma acted goofy. She leaned on the counter with her elbows braced and her chin in her hands. Then she swung her behind from side to side like a little kid. And the weird thing is she asked for a coke!"

"Emma *hates* coke! She says it burns her throat!" Anita injected.

"Right. I know! So, she usually gets an orange drink or a Gatorade." Susie shook her head, setting her blonde ponytail swinging. "But nope, she got the coke and just waited for me to pay for it instead of paying herself. I got my coke and when we started to leave, she said, 'Thanks, mister,' to the teenage boy behind the counter. And that's not all. Her voice *sounded* like a little kid."

"Oh, good heavens!" Anita burst out.

In a steely voice, Jenkins asked, "What happened next?" He leaned forward in his chair with his hands dangling between his legs.

Susie drew her legs up tight to her chest and encircled her knees with her arms. She laid her chin in the space between her knees and rocked her body. "I asked her, 'Emma, why are you talking like a kid?' and she said in that same kid's voice, 'Emma's not here right now. I'm Julia.'"

"Julia?" Anita cried.

"Bollocks!" Jenkins erupted from his chair, knocking it over as he stood.

"Yeah, Julia." Susie eyed her father while she talked. "I thought maybe I'd trip her up in whatever game she was playing, so I asked her how old she was." Susie stopped and let the tears in her eyes overflow. She wiped them away with the back of her hand.

Anita stood and came to Susie. She placed her hand on her shoulder, rubbing down her back. Pitching her voice low, she asked, "What did she say, sweetie?"

"She said 'six.'" Susie's voice broke. She tried again. "She said she was *six*!"

Jenkins asked, "How long did this behavior continue?"

"Long enough for me to say, 'Okay, Julia. When will Emma be back?'" Susie looked up at her mom and the tears ran over her bottom lids again. "She said in her normal voice, 'What's the matter with you, Susie? Why did you call me Julia?'"

Susie turned and wrapped her arms around her mom's waist and laid her head against her side. "I said, 'You just told me your name was Julia!' and she said, 'You are so silly sometimes, Susie,' as if she didn't know anything about what just happened."

"Good God!" Jenkins said, as he began to pace the length of the pool and back. "That answers it. We've got to get her into therapy."

"Yes, but we need to talk with her first to see if she can tell us anything," Anita continued to speak in a low voice. Her husband and daughter strained to hear her. She looked old and infinitely sad. "Oh, I so don't want to do this."

Jenkins flopped back down in his chair. His face was lined and gray. For once, he didn't look the dapper man who is in charge of his world.

Watching him, Susie wondered if he ever again would be. Was the secure world of his happy family crumbling around him? *Indeed, will any of us ever go back to the life we knew before? Before Weird Emma.*

He leaned forward with his hand extended to his wife. Anita reached for it, clasping it like a lifeline. Susie wished he'd hold out his hand to her, too. She'd darn sure take it.

CHAPTER FIVE

Before Monty came home Anita spent several hours looking up counselors and doctors on the internet. She researched them, their specialties, and what reviewers said about them. She chose three with the best comments about behavioral issues that had been improved with their help. She made an appointment with the first, and now on this sunny California afternoon, the day after Monty's arrival home, the four Montfords sat in straight-backed folding chairs waiting to be ushered into the doctor's inner sanctum.

"Don't be nervous, sweetie. It can't be all that bad." Anita reached for Emma's hand and brought her arm down to lay her hand in her lap, stopping her from constantly smoothing her hair away from her face.

"Yes," Jenkins agreed. "I imagine he will ask you questions you should be able to answer."

"Piece of cake, Emma," Susie added.

Emma offered a wan smile as the doctor entered the room. A big man with a florid face, his manner was all business. "What have we here?" he asked, while perusing the papers he held. His balding head gleamed in the glow from the florescent lights above his head.

"Who's the patient?" He looked at Emma. "I assume it's you. You look scared to death."

Emma looked away and slid farther down in her seat.

"Ahh, yes." He looked at the other three. "Not to worry. We'll have her acting appropriately in no time." He tapped the papers in his left hand with his right forefinger. "There's a lot of information in these forms. I assume you prepared them, Mrs. Montford?"

Anita nodded, looking skeptical, as if not daring to speak and have him turn that penetrating stare and accusatory tone on her.

"All right then. I'd like the three of you to wait outside while I speak to Emma alone."

"No! Don't leave," Emma burst out. "I don't want to be here by myself!"

Smugly, the doctor, who still had not introduced himself, said, "See. That's what I'm thinking. When things aren't going just how Emma wants them, she starts acting out."

He dismissed Emma with a smirk and turned to her parents. "I see this all the time. This is just another case of a poor little rich girl acting out in order to get attention from those around her. The bigger the audience, the larger the acting out behavior. A classroom full of students, and many of them her friends, gave her the opportunity to make the kind of scene she'd been waiting for."

"You're wrong, doctor!" Emma injected, her voice rising with passion. "I don't plan these things. They just happen."

He gave Emma a dismissive glance. "When things aren't just as Emma wants them, she gets angry," he said to the other Montfords. "And this claiming she doesn't know what's going on is pure fabrication."

"Oh, I say now . . ." Jenkins began, as the rest of the family sat stunned and seemingly unable to even utter a word.

Cutting in, the doctor finished with, "I don't believe I need to see her after all. This is a case of acting out due to the need for attention. Give her some rules, and discipline her if she doesn't follow them, and she'll be okay." He started for the door he used to enter the room but turned back. "Stay here and the nurse will be in with your check-out sheet." He opened the door and disappeared through it.

Jenkins breathed deeply, as if trying to keep from exploding with anger.

Emma began to cry, her upper body shaking with the almost silent sobs. Anita leaned over from her seat and placed her arm around her daughter's shoulder, offering a mother's comfort to a hurting child.

"Well, Mom, I bet you won't be giving this doctor a good review. Maybe not even a half of a star. He's as useless as, as . . ." Susie searched her mind to find just the right analogy, and triumphantly finished with, ". . . as tits on a bull!"

Emma forgot her tears and burst out laughing at the hilarious comment from her sister. "Susie you are such a nut!" She wiped the tears from her face with her fingers while Anita zipped a tissue from the box on the table. Emma took it and applied it to her eyes and cheeks. "I guess we can't let this idiot tell us what to do. Right, Dad? We will find another doctor, won't we?"

"You bet your wellies, we will."

Susie eyed her dad. "That another one of your English sayings, Dad?"

"Aye."

Later that afternoon, Anita pointed to the picture of a handsome, smiling middle-eastern man gazing at them from the computer screen. "This is the second doctor I thought we'd see. He's Dr. Aram and I've read all of his reviews. I should've read all of Dr. What's-his-name's reviews, too. The bad ones were farther down the page. I just read the first few, which were good." She shook her head. "Bad mistake, huh?"

"He certainly was a bad mistake. He was a real wanker, as wonky as hell," Jenkins concurred.

Anita pulled her cell phone from the pocket of her slacks and called for an appointment. No, they had nothing for the next day, Friday. They could work her in Tuesday afternoon at three if the doctor didn't get too backed up. Be there at three and anticipate the schedule being off. They were likely to have to wait, but Emma could be seen the coming Tuesday.

Tuesday afternoon the Montford family again sat in a doctor's waiting room, biding their time as they waited to be called back for a consult. Anita busied herself by memorizing lines for her latest film project.

Jenkins moved to the window and looked down on the bustling traffic on Wilshire Boulevard. He'd remarked on the way to the appointment that Dr. Aram's practice was located very close to Cedars-Sinai Hospital and was on the same street. *Good thing, that. In case we have a meltdown, we'll be close for hospital care.*

Emma and Susie had their cell phones in hand, and each was doing her own thing.

"Emma Montford?" the nurse called. Thoughts broken, they followed the attractive young nurse into the office where the doctor would receive them. It was a small conference room complete with an oval table and six chairs. The doctor entered a minute or so later.

"Hi, I'm Dr. Aram. What can I do for you today?"

Once dealing directly with Dr. Aram, Jenkins and Anita found him to be a pleasant man. He possessed a killer smile filled with gleaming white teeth around which his laughter flowed like maple syrup. It seemed to come easily to him to make funny remarks about just about anything: the sun giving him a deeper tan than was warranted; the fact that the gloves provided were too small for his huge hands; the stethoscope reminding him of the cobra snakes in his homeland. He had them all laughing and at ease in just a few short minutes.

Yes. I think I can say anything to this guy, Emma thought.

Wow! He should be a movie star. He's that handsome, Susie thought. *Or a comedian.*

Dr. Aram had taken time to read the notes Anita provided before entering the room, and now he discussed these with the family. Resting dark eyes on Jenkins and Anita, he asked, "So, as parents, you think Emma's behavior is different from that of just a willful teen . . ." He flipped through the sheet of notes and found that which he was seeking. ". . . 'acting out', as the other doctor suggested?"

"We're certain, my good man, that it's a great deal more than that," Jenkins replied.

"Emma?"

Emma turned her attention to the doctor when he called her name. When the conversation had taken a serious turn, Emma zoned out with an old *Entertainment Weekly* Magazine. Now, she looked at the doctor with her face full of dread.

Dr. Aram lifted the right corner of his mouth in a half-smile. "It's okay. Be at ease. Just a few questions, please, so I might understand more about your behavior. All right?"

Emma nodded and the doctor continued. "Do you know why you are here today to talk with me?"

"I guess so. You're going to try to fix me so I don't do dumb things."

"Mmmm." He uttered a non-committal acknowledgment, and then said, "Tell me what you know about your talking with a deeper voice and sounding like a boy."

"That's what I've been told. I can't recall any of it."

Susie, so far, had not been a part of the consult. Now Aram directed his penetrating dark eyes on her, as if he might see into her soul. *Here is where I'll get answers.*

"What can you tell me about your sister's erratic behavior? Can you give me some examples?"

Susie cut her eyes sideways at Emma before answering confidently. "Sure."

The doctor leaned toward her, evidently ready to hear anything that could help him to understand Emma's problems. Susie repeated the same things she'd told her mom, dad, and Emma: Emma had talked in a deep grownup voice and in a child's high piping tone. But she knew nothing about any of it a few minutes later. "Emma was really acting weird," Susie said, and shrugged her shoulders. "That's about it."

Dr. Aram dipped his head in a quick nod and reached for the phone on his desk. The line buzzed loudly until he punched the correct call number for his nurse. Within moments a middle-aged woman with a kind face wearing a light blue nurse's coat entered with a folder of papers, the 11 by 14s hanging out from its bottom.

Oh, crap! Emma thought. *Do I have to fill out all that junk?*

As if reading her mind, Dr. Aram hurried to enlighten them about the papers in the folder. "I have homework, as you call it, for you to do until I can see you again. It's important for the whole family to be a part of this. I want each of you, including you, Susie . . ." He paused to catch her eye and to ensure she was paying attention, ". . . to keep a log of any unusual behavior on Emma's part.

"I have to?" Susie whined. "That means I have to watch Emma night and day."

"You all do. There's a lot to look for. If Emma doesn't exhibit from among the lists of actions written here, then it may be something relatively easy to work with. We can only hope," he said, as he passed the packet of instructions to Anita. She dropped them into the depths of her big black bag.

His phone buzzed again and Dr. Aram said into it, "Please make an appointment with the Montfords for next week. Make it for . . ." he glanced at his watch ". . . make it for a forty-five-minute consult."

As he spoke to them about the things to look for in Emma's behavior, the sweet-faced nurse returned with the appointment time.

I wonder if my grandmother from England looked sweet like she does? Susie mused, while watching the grandmotherly nurse.

"See you next week and we'll look at your charts. Work hard on getting it done. It's necessary, young lady," Aram said to Susie, looking her in the eyes with his eyebrows arched.

I get it, already.

Dr. Aram held two sheets of paper in his hands, his head going back and forth between them like a spectator at a tennis match. He laid the papers on his desk and picked up the remaining two. Again the head swings as if comparing them. He laid the last two beside the first ones aligning them on his desk. "Amazing."

Bent over, he studied them again. "Well, they are all consistent." He swept his hand in front of him to indicate all of them. "You all did a good job with your homework." The killer smile flashed and the four Montfords returned it.

The mood in the room changed in an instant when the doctor announced, "It would seem Emma has a heightened awareness of sounds, smells, lights. Sometimes she is reclusive, wanting only to be alone, and other times she is vibrantly outgoing and social. At times she takes direction well; at others she seems confused and doesn't get it." He stopped and looked at his wide-eyed audience whose faces, once alight with hope, now wore fear.

"Your notes are quite telling." He slowly shook his head, his face sorrowful. "Emma is exhibiting signs of schizophrenia."

"No!" Emma wailed. "This can't be." Anita doubled over with her hands in tight fists against her designer shirt front.

"I'll be dad-gummed!" Susie said, using one of her mother's southernisms. "She not just being weird after all."

The doctor talked with them about his plan for counseling and explained the illness of schizophrenia to a greater degree, stopping often to ask Emma if she was all right. To demonstrate that yes, she could possibly have the illness, Emma's participation and answers varied enough to give them all pause and gave credence to Dr. Aram's diagnosis.

CHAPTER SIX

Anita was discussing the dinner menu with their cook the Friday afternoon after the Tuesday meeting with Dr. Aram. Madonna suggested chicken and Anita was saying, "Yes, your chicken piccata is without doubt the best I've ever eaten. All that lemony wine sauce with those big briny capers is just the perfect thing."

Anita turned in surprise as Emma, performing a half-skip, half-hop swept into the kitchen. "What on Earth are you doing, Emma?"

Bouncing on her toes, Emma announced, "I want hot dogs for dinner."

Madonna gasped and reached for the hem of her apron.

Anita, almost shattered, said, "What did you say?"

"I want hot dogs. I want hot dogs." Her voice got louder but that didn't disguise the sound of the little girl's voice tripping off Emma's tongue.

Anita shouted, "Susie, come here right now!"

Emma's eyes welled with tears and her sobs came fast and hard. "You, you, are scaring m-me," Emma stammered out in the same little girl's voice.

"What? What is it, Mom?" Susie's urgent voice preceded her into the kitchen. It did not block out the sounds of

46

Emma's distress however. She continued to stand with her hands by her sides, with tears streaming unchecked down her cheeks, mouth open and wailing.

"Is this the little girl you encountered before?" Anita asked Susie.

Listening for a couple of seconds, Susie moved to Emma. She put her arms around her and held her against her chest with Emma's head on her shoulder. "Julia?"

"They're being loud and angry," she said, pointing to Anita and Madonna, who wrung her apron in undisguised misery and dismay.

"They didn't mean it. It's okay, Julia. Let's go sit out by the pool." She led Julia away while Anita stood with her mouth open staring after them.

Poolside, Julia looked at the sky, at the palm trees at the far end of the pool, at the flowering plants in the yard. She seemed most enthralled with the red and orange birds of paradise blooms with their spear-like edges puncturing the green leaves from which they sprang. She ran about examining everything as if she'd never seen any of it before.

It came to Susie in a flash. *If she's Julia, she hasn't seen any of this before.*

Susie let her investigate all around the pool but drew the line when she asked if she could swim.

I don't know if she can swim. I'm not gonna be responsible for her getting in there and drowning.

Julia looked disappointed and began to trudge back to where Susie sat in a straight-backed lawn chair by a round metal and tempered glass table with three other chairs like it. Her dad had just bought the set at World Market. She plopped down and heaved a long sigh.

Susie said nothing and waited to see what Julia would do next. The strong afternoon sun beat down on them as it headed toward sunset. Susie wiped sweat from around her hairline with her forefinger and idly glanced at the residue as it spread to wet the entire end of her finger.

Lifting the heavy whitish-blonde hair off her neck, Emma remarked, "It's too hot out here. It must've been your bright idea to come out and roast in this heat, Susie."

"Come on, Emma. We've got to go talk to Mom right now." She grabbed Emma's hand and tried to pull her from her chair.

"Why?" Her voice was bright with surprise and uncertainty.

"You were that little kid, Julia, again just now."

Blue eyes wide, Emma repeated, "Julia? I was?"

"You sure were. Mom and Madonna must've said something to hurt your feelings because you were crying. When I got there, you said they were mad and yelling at you. You also said they were scaring you."

"Jesus Christ!" Emma leaped from the chair, snatched a pool noodle from the adjacent table top and threw it as far into the pool as her strength allowed, its yellow length flashing in the afternoon sun. She whirled and faced Susie. "I don't remember *any* of it. Dammit, Susie, what am I going to do?"

Susie gave an elaborate shrug. "Beats me. Let's go see what Mom says."

Their mom stood at the glass door watching them and moved aside as they entered the kitchen.

"It's me, Mom," Emma said, her voice breaking in anger. "I guess you can't tell unless I say or do something."

"Come here, honey." Anita held out her arms and Emma scooted into them. She laid her head against her mom's breasts and slipped her arms around her waist. They stood, swaying together, Anita offering comfort to her child, who appeared to sorely need it. Susie joined them, stretching her arms to encompass both. The three stood holding on to each other for a long minute while Madonna turned the chicken in the pan and added capers and white wine to the lemon sauce.

Alone together in their bedroom, "If that's how someone with schizophrenia acts, I sure don't want it," Anita told her husband.

"I'm not certain it is that," Jenkins said as he unbuttoned his shirt. He sat on the cream silk coverlet and bent over to unlace and remove his shoes and socks. Standing, he slipped his trousers down and off. "I need to see more of her behavior to be sure. At times she acts bizarre, as if she is unaware of anyone or anything around her."

"Yes, I think the kids call it "spacing out" or "zoning," and she does seem to have a different personality during those episodes." Anita put her white slacks and the sleeveless blouse covered in red and orange full-blown cabbage roses into the hamper used for soiled clothing. She floated a short diaphanous, sky-blue nightgown over her head and down her body.

"Cor, you are such a sexy bird," Jenkins said, as he reached for her.

Together, the family had two additional visits with Dr. Aram and Emma had one with him alone. While they liked the doctor a lot and each thought him to be a good counselor, they discussed his diagnosis and felt Emma's problem to be something other than schizophrenia. All were determined to get a true diagnosis, and so the search for the right doctor continued.

The Montford family sat in the waiting room of Dr. Irit Levy's elegant Wilshire Boulevard office. Susie ran her hand over the teal fabric of the settee on which she'd chosen to sit. She watched the color change from dark to light as she swept her hand in opposite directions. "Sweet," she said, nodding in approval.

Jenkins Montford stood and paced along the wall opposite the windows which faced the tops of the palm trees lazily waving their fronds. He didn't look at the palm trees, or even the windows. His eyes fastened on the diplomas and certificates prominently displayed and hanging in tasteful sets of threes. He saw Dr. Levy graduated from Yale with a degree in Behavioral Sciences. She'd gone on to do graduate work and to graduate from Harvard with a Masters' degree in one year, based on the dates of her Yale graduation.

Dr. Levy is one smart bird," he allowed, lapsing back into the Cockney dialect he learned in London after leaving his proper upbringing. "She graduated from Yale in four years and got her Masters from Harvard in one additional year."

"How encouraging," Anita said. "Where'd she go next?"

"She must've been trying to decide where she wanted to spend the next four years of med school because she went back to Yale."

She spent four years at Yale, went to Harvard for a masters' and then went back to Yale for medical school?"

"Her degree in psychiatry is from Yale."

The girls watched this interchange between their parents. "Good gosh, how many years does it take to be a doctor, anyway?" Susie asked, frowning and shrugging at Emma.

Emma hadn't spoken since they left the car parked in the public underground garage and walked the two blocks up Wilshire to Dr. Levy's office. She didn't speak now.

"She still wasn't finished. She had a residency program to do before she could become a full-fledged doctor," her dad said.

"This resi . . ." She stopped and tried again. ". . . resitcy program takes how long?"

Laughing, Anita said, "It's a *residency* program, sweetie. And it takes another four years."

"Where did she do it?" a quiet voice asked.

They all looked at Emma. Susie threw an arm around her neck in a mock choke-hold. "Glad you could make it, Emma!" she laughed. "Good to have you with us."

There was no response,

"Behave, Susie," her mom reprimanded.

Jenkins looked at his troubled daughter and gently said, "It says on this one," he pointed to a certificate farther down the wall," she did her residency at UCLA. So she's spent some time out here. That'll make it easier to talk with her since we'll at least have knowledge of the area in common."

A perky young woman who looked like a movie star with her tanned skin, her golden curls, and a dynamite figure appeared without noise, even though she wore perilously tall high heels. The thick, low-pile carpet absorbed any sound she may have made. "Doctor Levy will see you now. Follow me, please," she invited with a wide, white-toothed smile.

Anita and Emma rose from their chairs. Emma hung back, but Anita took her arm and said, "Come on, Emma. We'll all be together. We can do this." Susie was already at the door waiting to peer inside.

"I don't think I want to go in there. Maybe we should just go home," Emma said to Anita.

That's strange. Her voice sounds so young. This isn't the way Emma normally sounds, Anita thought. *Is it*

Julia? Still holding Emma's arm, Anita led her forward to the entrance to the doctor's inner office.

The office assistant opened the heavy mahogany door and held it open as the Montfords entered with Jenkins leading the way.

A woman stood behind a surprisingly small open desk that looked more like a table. It appeared to be cherry wood. The doctor was small, probably five feet, and quite thin. Impeccably dressed in sensible low heels, a knee length navy pencil skirt and ivory long-sleeved blouse, she wore her hair, a mass of dark curls, in an up-do swept to the back of her head.

Moving to the front of the group of four, Anita offered her hand to the doctor, who walked around the end of the desk to take it. Looking only at Anita, she said, "Mrs. Montford, I'm Doctor Irit Levy."

Remember to be relaxed and pleasant, Anita thought as she clasped the doctor's small fingers in hers.

Doctor Levy took her eyes from Anita's and offered her hand to Jenkins, whose large hand enveloped hers in a single shake.

"Hello." The doctor scrutinized Jenkins' face and movements as he inclined his head, almost a gallant bow. "My pleasure." He straightened, removed his hand from hers and turned to the girls who stood waiting.

Dr. Levy approached the girls. "Glad to meet you. You're Susie, I see."

Susie raised her eyebrows.

"No, I'm not psychic. I know there are two girls in the family and you appear to be the youngest." Dipping her head toward her shoulder, her lips still spread in laughter, she greeted Emma.

"Welcome, Emma. You and I . . ." she turned and her right hand swept the room, ". . . and, indeed, all of us, will learn a lot about each other as we find out what is happening with you. Okay?"

Emma's eyes were glassy as she looked down at her fidgeting hands. She raised her head and looked out the window at the brilliant azure sky dotted with green tree tops. Her chest lifted with the deep breath she drew into her lungs. Exhaling at a turtle's pace, she finally said, "I hope you can fix me."

Dr. Levy strained to hear her. "Well, we're going to work hard at this." The doctor smiled again, alabaster teeth gleaming as she beamed confidence at each Montford. "Now, all of you take seats and we'll get to know each other." She took a seat in the circle of chairs spaced about a foot apart to the right of the table desk. The Montfords followed, each settling into a comfortable chair with a deep seat and wide arm rests. Emma sat beside the doctor.

"So, just to be certain," the doctor began, "you *have* seen two other doctors before coming to me?"

"Yes, we have," Anita confirmed. "I would think there is nothing wrong with that. In this case, we are getting, with you, a *third* opinion."

Levy assessed Anita and replied, "The third time is often the charm. Let us hope that is our result."

Her parents exchanged startled glances when Emma announced, "I am so relieved. I have a good feeling about this, Dr. Levy, and if talking with you will help with my problem, then I'm all for it."

Jenkins' grin spread across his face. *Ah, Emma sounds so adult.* Then he sobered with the thought: *She may not be Emma.*

"Then we're half way there, Emma." Dr. Levy laid her hand on Emma's forearm. "You feeling free to talk will make the whole process easier for all of us."

Levy placed a cream-colored throw pillow behind her back. "This is the price I pay for being child-sized." She raised a rueful eyebrow.

Addressing Anita, she started the session. "When you called, you indicated Emma spoke in more than one voice and she was unaware of what she said or did at those times."

"That's right."

"I want to hear about that from all of you. But first, I want to find out about you as a family." Nodding to Jenkins, she said, "Mr. Montford, tell me about your job."

Jenkins crossed his legs and smoothed the seam in his trousers. He looked at Dr. Levy and spoke with assurance. "I sell goods and services to foreign countries that help them compete, and succeed, in the economics of the marketplace. In other words, it keeps these countries from always having their hands out, seeking aid from the US, the UK, and the rest of the West."

"Then you are away from the family at times. How often are you away?"

"Oh, about half the time, I'd say." He looked at Anita for confirmation. She nodded.

Turning her gaze on Anita, Dr. Levy asked. "Mrs. Montford, do you work?"

"Yes."

"What is it that you do?"

"I'm an actress, or as is preferred now—an actor."

"I see. I thought I perhaps recognized you. Are you often out of town while filming?"

"No. Not often. Mainly I work on the lot or close by."

"So, you are with the girls more than your husband?"

"Yes."

Levy looked from one parent to the other. "Who stays with the girls when you are both away?"

"A live-in housekeeper. She prepares their meals and sees to the upkeep of the house," Anita responded.

"Her name is Madonna and she's a great cook!" Susie added. Seeing the frown her mom leveled at her, she was quick to add, "Sorry, Mom. I'll be quiet now."

"Tell me more about your family and how your routines work."

Continuing with her curt answers, which bordered on the defensive, Anita said. "Javier is my driver. He usually takes me to the set and returns to get me after the filming is finished for the day. That means he's available to take the girls wherever they need to be."

"That's good. How about the girls' grandparents? Are they a regular part of their lives?"

"I'm afraid not," Jenkins answered, as he uncrossed his legs and re-crossed them in the opposite direction, "My parents have long been deceased and are buried in the churchyard of our family's small church in Yorkshire, England." He gestured to Anita.

Anita said, "My parents were killed in an automobile accident when the girls were too small to remember them. Neither Jenkins nor I have any siblings, so Emma and Susie have no other close relatives."

"It's your immediate family—you four—plus Madonna and Javier, who make up your every-day world. These five are the ones Emma is with most of the time now and the most likely to notice anything different. Am I correct?"

Nodding and murmuring "Yes," the Montfords agreed.

Levy swept her eyes from Anita to Susie, who sat beside her mother. "Susie, do you think either Madonna or Javier have witnessed Emma when she is speaking or acting differently?"

Susie's eyes narrowed and a line appeared between them as she gazed into space. "Not that I can remember."

Addressing the parents, the doctor asked, "Have either of you seen Emma when she didn't seem herself?"

Glancing at each other again, Jenkins said "No," while Anita nodded, her burnished gold curls in artistic disarray. "Yes. Once," she replied.

"Susie, you and your mom are the only ones in the home that have."

Interrupting Levy and seeking Anita's eyes, Susie responded. "Oh, we need to count Madonna. I remember now she did see Emma the same time you did, Mom—that time in the kitchen when Emma was Julia."

Levy nodded. "Okay. With Emma's permission . . ." she stopped and looked to Emma, who nodded in return, ". . . I'll ask you to tell me what you've seen. You don't have to tell the whole circumstances, just who Emma appeared to be, if you were able to ascertain that."

Squirming a bit in her seat so she was an inch or two closer to Emma, Susie said, "I really don't know who, or how many, I've seen. At first I thought Emma was just being goofy. There were a couple of different times when her voice definitely didn't sound like her. She didn't act like herself then, either." Susie looked at Emma, her eyes asking her forgiveness. Tearing her gaze from Emma, she finished, "I think I'd better think about this first, and make sure I have everything straight in my head, before I get it all wrong. I don't want to tell you something that isn't right."

"All right. That's fine, Susie. We'll find out more next time." She turned to the quiet girl beside her. "Emma, how are you feeling about this? Is there anything you'd like to say?" She leaned out from her seat to catch Emma's eye. "I'd really like to hear your thoughts today."

"Well, I don't know when I do these things, so I just take Susie's word for it. I know Susie wouldn't lie to me." Her chin dimpled and wavered, "At least not about something like this."

Levy studied Susie. At last she spoke. "No. I believe you're right, Emma."

She looked at the simple school room clock on the wall. The Montford family's time was up. As they prepared to leave, Dr. Levy hit a button on her intercom.

"Mindy, can we squeeze in an hour tomorrow for the Montfords?" She paused but a moment. "Yes, all four." She listened, sitting erect with her navy heel-shod feet placed primly together below her desk. "Good. I don't mind. We'll manage it. Thanks, Mindy."

She remained seated and looked up at Anita and Jenkins who stood ready to go. Anita's big black bag dangled from her shoulder.

"I do need to see you as a family again as soon as possible. I understand you have to leave right away to return to China, Mr. Montford. I can squeeze you in for an hour tomorrow after my regular office hours at five."

Jenkins looked at Anita for confirmation. She said, "Yes, we can do that. I'll have to call the director and see what they can do to rearrange the scenes I'm in that are on the schedule for late tomorrow afternoon. I don't think it will be a problem."

Dr. Levy stood and shook hands with first Anita and then Jenkins. "Then I'll see you tomorrow at five."

CHAPTER SEVEN

The Montfords were silent as they left Dr. Levy's office and walked to their car. As Jenkins pulled out into the busy Wilshire Boulevard traffic, Anita looked straight ahead and each girl looked out her side window. Jenkins turned off Wilshire onto North Virgil. Susie slipped her hand into Emma's and it remained there as the road turned into Hillhurst Avenue. She knew they were close to home now, but Emma still clasped her hand. They crossed Los Feliz Boulevard and began to climb the twisting road into their neighborhood.

Emma let go of Susie's hand. Leaning forward as far as her seatbelt would allow, she announced, "That wasn't so bad. Dr. Levy may be able to help me."

Loss shot through Susie. Emotions battled within her. She was Emma's companion and now it seemed she was her caretaker. She wasn't sure how she would feel about Emma spilling her guts to someone else.

It was such an unexpected statement from Emma that her parents began talking as one. Jenkins took the narrow road with homes built right to the edge more quickly than he should, often scraping a curb as he dodged approaching cars.

"My daughter is finally talking and she's not afraid to do it," Jenkins declared, parking the car in their driveway.

"Yay, Emma!" Susie said, jabbing Emma's arm with her elbow. Then everyone spilled out and hurried into their home, except for Jenkins. He went to the right front tire to make sure he hadn't harmed it with his reckless driving. He found it scarred, but functional.

"Girls, I told Madonna not to make dinner tonight, so go to the bathroom and wash your hands. Then come help me put sandwich makings on the table. We'll talk while we eat." Anita set her shoulder bag on the hall table and headed to the kitchen.

She thought Emma seemed to be acting normal. Normal for the real Emma, that is. Jenkins entered as Anita watched the girls head down the hall to their bathroom. She put her arms around his neck and he swept her into his arms. He kissed her long and deep. "I at least have some hope now, my love."

"Me, too."

Sitting around the long bar in their kitchen, the momentum carried them through making their sandwiches. They split thick crusty rolls, and placed mounds of ham, turkey, cheese, lettuce, and tomatoes inside. Sweet potato chips spilled from the bag as eager hands reached for them. A plate of fresh fruit slices glistened in the center of the bar. Susie swigged her coke and Emma sipped her orange drink while their parents shared a bottle of Pinot Grigio.

Nibbling on an apple slice, Anita spoke around it. "Well, I thought, on the whole, the meeting went well."

Susie chimed in, "Yeah, I kinda liked the doctor. I just hope she can do what she thinks she can."

Looking closely at his older daughter, Jenkins asked. "What did you think, Emma?"

Emma had the entire top of the twelve-ounce bottle of orange drink in her mouth. She drank it as would a small child, with her lips sealed around the tip. She set it down and picked up a sweet potato chip and examined it, turning it over in her hands and pinching off a flake.

"Emma." Jenkins repeated. No answer. He raised his voice. "Emma!"

Busy picking the tomatoes out of her sandwich, Emma seemed to not notice when Jenkins reached over and laid his hand on her arm. "Emma. Answer me!" he demanded.

Susie sat with her sandwich raised, her eyes wide, and watched the interplay. She knew it wasn't Emma her dad was speaking to.

Finally looking up at him, her eyes wide and guileless, Emma answered him confidently. "Emma can't talk right now. She's gone for a while." She sounded like a much younger child.

"Who are you?" Anita asked, her voice shaking with every word.

"I'm Julia," she said, irritated, and her tone saying, "What's the matter with you. Don't you know who I am?"

"See, I told you!" Susie exclaimed.

Anita turned her trembling mouth to Susie. "How long will this last?"

Julia—Emma—took a bite of her sandwich, placed the end of her drink bottle in her mouth, and washed it down.

"I'm not sure. None of them have lasted long. Remember she came back to herself at the pool after a few minutes out there. I think she'll be all right soon."

Emma slumped and suddenly began to rapidly blink her eyes, after which she glared at them. "Why are you all looking at me like that?"

Anita looked at her, love and pity showing in her eyes and in the lines of her face.

"Oh no, I did it again, didn't I?"

"Yep. I'm sorry, Emma." Susie leaned into her and gave her a one-armed hug.

"What did I do?" Her face was full of anguish.

"You were that little kid Julia again."

"The six-year-old girl?" Emma asked. Her voice rose as fear and dismay set in.

"Uh-huh."

Emma closed her eyes so tightly her long eyelashes almost disappeared. They all watched her as she slid from her stool. Her eyes popped open and her lips curled. She looked around the dining area as if seeing it for the first time.

"Well, shit!" she vehemently said. "What's going on here?"

The three stared at her in horror. The voice coming from Emma sounded like a young teen boy.

"What you looking at? You ain't never seen me before?" The voice chuckled using Emma's mouth. Looking at Jenkins flushed face, he vowed, "Ya better get used to it, Pops, because I'm gonna hang around here to keep an eye on my girl Emma." He winked at Anita, causing her to jerk back in alarm, recoiling from that as much as from the words coming from her daughter's mouth.

Her voice surprised out of her, Susie quickly regained it. "What's your name?"

"Ralph." He looked Susie up and down. "Hey, you're pretty hot. Ya wanta be my girl?"

While her parents sat on their stools perfectly still with their lips parted and hanging on every word, Susie took her time responding to Ralph. "Maybe. Let's first see how good you are to Emma."

"I'm always good to Emma. I'm going to take good care of her. Just wait and see."

He looked at the food spread before him. "What have we got here? Sandwiches and chips? Great! I'm starving."

Still standing, Ralph took a bite of Emma's sandwich and chewed it quickly. He opened his mouth and took another bite, chewing it with his mouth open while shoving in several potato chips. He paid no attention to the three who sat mesmerized, watching him as he took yet another bite of the sandwich. As it touched his lips, Ralph ducked his head and shook it as if slinging water from Emma's long hair after surfacing in the pool.

"What?" Emma asked, looking at them over the bun bursting with meats and lettuce. "Everybody is staring at me."

"It happened again, Emma." Susie struggled to talk around the frog that had taken up residence in her throat. It came out in halting jerks, far from her usual exuberance. "I'm so, so sorry."

"What did you see? Did I do something crazy?" She laid the sandwich on her plate.

Her parents and her sister all looked uncomfortable, as if trying to think of something to say. Finally, Susie spoke. "I don't know why Julia came, but she was first. She seemed happy. Things were going fine, except it was really weird. Then Ralph came. I think Ralph came because you got upset when you found out Julia had been here." She paused while everyone gave her their attention. She shrugged her shoulders. "I don't know if any of that's true, but it makes sense to me."

"It could be, Susie," Anita allowed. "I certainly don't have any kind of explanation of why two completely different personalities—I guess they are called personalities— came one right after the other."

"Well, Mom, at least now you've seen what it's like." She looked up at Jenkins. "You too, Dad." Her voice broke as she whispered, "Everybody knows but me."

She regarded each of her family members. "I guess you think I'm crazy, huh?"

A stern expression firmly in place, Jenkins replied, "Not at all, Emma. We're just beginning to see whatever is causing these incidents. We have a lot to learn, but you are *not* crazy!"

Emma asked meekly, "Am I still me?"

Anita slid off her stool and rushed around the bar. She held Emma's head against her bosom, stroking her bright blonde hair. "Of course you are still you, sweetie."

"Will I ever get better?"

Jenkins left his stool and laid a hand on Emma's shoulder. "Yes, you will, Emma. We must have faith that Dr. Levy will find out what's wrong. And, by God, we're going to resolve it. We all need to work on this together in whatever way we can."

Lying together as much to receive comfort as to assuage their mutual desire, Anita and Jenkins held each other, savoring the closeness shared after making love. Their legs entwined and they lay facing each other. Their bodies were sated, but not their minds. Feeling the need to discuss how Emma's condition could have begun, both were fearful of making a much-loved spouse angry.

Jenkins thought *it has to be said, so I guess I'd better start.* Laying his head farther back on his pillow allowed him to see Anita's eyes as the big palm tree outside their window played shadows and light across her face.

"I don't know how to say this, my darling, but is there any chance that while I was away one of the staff here may have either beaten Emma or locked her away at times? Or done anything else you can think of? Anything that might have contributed to her needing a rescuer in the form of another personality?"

Gazing into the distance with eyes unfocused and seeing nothing, her thoughts whirred like helicopter blades. She brought her eyes back to her husband. "I don't think so. You'd think I'd know about that."

Jenkins gently asked, "Did you, perhaps without thinking during punishment for some infraction, strike her too hard or anything like that?"

Anita recoiled, pulling away until she was out of his arms and legs. "Of course I didn't, Monty! Why on earth would you ask me such a thing?"

"I'm sure Dr. Levy will ask you the same."

She fired back, "It didn't have to be that kind of abuse, Jenkins! It could've been sexual abuse. Did *you* ever sexually abuse Emma?"

"Dammit, Anita! You know I didn't!"

Anita brought her hands to her face. With the right, she rubbed her forehead. A bad headache was starting there. Slow and low, she added, "Monty, I never thought for one instant that you did, but I just . . . I had to ask."

"I expect the doctor will ask all of us these questions to see if anyone can shed some light on how this started."

Susie entered the kitchen yawning. Her dark blonde curls resembled a bird's nest and she still wore her pajamas which sagged comically in the seat. Anita sat at the bar drinking a cup of black coffee and eating an egg white omelet.

Susie took one look at the unappetizing fare. "I'm just gonna have some cereal." She yawned again and opened the pantry, searching through several boxes of cereal to find one she thought she might want to eat. *Anything's better than an egg white omelet!*

"Good morning to you too," Anita said around a bite of wheat toast.

"Oh, sorry, Mom." Her returned greeting was drowned out as she leaned into the big silver side by side refrigerator in search of milk. "Where's Dad?"

"He's out by the pool talking business. I guess it's a call from China. They want him back there now. He's trying

to stall for time so he can spend a couple more days here."
She took the last bite of the omelet and looked around.
"Where's Emma?"

"I think she's still asleep. You know what, Mom?"

"What?"

"I think this business makes her tired, because she
always sleeps well after she's suffered one."

"Hallelujah! At least there's one good thing to come out
of this."

Anita's sarcasm garnered a small laugh from Susie. She
slurped her cereal, turning her bowl up to drink the last
drops of milk.

"Susie!" her father exclaimed, as he entered the kitchen.
"You must stop that. You are old enough to be a young
lady now with responsibilities, so you must act like one.
No more turning up the bowl and drinking from it like a
puppy. I'm counting on you to behave as a grown up while
I'm away. You must help Emma and your mother, and you
can't do that if you are acting like a hooligan."

*That's your favorite word, Dad. I bet you were a hoo-
ligan when you were a kid. IF you ever were a kid.* "Yes,
Father," she said instead.

Jenkins sat at the bar. "Susie, I want you and Emma to
work together to try to remember any episodes she's had
on any subject at any time. As you remember them and
tell her about them, see if she remembers anything at all.
Keep track and write them down." He half-smiled. "That
should keep you busy and out of trouble until time to go
back to the doctor."

"Okay. I think I'll go check on Emma."

Anita called after her as she started down the hall, "Be
sure to pick up in your rooms so Madonna can clean them
today."

"Okay, already!"

Emma assumed she had no reason to get out of bed and lay propped against two pillows while she checked her emails on her laptop. Yes! There were emails from several of her friends. She clicked on Jessica's and began to read.

> Hi, Emma. We've all missed you this week. What's up with Sister Magdalene dragging you from class? I heard she really did take you to see Sister Mary Agnes. Did you get expelled? I know Susie hasn't been back, either. What happened????? Write me and let me know! I. Miss. You. Girl!!! Jessica

Awesome! They miss me.

Emma was opening another message when Susie rapped three times on her door before swinging it open and barging in. She flopped down on her stomach beside Emma and braced herself on her elbows. "Mom says we have to straighten up our rooms so Madonna can come in and clean them."

She looked all around Emma's room, her head swiveling from one neat corner to the next. "Crap! You hardly have anything to do. How do you keep your bedroom so neat?"

"I don't throw everything on the floor like you do."

"Now who would've ever thought of that?" She peered at the laptop screen. "Whatcha reading?"

"An email from Jessica."

"Boy, I'll bet she's wondering what's going on."

"True. I have to decide what I'm going to tell her. I imagine all of them are much the same, all wanting to know what's happening." She grinned at Susie. "Maybe I'll just write one answer and copy it to all of them."

"Makes sense to me," Susie agreed. "That's definitely what I'd do." She rolled onto her back and got up. "I guess

I'd better get a shower and get dressed. You and I gotta talk before our meeting with Dr. Levy this afternoon."

"Don't remind me," Emma said, as she put aside the laptop and got out of bed.

With both parents busying themselves after lunch, Susie and Emma cleared the table before finding a place for their talk. They went outside to a small patio under the jacaranda trees. Two benches were placed there for sitting and relaxing in the shade on a typical warm early fall afternoon. It was a perfect spot for quiet, but earnest, conversation.

Emma sat on a bench and curled her legs to the side. "Oh, I love it out here when the jacarandas are in bloom."

"Yeah. I love those purple flowers, but I sure don't like fishing them out of the pool."

Emma frowned and glared at Susie.

Susie hurried to say, "Jacarandas are nice and they make it really cool out here in the shade."

Emma's face morphed into a vicious-looking mask. "Jacarandas are nice. Jacarandas are nice," she mimicked in an older teen boy's voice. "Fuck the damned jacarandas!" She jumped up from the bench, arms swinging at her sides. "I'll just cut the god-damned trees down." She looked around. "Where's the ax?"

Susie stood with her brows drawn together in dismay and tried to make sense of what she was hearing.

Emma strode around the corner of the house, heading for the closed garage door. "I know it's in here somewhere. Just let me get my hands on it and those damned trees are dust."

Susie shot forward as if fired from a cannon. "Wait. Wait! Just wait a minute." She zipped in front of an Emma she didn't know and put her hand up like a traffic cop.

She said the first thing that popped into her head. "Let's don't chop the trees down right now. We'll never find that darned axe. Dad hid it so nobody could cut themselves with it."

"He's not *my* dad. He doesn't tell me what to do. If I want to cut the damned trees down, I will, and he can't stop me. Now, get out of my way so I can find the fucking ax."

In desperation, Susie tried to think of something to distract the person whose angry voice came from Emma's mouth. She could think of nothing that she thought might work so decided to return to the original topic in hopes of Emma returning.

"What's wrong with the jacarandas, anyway? Why would you want to cut them down? For instance, what makes them different from the eucalyptus trees?"

The barrage of questions seemed to confuse the person who acted and sounded like a young man. He looked from Susie to the jacaranda trees. Then his gaze swung to the eucalyptus trees before returning to Susie.

"What the fuck are you talking about?"

"Oh, let's forget about the trees. Let's talk about you."

The 'other' Emma opened his mouth, but Susie cut him off.

"Come on." She grabbed his hand and tugged. "Let's go sit by the pool and you can tell me all about you."

Thinking as fast as her legs were moving, she dragged Emma's alter personality toward the pool so quickly that she stumbled over her own feet. Catching her balance, she continued pulling the resisting alter until she pushed him into a canvas chair. She grabbed another nearby, pulled it up and sat so that their knees were almost touching.

"Now, tell me about you. You sound older than Ralph."

"Damned right. I'm Sam. That piece-of-shit Ralph is just a hanger-on. When I get rid of that bitch Emma, I may just get rid of him too."

Even with the warm sun beating down, Susie shook with the chill that rushed through her.

"Sam, I think you need to be careful. You wouldn't want to do anything to get in trouble, would you?"

Emma's blue eyes took on a hard glint as Sam appraised Susie. In a silky voice, he asked, "Are you friend or foe? What difference is it to you what I do?"

Unsure how to answer, Susie thought as quickly as she could. *I know I need to stay out of this, but I've got to answer him.*

"I just want you to be safe, Sam."

Emma's face split with a malicious smile. "Safe, huh? It's Emma you should worry about." Sam held the smile before it began to fade. With the smile gone, Emma's body relaxed. She briefly closed her eyes, the eyelids jumping as her eyes moved beneath them before becoming still.

Opening her eyes she asked, "What are you doing?"

Susie jerked her head in surprise and let out the huge sigh she didn't realize she was holding. "Oh, dear God, Emma, you scared the crap out of me. I didn't know who you were, but I was trying to figure out what I could say to you to keep you from cutting down the jacaranda trees."

Emma's face paled in the afternoon sunlight. "What?"

"Yeah, you got pissed about something and said you were gonna cut them down."

"What happened?" Emma pushed back her canvas chair and stood. She lowered her head, as if she might find answers in the tiles surrounding the pool and began to pace.

"You just out-of-the-blue turned into somebody else and got mad. I'm not sure if it was Sam all along, but he's who we ended up with until just now. I can't think of anything to cause it except we were talking about the purple blooms on the Jacarandas and how pretty they are."

"Hmmm, something's there, Susie. It tells me I should know about this." She shook her head. "But, I can't think what it might be." She returned to her seat and sat down.

"You okay?" Susie's face revealed worry and compassion.

"We started out to talk about what you've noticed me doing when it really wasn't me, right?"

"Yes. That's what we came outside to do." Susie sat again in her chair, which she had placed ninety degrees to Emma's. "We can still do that."

"Okay," Emma said. "Tell me everything you can think of." She braced on the chair's arms and leaned toward Susie, as if waiting for the whistle to blow for the start of a race.

Susie looked at the tense set of Emma's shoulders and knew this was going to be hard for Emma to hear. "Well, let's see," she began. "There was the time you talked about us staying away from the gardeners."

"And I spoke with a deep voice."

"Yes. And you know about ordering the coke at Griffith Park when you told me you were Julia."

"That time you said I sounded like a little girl?"

"Yes, you did. When you are Ralph, you sound just like one of the boys from school with your voice cracking. By the way, Ralph wants me to be his girlfriend." Susie shook with a fit of giggles.

"Stop it, Susie! We're supposed to be serious so I can know what I say and do when one of these other people take over, or whatever they do."

"Well, I thought you wanted to know everything. Dang, Emma, don't get so uptight. I'm just telling you what I've seen or heard when I *know* it's not you."

"For sure," Emma answered, unconsciously using the valley girl talk she claimed to dislike.

Susie leaned against the back of the chair with her arms crossed in front of her chest. "I've seen Julia a few times, but I didn't know it then. She just acts like a little kid. She skips along. She stops and looks at flowers and stuff like bugs. She said 'Yes, ma'am' to Jessica, for Pete's sake."

"Oh, no," Emma groaned.

"I'm sorry. I should've asked you what was going on when you did that stupid stuff, but I just thought you were being stupid!" Susie's lips turned down and she hung her head, looking at her hands turning to fists in her lap.

Emma stood and pulled her into a hug. "You couldn't know, Susie. It's all right. You have to know I don't blame you."

Susie smiled at her sister, her lower lip trembling so it was a little lop-sided. "Thanks, Emma. You know, you really are my best friend, and I love you."

"Yes, I know. And I love you, too."

The Montfords arrived to find Mindy on her way out at the close of the day's work. Dr. Levy met them and invited them into her office.

"Good afternoon. Please take a seat and we'll get started." She waited for them to settle down, offering the customary pleasantries about the weather and traffic. Then the session began.

"The first thing I want to do is to talk with you privately, Mr. Montford, since you will soon be leaving the country. We'll meet in the small conference room and everyone else can stay in here. We won't be gone long."

She led him to the conference room and motioned to one of two chairs placed at a bistro-sized round table.

Jenkins sat, leaned back and crossed his legs. He appeared to be quite at ease.

Dr. Levy sat opposite him. Her tone and demeanor became quite professional and straight-forward as she addressed Jenkins.

"As I begin my sessions with Emma, I'll learn more and more about what she remembers." Her deep brown eyes drilled his before she spoke again. "Normally I wouldn't be so abrupt, but with this possibly being the last time I see you for quite some time, I have to ask you now. Remember, this is privileged information and critical to getting to the cause of Emma's strange behavior. In that regard, I ask you to be completely honest in your answers." Pausing for only a single heartbeat, she threw back her head and asked her first question. "Have you abused Emma in any way? Emotional abuse? Physical abuse? Or sexual abuse of any kind?"

Jenkins didn't break eye contact. "I expected that question. It's only right you should ask it. Anita and I discussed this last night. My answer was then, and is now, no. No, not in any way did I abuse my daughter."

"Did you have any suspicion at all that Emma was exhibiting signs of more than one personality?"

"None at all. Whenever I was home, she seemed to be her usual self."

Dr. Levy looked down at her notes. Looking up again, she affirmed, "Something happened to Emma to get her to this state. Eventually she will start to remember flashbacks of whatever happened in whatever form it took place. We hope the identity of the responsible person will be revealed." Again, she held his eyes with hers for several moments. Rising she said, "Thank you Mr. Montford. You can rejoin your family now and please ask Anita to come in."

Taking but a few minutes, she asked the same questions of Anita, searching for some measure of strength or weakness on the mother's part.

"I don't know anything. I didn't see anything. I wasn't aware of this strange behavior from my daughter," Anita said in a steadily rising voice. "Don't you think I would've done something if I had known what was happening?" Her tone was frosty enough to form icicles.

Dr. Levy's impression was Anita truly didn't know anything but was resentful that anyone might suspect she did. *I'll have to choose my words with this one. I think she feels guilty that she didn't see or suspect anything. I wonder why.* "I should think so," she answered. "Thank you, and now let's get back to Emma."

The rest of the session was devoted to completing a mandatory questionnaire designed to diagnose borderline personality and major depressive disorders as well as all the dissociative disorders. It took about forty-five minutes to complete with Emma. Three answers from which to choose were: "Yes," "No," and "Unsure." Emma had "Yes" answers on questions regarding her physical symptoms, like headaches, but had predominately "Unsure" answers to emotional symptoms, like hurting herself and thoughts of suicide, to lost time she couldn't account for, to objects she possessed that she didn't recall buying or receiving. Included was a section on abuse to determine if she had been sexually abused, a common occurrence in those diagnosed with Dissociative Identity Disorder, commonly referred to as DID, which Dr. Levy was beginning to suspect the diagnosis would be. From Emma's answers, Dr. Levy would ascertain an estimate based on her experiences with other clients whether in-depth sessions with Emma were called for. Before even seeing her answers, she expected they were.

Dr. Levy told Susie that she would need to speak with her later, but for now she didn't want what Susie knew to in any way color her findings from Emma's answers. They scheduled Emma's first solo appointment for the following Monday and they all departed the building together.

That evening the Montfords had dinner consisting of a simple green salad and a baked pasta dish oozing creamy soft cheeses Madonna made from scratch using one of her secret family recipes. It was a favorite, and all ate heartily, even Emma, who had gone through the exhaustive interview which delved into her memory and found it almost depleted. Dr. Levy told Emma at the end of the session not to worry about the 'I don't know' answers because they would find them during the therapy sessions. Emma clung to that with a hopeful heart.

CHAPTER EIGHT

It was nearing quiet time before bed and the girls decided to burn off some energy in the pool. The setting sun sent billows of gold into the clear water as Susie dove in. She surfaced just as Emma, in the deep end, threw the basketball-size pool ball into the air and then batted it at Susie on its way down. The force sent it ricocheting off the back of Susie's head. She yelped and dove down deep below the surface. She swam away but quickly turned around and rose up between Emma's legs, lifting her high and then dumping her face first into the water. She came up coughing and spitting.

"No more! No more. I give," Emma spluttered.

"All right then," Susie crowed. "Tell me I'm the boss of this pool!"

"I said I give."

"And I said for you to tell me I'm the boss of this pool."

Emma's face changed dramatically. It now wore an ugly scowl.

"You'll eat shit and drown before I'll tell you that. You're a pain in the ass like Miss Pollyanna Perfect."

Thinking fast, Susie asked with dread growing, "Who are you? What's your name?"

Emma's body seemed to grow as she inhaled and took on the persona of a teen boy puffing out his chest. "I'm Sam. You know who I am."

"Hi, Sam. Sure, I remember. I'm Susie. You're a pretty big guy. How old did you say you were?"

"I'm eighteen. And one of these days Miss Goody Two Shoes is going to know that she's not the most important person on earth." The words coming from Emma's mouth were a growl, spoken with contempt, and sounded just like a disgusted teenage boy.

"Wow! You sound mean." Susie treaded water, waiting.

"Nah, I'm just tired of this bitch. I'm ready to be the leader."

A question was forming in Susie's mind, but she never got to ask Sam what he meant about being the leader.

"Okay girls, time to come in and get showers," Anita called from the open doorway.

"Coming," Susie yelled back. *This guy scares me. I need to find out more about him. You've got lousy timing, Mom.*

"Are you coming with me, Sam?" She turned to look at Sam who was occupying her sister's body.

"Who's Sam?" Emma asked, holding on to the side of the pool and narrowing her eyes at Susie, even though the sun wasn't shining into them.

"Nobody. I'm just messing with you."

Susie flipped from her back to her left side, stayed there about a minute, and flipped onto her right side. She did this again and again. She looked at the large red numerals on her digital alarm clock. It read 2:18 AM.

She wondered if she was ever going to go to sleep, but couldn't stop thinking about Emma. Tired of this whole thing already, she simply could not tell Emma about Sam this afternoon in the pool and make her cry again.

She knew they were at the very beginning of the journey and they were all required to travel it with Emma. That meant that at any time she, and her mom and dad, could witness any one of the parts taking over Emma's body and thought processes. Since the two meetings they'd had with Dr. Levy where they learned more about the illness, they had all seen some other part come forward. And now they could no longer think it was due to Emma being goofy.

Susie flipped to her back and squeezed her eyes shut, thinking she couldn't even begin to guess how this was all going to come together and how it would turn out in the end. But, sleep was necessary so she took long, deep breaths and eased them out while she counted to ten. In less than a minute she was forgetting to count, her breathing returned to normal, and she slept.

It was nearing ten o'clock the next morning when Emma tapped on Susie's bedroom door. Receiving no response, she went in and perched on the bed beside Susie. She shook her shoulder and Susie jerked awake.

"It's time to wake up, sleepy-head!"

"What time is it?"

"Ten o'clock."

"Darn. I'd planned to send emails to a bunch of my friends this morning. Skipping school is great, and I want to rub it in that I'm doing it and they're not." She giggled. It was a nasty little laugh, and was *so* Susie.

"You can do that later. Come on, let's get something to eat."

Susie filled a bowl with raisin bran and added milk. Emma made herself a tomato and avocado sandwich on wheat raisin bread. Susie sat at the bar and lifted up a big spoonful of cereal. She was shoveling it into her mouth when Emma set her plate on the bar and climbed onto the tall chair. Tomato and avocado slices hung out all around the rim of the bread. Plus, it was *raisin* bread. Susie drew in breath, gasping and almost choking on her mouthful of cereal. She started violently coughing and Emma got up and smacked her hard between her shoulder blades.

"Are you okay?" Emma pounded her back again.

Attempting to get her coughing under control, Susie cleared her throat a last time. "Yeah, I guess so." *What am I going to say to her about that sandwich? Good gosh, she hates raisins.*

Emma returned to her seat and stared down at her sandwich. "What is this? I don't eat this stuff." She looked around the kitchen as if searching for someone who could have made it for her. Susie knew it wasn't Emma who made the sandwich but didn't know which part hidden inside her did.

"What's going on, Susie? What's happening to me? I'd never eat avocado. Never! Is this one of those things I do when it's not me?"

"Uh, yeah. I guess."

"Then I'm ready to get to work with Dr. Levy. I've got to do something!"

"All right. But don't think about that now. Let's get you something to eat." She hopped off her chair and rummaged in the pantry. She held up a box of Honey Nut Cheerios®. "How about a bowl of these?"

"Okay." Emma took the box of cereal and set it on the bar, got a bowl from the cabinet and milk from the refrigerator, and set it down by the Cheerios. Susie picked up her bowl and looked down the hall to be sure no one was watching. She giggled and dashed to the sink where she tipped the cereal into the garbage disposal and rinsed it down.

"There. That was too soggy. Hey, Emma, hand me the Raisin Bran before you sit down. Now, we'll both have fresh cereal."

As the girls sat together eating, Susie continued, "Aren't we the luckiest kids in the world? We don't even have to go to school! Let's ask Mom if her chauffeur can take us shopping. We can goof off at the mall . . ."

"Ah, that's just what we want to talk with you about," their dad interrupted. Jenkins appeared behind them with Anita at his side. "Finish your cereal, girls, so we can talk."

"They're not going to eat, Jenkins. They're more interested in what we want to tell them." Anita moved to the bar to stand behind her daughters. She put an arm around each girl's outer shoulder. "Your dad and I've been talking about how you're going to be educated." She turned Susie's shoulder so she faced her. "I meant it, Susie, when I said you wouldn't be going to that school if Emma couldn't. So, we had to come up with another plan."

Jenkins went around the end of the high bar table and stood facing them on the other side.

"We looked at all kinds of options and the one we think will work the best is for you to have a tutor and be homeschooled."

"Yes, at least for the time being," Anita affirmed.

"Mo-om!" Susie wailed. "I'll never see my friends!"

"Who was that who was just now saying she was lucky not to have to go to school?" A raised eyebrow accompanied Jenkins' question.

"That's different, Dad. I meant for *now*. Of course, I know I'll have to go back to school some time."

"That's the point, Susie," her mom said. "*You* could go back to school, but Emma can't. At least at this time. Right?"

"Yeah, I guess not." Susie suddenly brightened, her wide smile in place, and elbowed Emma. "The Devil's Den has spoken and you can't go back because you called Sister Magdalene a bitch." She hung on Emma's shoulder and laughed. "You go, girl! I wish I'd been there to hear it."

"Calm down, Susie." Jenkins bent and looked into Susie's face. "We've made the decision and you *will* have classes here at home. You and Emma will start regular school classes perhaps as early as Monday."

Anita laid her hand against Emma's cheek. "And what do you think, sweetie?"

"As long as I get to have my sessions with Dr. Levy, I'm all for it. I don't want to get behind in my studies." She looked at Susie and pleaded, "Just say yes, Susie. I'd really like having classes with you."

"All right." Susie lifted her eyes from Emma's face and pinned her parents with her gaze. "If we have to." Her eyes returned to Emma and another huge grin dominated her face. "You still want to go shopping today?"

It was luck that the usually sharp Susie didn't pick up on the vibes emanating from her parents or she and Emma perhaps could've had a much bigger day than simply shopping at the mall. Relief was etched on both parents' faces. They were likely so pleased to not have an obstinate rebellion against homeschooling that they would've given the girls just about anything they wanted, *if* they'd asked.

The chauffeur drove the girls to the other side of the 101 into West Hollywood. There Javier pulled into the parking garage of The Grove, the highest-rated upscale shopping mall in the Los Angeles area. Javier's orders were to park the car and stay near the girls while they went from shop to shop. He did, watching them as they entered one of the trendy little stores specializing in the latest styles in teen clothing. Both exited with a bag each. Javier continued to watch from his spot in front of Barnes & Noble® as they boarded the trolley, its tracks weaving through the wide street that formed the center of the outside-entrance shopping mall. He decided to go inside to the coffee shop located on the second floor. From the outside balcony, he could see a good portion of the trolley's route.

Javier took a sip of his latte and set his cup on the table. He picked up a beignet and bit into it as the powdered sugar spilled down his black shirt front. Idly watching the people below, his attention was drawn to a group gathering outside one of the boutiques. Suddenly, there was pushing and shouting and he glimpsed Emma in the middle of the melee.

"Good God," he uttered, as he saw Emma swinging what looked like a pair of boots at the people trying to take them from her. Susie was being held back by a security guard as she tried to get to Emma.

Javier took two steps at a time down the stairs and burst out the door into the street. He sprinted as best he could around and through the curious onlookers until he stumbled to a stop by the second security guard, who had managed to restrain Emma with her hands behind her back.

"Javier!" Susie yelled, her body sagging with relief. "They think Emma was stealing the UGGs®. She just was not thinking and walked out the door with them in her hands. Tell them," she nodded to the security guards, "that we're with you and that you need to take us home."

Before Javier could say anything, Emma shrieked in a southern accent, "Leave me alone, you assholes! If I'd really wanted your damned shoes, you'd never have known I had them." She then kicked the boot that had fallen to the pavement during the tussle with the guard.

Javier raised his voice. "Be quiet, Miss Emma." To the security guard he said, "Sir, my name is Javier and I'm the chauffeur for these two kids. That's Susie over there," he indicated Susie with a sweep of his hand. "And, that's Emma." He pointed to her with his left forefinger. "I'm not sure what's going on, but I hope we can settle it quickly."

Reaching in his wallet, he brought out his drivers' license and attempted to hand it to the guard who held the still complaining Emma. "Let me go, damn you," she screeched as she tried to pull free, aiming a kick at his groin.

The guard deflected the kick with his hip and jerked his head in the direction of the store's door. "Let's go inside and get this straightened out."

The five muscled their way through the gawkers and entered a small room in the back of the store that contained an oval table and six chairs. Leaning forward with both hands flat on the table, Javier said, "I'm their driver and I know both of these girls. But, I don't know what is happening with Miss Emma. I've never seen her act this way before. I can't explain this strange behavior."

The guard bent down to Emma who sprawled in a chair with her legs stuck out before her. Her jaw was set, her face sullen. "What do you have to say for yourself, young lady?" Unresponsive, Emma glared at him.

Susie explained, "My sister sometimes gets these moods when she might not think straight, and then she gets angry when she is accused of doing something wrong. It's like she can't help it. But, she'll be fine in a few minutes. Can we just pay for the boots and go?"

Javier was quick to offer his help. "I'll be responsible for them and take them straight home."

The store manager entered while Susie was explaining Emma's actions. Now, he spoke. "The boots cost $160 plus tax. You'll have to pay for them before I can let you leave."

Susie opened her purse and sorted through a folded wad of bills. She peeled off $200 in twenties and slapped the bills on the table. "Keep the change."

During the ride home, Emma sat with her arms crossed in front of her chest and her face was furrowed with fury. She murmured to Susie, "Those sons-a-bitches can kiss my ass."

Susie's insides quaked. This was the longest any of Emma's episodes had lasted. She had to know. "Who are you?"

"Are you shittin' me? You been gittin' in the liquor cabinet? You know who I am."

Susie frowned. "Who?"

With her voice rising and the drawling getting lengthier, she turned her own frown on Susie. "I'm Christine! Are you stupid or somethin'?"

"Oh," was all Susie could think to say.

"I didn't want those friggin' boots, anyway. Why'd you give 'em money for 'em?" She frowned at Susie, her lovely face drawn into a mask of disgust.

"I was trying to keep you out of trouble, Em—I mean Christine." *God, I hope that doesn't set her off.*

It was too late. "You almost called me Emma. Don't call me that. I *ain't* Emma. Emma's a pretty nice kid, but then who wants a baby goat?" Christine brayed laughter at her own joke and punched Susie's upper arm.

From the driver's seat, Javier watched the interchange in the rear-view mirror. He sorrowfully shook his head.

"Okay, Christine."

Once home, Emma returned, pulling herself from whatever depth she had receded into when Christine came forward. Javier and Susie informed Jenkins and Anita about the incident, revealing as much as they knew. Emma hung on to a chair back and listened to what she had no idea she'd done.

Their father directed, "Susie and Emma, go to your rooms, and while it is still fresh in your memory, I want each of you to think of ways you could try to handle a similar situation when it occurs again." No one seemed to have any doubt at all that it would, indeed, occur again.

Once the girls were out of the room, Jenkins explained to Javier that Emma was seeing a therapist because of her unexpected behavior. He asked Javier, given what he had just experienced, if he would be willing, as an addition to his duties, to drive Emma to and from the appointments.

"Yes, I think I should. I've always liked your children. Whatever it is that Miss Emma is going through, I hope her doctor can help her."

"You've already been a large help by taking control of the situation today. I thank you for that," Jenkins said, as he offered his hand to shake.

Javier shook his boss's hand, firmly pumping it up and down.

Anita reached for Javier's hand and took it between hers. She raised her face, gratitude showing in her moist eyes as she told him, "I've been away from the set too many days already. So, starting tomorrow you'll need to drive me to where we're filming. It's possible that I may be there all day." She shrugged, and continued, "But again, it might be only a portion of it. I suppose it will depend on how much I have to make up and the other actors' schedules." She placed her palm against her forehead and moaned, "God, I hope I don't lose my part in this movie because of missing this much time."

CHAPTER NINE

After their last office visit with Dr. Levy, Anita and Jenkins talked long into the night, wrestling with what to do with their girls' education. Even with Emma getting care, it would take some time before improvement showed its bright smile. Since she wasn't allowed to return to school until improvement could be documented, allowing Susie to stay home with her meant both daughters were going without a proper education. They had agreed and told the girls they felt homeschooling would be the best solution.

Anita suggested they find a provider service that would conduct a search for the right teacher and then oversee her teaching. "You know, make her answerable to somebody so she truly does teach what's required."

"It would have to be an accredited provider service in order for me to even consider it." Jenkins patted her thigh as she sat with legs drawn up and feet braced against the mattress.

"Oh, it will be, I assure you. I wouldn't put my babies in just anybody's care." She reached for her iPad lying on the nightstand.

That next morning while the girls slept late, Anita made several phone calls to accredited services providing certified teachers who came to an individual's home and taught the equivalent of the Los Angeles school system's curriculum and that of St. Michael's specifically. She chose one which had a good address in a better section of the Los Angeles area and who fulfilled all her and Jenkins' requirements. What made it even better was the address of the service provider was within three miles of their home. Anita hoped the teacher was lucky enough to live close by, as well. And now their girls had been matched with that teacher.

Early Saturday morning Javier had the car ready to chauffeur Anita to the set for the day's filming. Anita made sure she had everything she needed, giving a last look around her bedroom. She tiptoed into the hall and silently opened the door to each of her daughter's rooms, peeking in at them before she left for a full day away. Emma lay on her side with her light, pink coverlet covering her shoulders and one hand under the pillow supporting her face, looking much like a sleeping princess. Susie lay on her back, covers tangled, blue pajama-clad legs askew, mouth open and snoring slightly. Anita grinned. *I'm going to have to work hard to make that tomboy a lady.*

"Okay, Monty," she said to her husband as he sat at the kitchen bar reading the American print Chinese paper from Beijing. "I'm on my way. I'll be back tonight as soon as I can."

"All right, my love. I know you have to go. I'll book my flight for tomorrow and take care of that and any other

China issues today." He squinted at Anita and pursed his lips.

"You look quite alluring. Come here," he coaxed. Cupping her buttocks, he squeezed the firm flesh. "Tonight's our last night together. Hurry home." He added another squeeze and Anita dropped her face to his for a kiss that exuded more passion than the early hour and circumstances could well bear.

"Ready, Mrs. Montford?" Javier asked, as he held the door open for her to climb into the backseat of the town car.

Anita took his outstretched hand, holding it a few moments as she said, "Again, I want to thank you, Javier, for looking after my girls and for being such a faithful driver for me."

The chauffeur briefly ducked his head and looked down while red crept up his neck. "It's my pleasure, ma'am."

Anita found the place on the set she was to report to. Her heart rate accelerated and her breathing sped up as the sheer joy acting brought her kicked in. *God, it's good to be back. I missed this.*

"Dammit, Anita! Where've you been? I've had to shoot around you for the last four days." The assistant director stood in front of her with his eyes hard and accusing, tapping his daily call sheet against his leg.

Taken aback by his tone as much as by his ignorance of why she was absent, Anita fired back, "Well, hell, Curt! Didn't anyone tell you I had a family emergency? I *couldn't* be here!" She didn't check her emotions at the door to the lot and now her face was red, her temper flaring.

"No! Nobody told me a damned thing. And watch your tone with me. I'm not a mind reader." He gave her his back and threw over his shoulder, "You better get your ass in gear and be ready for the next scene we're filming." He stalked off in the direction of the canteen.

Shit! Now I've made an enemy of the assistant director. And on my very first day back. I'll have to make amends somehow.

Jenkins Montford carried his coffee cup out to poolside and set it on the round faux glass table. They'd never replaced the inexpensive little tables with heavier real glass tops after the girls were large enough for glass not to be an issue. *Maybe we better keep these fake ones forever. After all, Susie is a clumsy bear still.* He smiled as he thought of his second daughter. *I wish she knew how much I adore her for just being her fun self.* Remembering his childhood, when a walk on the English moors brought hope of encountering some small animal to break his loneliness, Jenkins came to revel in the playful interplay between his daughters.

After comparison shopping for prices on the internet's search engines, he soon had the ticketing desk for United Airlines on the line. He could have made a reservation with China Air, however, he felt patriotic enough to his adopted country to pass on calling them.

"Good morning. United Airlines. How may I help you?" The Asian ticket agent spoke with an almost perfect American accent. He had to laugh. *Probably born and raised right here in LA's Chinatown.* He wound up with a flight leaving the next morning at 11:30, a direct non-stop flight arriving at 3:10 P.M. Monday afternoon in Beijing. The Beijing airport was huge, and after going through customs and taking a taxi the thirty or so miles in to the conference center in the city, he'd be lucky to get any work done that day.

"Aw, Dad, you gotta go back tomorrow?" Susie whined as he ended the call. "You just got here."

"Yes. It's been nice having you home, Dad," Emma added, aiming a lovely smile at him.

"We even acted like a normal family," Susie declared, "A dad, a mom, and two kids. Hey, we're the All-American family!" She turned to slap Emma on the back and instead read the hurt expression on her face. She knew just what it was. "Oh, Emma! I'm such a jerk. I didn't mean anything by saying we acted normal. We *are* normal, dang it!"

Emma smiled and blinked back her tears. "I know, Susie."

Their dad watched this exchange. He said, "I've enjoyed being home with my girls — all three of you. You two make me happy that you're mine. I'll miss you while I'm gone. But, I want you to know that I truly believe you'll both be fine." He put an arm around Emma, drawing her close, and laid a kiss on her forehead. "We're in this together and we'll make it work out for us all."

With his other arm, he beckoned Susie to him and drew her to his side. "I never knew having children could make my heart feel this way. I love you, girls." He drew back, letting them go, and looked first at Emma and then Susie. "I want you to know that. And remember it."

Susie shot both arms out and encircled her dad's waist. She looked up at his handsome smiling face and returned his smile. Ducking her head, she laid it against his chest. "I promise to remember it, Dad," she said, a good deal more somber than usual.

The sedate Emma hugged her dad from the side. "I'll remember it, too, Dad."

The girls had their ubiquitous cereal for a late breakfast and then changed into their bathing suits. Emma wore a navy one-piece with straps across the back and high cut legs. It hugged her body which, now at fourteen, had curves in all the right places. She was striking and to see her dive into the pool with long legs flowing was a portrait of sheer beauty.

"Hey, you look great in that suit, Emma. You look like an Olympic swimmer." Susie noted her own faded bikini. "I think this old thing used to be some color of blue. Or green." She giggled. "Who knows what color it once was?"

"Well, you might consider pitching that one, Susie," Emma said, pointing at Susie's bosom. "You're busting out of the top and the bottom hardly covers yours anymore."

Susie looked down at herself. She turned, craning her neck so she could see her backside.

"You may be right, Emma. My butt sure is hanging out back there." They cackled with laughter and Susie jumped in, making a huge splash. Emma splashed back and soon they were chasing and dunking each other.

They spent a good portion of the day hanging about the pool. They swam, played Marco Polo, and sunned on the side of the pool's seafoam green and indigo blue tiles, remembering to apply sunscreen often.

"I gotta pee," Susie announced soon after they'd once again slipped back into the pool.

"You get out right now! Don't you dare pee in this pool," Emma ordered.

"But, I always did when I was little. Why can't I do it now?"

"Gross, Susie! I'd never have gotten in that water if I'd known that. You're disgusting."

"All *right*! I won't." She splashed water on Emma while asking, "Want me to get us a snack while I'm in there?"

"Only if you wash your hands after you pee. And stop splashing me!"

Susie climbed up the ladder and out of the pool. Emma lazily floated on the surface until Susie brought the food. Emma climbed out and snagged Susie's towel, a green and blue one with seahorses cavorting across it.

"That's my towel!"

"You used mine," Emma returned as she wrapped the towel around her budding figure and sat down to eat.

Susie looked at the towel wrapped around her waist. "Oh, I guess I did. It's all good."

The sisters ate the slices of cool cantaloupe and sweet watermelon interspersed with peanut butter filled pretzels.

Lifting a dripping piece of red fruit to her mouth, Emma remarked, "This watermelon will make you have to pee again. Remember, you'll be in big trouble if you pee in this pool!"

"Okay, okay, I won't," Susie promised.

They sat together companionably eating and talking, not wanting to waste one minute of this freedom before their homeschooling began in a couple of days.

Their dad watched them through the glass panes in the French doors that led from his and Anita's bedroom to the pool. The sunlight gleamed against his teeth as his smile widened.

Anita's scenes were over by six. She had to pay close attention to everything happening on the set so Curt wouldn't single her out for reproach. It was miraculous that she'd managed to learn her lines while waiting for camera setup, microphone placement, and the other actors to be ready. Only once had she flubbed her lines so badly that she was berated by the assistant director. Her lines were: "I'll be back soon, my darling. I'm just popping out to have lunch with Yvette and Mary Ann. Could I bring you something when I return?" What she said was: "I'll be back soon, Monty. I'm going to have lunch with Emma and Susie. Would you like something, my darling?"

"Cut. Cut!" Curt yelled. "Where's your head, Anita? Up your ass?" He looked at her with eyes even colder than before.

Appalled that she'd let her emotions and worry about her family intrude into her work, Anita could only apologize and move on. She shook her head, trying to clear the thoughts of home from her mind.

"I do apologize for my mistake, Curt. I've got a lot on my mind, but it won't happen again."

With brows drawn together and mouth in a tight line, Curt replied, "It better not."

Later, speaking quietly, and only to herself, Anita vowed, "I'm going to make time to speak with Curt about Emma, and about Monty going back to China, and the homeschooling. I expect him to be only moderately sympathetic, but I know I have to pull it all together in order to keep my job. I suppose I'll simply say Emma has some emotional problems and is going to a therapist." *Or behavior problems. Oh, I don't know what I'll say.*

It was after seven o'clock when Javier stopped the car in the driveway and hurried to open the door of the town car so Anita could get out. She did so, saying as always, "Thanks so much, Javier."

Monty sat watching the evening news on the huge wall-mounted television at the far end of the rec room. Anita entered and put down her things on the kitchen counter. The open floor plan allowed him to see her kick off her heels as she stood by the kitchen table with its high stools.

"How'd it go?" he asked softly.

"Okay, I guess. Curt, the assistant director, was on my case. Can you believe no one gave him the word that I was dealing with a family emergency?"

"Oh, is that what the little bitch is? A family emergency?" The last part issuing from Emma's mouth was drawled in the mocking tone of a deep-voiced male. "I'm sure she'd *love* to know that."

Jenkins was moving toward Anita and they both turned toward the girls' bedroom hallway at the first sound. They saw Emma standing there in pink shorts and a pink-flowered tank top with a mocking smile spread across her lovely face. Susie stood behind her, eyes big as she stared at her sister.

"Sam?"

Emma whirled around to face Susie. "Yeah, what?" she asked in Sam's voice.

"Can I talk to Emma now?"

"Why would you want to talk to her when you've got me? She's such a do-gooder little bitch. Always wanting things to be perfect." Stopping, and breathing hard, he continued, "You know what?"

"Wh-what?" Susie stammered.

"I'm getting very tired of Emma. She thinks she's the most important person in our group and she's definitely not. You'll see that pretty soon." He placed a hand on either side of the door frame and hung between them as he glared at Susie, Emma's face incongruent with what lay upon it.

If it wasn't so serious I'd have to laugh at Emma trying to be so tough.

In an instant Sam changed. With a sly grin and blue eyes twinkling he said, "If you want her, you got her." He banged Emma's body hard against the door frame, hitting her head.

"Owww. Oh, that hurt!" Emma exclaimed, raising her hands to her head and bracing her forehead in her palm. She seemed to deflate as she continued to cup her forehead in her left palm while rubbing her right temple with her hand. Dropping her hands and looking behind her, she saw Susie.

"Why'd you push me, Susie?" Her face and voice were full of hurt.

"Oh, sweetie, Susie didn't push you," Anita said, rushing to enfold Emma in her arms. "It was an accident."

"Oh, I didn't know. I just assumed it was Susie acting like Susie. But, boy, does this hurt. How'd I do that, anyway?"

Susie joined her mom in hugging her.

"Uh, why are you hugging me?" she asked, as she looked at her mom and then at Susie.

Into the silence, Jenkins cleared his throat.

Emma looked at her dad and back at the two with their arms still around her. "Oh, God," she moaned. "What did I do?"

Jenkins said as calmly as possible, "Sam came again. It was he who pushed you against the door frame."

Emma nodded, shoulders slumping as she sought a seat at the tall table. She pushed Anita's high heels under it with the toe of her sandals and then sat on one of the stools.

"What we've learned from this is Sam wants to do some kind of harm to you in some way, Emma." Her father came to her and put both hands on her shoulders, gently massaging her tense muscles. "I don't know what may happen."

He was silent, thinking for a few moments. Continuing, he said, "We have to take this seriously, and we can only hope Dr. Levy can get that part under control." He stopped and gazed at Susie. "What this means is you must be vigilant at all times whenever Sam comes out, Susie. You're with Emma more than anyone. We, and you, have to make sure that Sam doesn't hurt Emma. Pushing her head against the door was bad enough."

Anita interjected, "Oh, Monty, is that too much responsibility for Susie? She's only twelve."

"I can handle it, Mom. Emma's my best pal as well as my sister. I want to help her. I'll sock that big bad Sam right in the nose!"

Emma started laughing low in her throat and it grew louder until she was laughing aloud and hanging onto Susie's shoulder to keep from falling off the stool. "Susie, you are such a nut," she finally got out. "If you sock Sam, you'll be hitting *me*! That won't work!"

Susie looked bewildered as Emma laughed, but now her eyes lit and a grin slid across her face. "Got it! I can't hit Sam. But, I sure can tell him off! I will do that the next time he comes out." She looked around and sniffed. "Something smells good. I'm hungry. Is it time to eat?"

Later, when all were in bed and the night noises abated, Jenkins and Anita shared their day. Jenkins said, "Yes, it's a good idea to talk with Curt about what's going on. If he doesn't care and is not willing to give you a little slack, then screw him. Go to the director instead."

Anita trailed her hand down the side of Jenkins' face and traced his lips with her fingers. She raised her head from where it lay on his shoulder and placed her lips on his. They were both satiated in the aftermath of love-making and were feeling quite mellow, trying to let go of bothers, but they had a myriad of problems facing them.

"Are you completely packed with everything you need and ready to get up and go, Monty?" Anita pushed herself up and bent over him, her hair loose and wild, just the way he liked it.

"Yes. Everything is by the door." He put both hands in her long curls, feeling their softness. "All I have to do is take a shower and get dressed and I'm on my way." Dropping his hands from her hair, he braced on one shoulder and pushed aside the straps of her sheer nightgown.

"Ahhh," she sighed. "Did you set the alarm?"

"Damn!"

Emma got out of bed and rummaged in the medicine cabinet in the bathroom she shared with Susie. She was looking for something to help her menstrual cramps. She pushed aside the Midol and ibuprofen, the acetaminophen and drops for red eyes, searching for the item that lay on the back of a shelf.

"Got it," Sam said. He laid out Emma's right arm on the vanity counter and took the single-edged razor blade in his left hand. He drew two shallow slits across the blue veins on the inside of Emma's right wrist. The blood welled up along the two slits.

"All riiight!" Sam exclaimed. He liked his handiwork so well he decided more was needed. He drew another line in the blood that covered Emma's wrist and watched it run down the sides and puddle on the countertop.

"There, that should show the bitch who's boss!" He ran water over the blade and returned it to the cabinet and then closed the door. He stood staring at the face in the mirror.

Emma found herself staring at her white face in the mirror above the sink. She dropped her eyes to her dripping wrist and recoiled, her hand flying up and slinging red drops across the mirror. All color left in her face bled away as she watched the drops drip down the glass.

"My God. What am I going to do?" Her horrified whisper was wholly inadequate to convey her feelings. Such turmoil had her head reeling and her stomach in knots. She took several deep breaths and slowly released each one. Her heart continued to hammer against her ribcage. She looked into the blue eyes looking back at her and knew they were hers. Emma's.

In a ragged whisper, she told herself, "I know it was Sam who did this." She lifted her wrist and watched the slits as they began to clot. Only a little blood welled at the site of the deepest cut. "And one day he's going to kill me. I know it."

While opening the medicine cabinet in search of bandages, Emma saw a flower on its fancy gilt edge contained a drop of blood. She shuddered. "Somebody's got to help me." Fear and anger brought on helpless tears. Speaking to her reflection again, she muttered, "At least I can clean up this mess before anyone sees it."

She continued to bandage her cuts, and when finished she did a thorough wipe-down of the blood-spotted mirror and edge, and then cleaned the counter and sink. *I wonder what Dr. Levy will make of this. We've got to get rid of Sam!*

Back in her room, Emma searched for a top that might minimize the bandage on her wrist, hoping no one would notice it. She pulled an orange crinkled blouse from its hanger. *Where on earth did this come from? I'd never buy anything as ugly as this!* But it did have something going for it. It had long floppy sleeves that fell almost to her knuckles. *I'll wear this tomorrow.*

CHAPTER TEN

Monday morning brought change to the Montford household. Anita had arranged for it in the person of Zelda Bass.

Likely to cause more friction with Curt for not being on time, Anita shrugged off her unease and told Javier she'd be late leaving for the set. Thus, she was home when the homeschooling teacher rang the doorbell. The wafting notes of "Born Free" swept the room and Anita hurried to open the door.

She looks like Mary Poppins was Anita's first thought. A woman, appearing to be perhaps in her mid-to-late twenties, stood before her in sensible black heels and a mid-calf navy skirt. A fringed shawl wrapped her shoulders. Her blondish hair was piled atop her head, tendrils escaping from their confines as if ready to take flight. She thrust her hand forward. "Good morning. Mrs. Montford?" Anita offered a smile along with her hand. "Yes, I am. You must be from the teacher's agency. You're Zelda Bass?"

"Yes, I'm Zelda. I have to tell you this is my first job with this company, and if you don't like me or my work, I'll be on my way. No problem." She flinched and shut her eyes, offering a weak smile as she opened them.

"Certainly not now, Zelda. You just got here. We'll see what the girls say after today's lessons. Maybe a week would be better. Come on in and we'll give it a try." *Oh, Lord. Have we done the right thing?*

She opened the door wide and pointed the way into the rec room where she'd put together a classroom with four card tables forming one large workspace. Three folding chairs with padded seats, three computers and a printer that Jenkins had set up before bed last night sat with the table. A smaller table made of plastic in the primary shades of red, blue, yellow and green held typing paper, pencils and pens, a stapler, paper clips and such odds and ends. It, along with a chalkboard with chalk, an easel with a large pad of paper and a variety of Sharpies she'd liberated from the girls' old playroom completed the classroom.

"Wow! It looks like you've thought of everything." Zelda walked to the table with the computer that faced the other two and laid her bag atop it. "This'll work just fine." She turned back to Anita and gestured to the bag. "In here I've got the curriculum and the instructions for where each girl should be right now with their studies. Of course, it will be a little different from their curriculum at the Catholic school." A dimple appeared in her right cheek. "There won't be any religion classes."

A whirlwind swept into the room. "No religion classes? That is so dope!" Susie danced across the room, toes turned in and heels flying high like a flapper from the Roaring Twenties. Emma appeared behind her and Susie stopped her dance and grabbed her hands, pulling her into the classroom.

"We can't get no religion classes," she sang to the Rolling Stones tune "I Can't Get No Satisfaction."

Emma pulled free. *It would be just like Susie to notice the bandage on my wrist.* "What on earth are you on about, Susie?" She looked up and saw her mom with a strange woman who was oddly dressed by today's fashion standards. "Are you our teacher?" she asked, her eyebrows rising toward her hairline.

Anita chose that moment to check her watch, "Oh, my God, I am so late," she moaned. "Curt will be furious." She beckoned to Emma, who sidled over to her mother, still looking at the other woman.

"Yes, this is your teacher, Ms. . . ." She turned to Zelda who stood beside her with her hands clasped together. "Are you a Miss or are you married, Zelda?"

"Miss. I'm single."

"Yes, this is Ms. Zelda Bass and she *is* your teacher. I've got to run now." She headed for the front door where Javier waited. "Oh, that reminds me," she said, looking back over her shoulder, "Javier will be taking you to see Dr. Levy today at four o'clock, Emma. Then he'll come get me and you two can tell me all about your day." She blew kisses to each of her daughters and then stepped through the door and into the waiting limousine.

The three stood looking from one to the other. Ms. Bass said, "Right. Okay, girls, take a seat and our school day can begin."

Ms. Bass began the session by telling the girls a bit about herself. She admitted this was her first job teaching in the home environment. In answer to Susie's statement that she sounded like she was a southerner, she replied that she was from Montgomery, Alabama, but she'd been in the Los Angeles area for close to five years. She'd worked as a waitress, a store clerk, and in data entry while completing her degree in Secondary Education from USC.

"Where'd you get the name Zelda?" Susie wanted to know.

"Zelda Fitzgerald, who was the wife of the author F. Scott Fitzgerald. She was born and raised in Montgomery, too."

"Did you know her?"

"Lord, no, Susie," Emma burst out. "That was a long time ago."

"It's always okay to ask," Ms. Bass said. "That's how we learn."

"Then please forgive me," Emma said, "but I have to ask you. Are you a member of a particular church group or something that requires you to dress like that?"

Emitting a giggle born of embarrassment, Ms. Bass explained. "No. I was uncertain how to dress for an in-home teaching assignment. I understand so many of the clients have religious beliefs that truly don't allow the type of clothing most young people wear today. I just wanted to be acceptable." She pulled at the fringe on her shawl. "I haven't any winter things unpacked and was afraid I might get cold, so I pulled this off the table by my bed and threw it on."

Susie's eyes lit up. "Cool."

"Makes sense," Emma concluded.

"Now let's get to work."

They spent the balance of the morning uploading and downloading files onto their computers so they might have the approved curriculum provided by most of the homeschooling networks in the Los Angeles area. Zelda also downloaded the Los Angeles County school curriculum guidelines and work pages for all of the course work required by the county so she could compare them.

At lunch time they sat down to a chicken casserole and a green salad Madonna unobtrusively made for them while they were busy at their computers.

As they sat at the kitchen bar where the family ate informally, Susie and Emma chattered together. Noticing their teacher wasn't talkative Emma ventured to ask, "Ms. Bass, is something wrong? You're really quiet."

Zelda picked at the lettuce leaves in her salad with her fork before answering. "Not really, Emma. I have to work out some things and see where it goes."

Susie slugged down the last of her iced tea. She set her glass beside her plate and then pointed to Emma's floppy sleeve. "Get your sleeve out of your salad dressing, Emma. What 'd you wear that stupid blouse for, anyway?" Fear speared Emma to snap, "Nobody asked you for your fashion advice, Susie! Leave me alone!" She hopped off her stool.

Susie sat with dropped chin and big eyes while she and Ms. Bass watched Emma storm off to the bathroom. Surprise, and something else, played across Zelda's face before she was able to shut it down.

"How are you, Emma? Ready to get started?" Doctor Levy's question accompanied her welcoming smile.

"Yes. I'm *so* ready to work on fixing me."

Emma sat on an off-white sofa with both small and large pillows in rainbow colors. Sinking back into its softness her body visibly lost its tension as her limbs loosened.

Doctor Levy spoke quietly, "When we met the first time, I told you the three major reasons one develops Dissociative Identity Disorder. I'm thinking that might be what you are experiencing. We'll find out more as we go along. Do you remember what the three were?"

"Yes. It involves abuse."

"Do you remember what kind?"

Emma pursed her lips, sucked in the upper. *I know this.* Licking her lips, she answered, "Verbal, physical, and uh, sexual."

"You are a quick learner, Emma. Let's work on finding out what happened to you."

Emma stared down at her fingers twisting in her lap. "Could it still be going on?"

Dr. Levy's small bosom rose with her sigh. "Let's hope not, Emma. It is possible. But, it's more likely that whatever abuse you suffered was inflicted years ago and you're just now remembering it."

An exasperated sound, half-moan, half-sigh, escaped Emma. "So, what are all these people inside me . . . ?"

"Parts," Dr. Levy interrupted. "*You* are the only real person."

"Okay. What are all these parts inside me really doing?"

"They're actually called "alters." Each one has a different mission. Each is there to help you deal with whatever it was that happened to you. The reason you can't remember is a *saving* or *helping* part was there when the abuse happened. The mission was to take the abuse from you and to have it happen to them instead of you. Your mind literally could not handle it, so it created other alters to take your place."

Dr. Levy leaned forward with her elbow braced on her crossed knees, pen in one hand and notebook in the other. "It's all right that you don't remember it now. We're going to talk a little more about what, if anything, you do remember . . ."

"But, I don't remember anything!" Emma cried.

"You will, Emma. What I was saying is that we will talk a little more today and then at our next meeting we will introduce hypnosis." She stopped to get Emma's reaction. Emma sat still with her hands in her lap, seeming depleted after her outburst.

Levy continued. "I will hypnotize you. It's very easy to do and it's not harmful or painful at all."

She was rewarded with Emma's peaked interest as she raised her eyebrows. "What happens then? Do I just start to tell you stuff?"

"Yes, you do." She hesitated a moment while she chose her next words. "And we should be able to bring forth at least one or more of the parts you've been told of by your family. Do you remember who they've said they witnessed?"

"As if I could forget." She suddenly stood up and took a few steps. "Is it okay if I walk about? I get antsy sitting still for so long. I just need to move because I feel like something is holding me down on the sofa."

"Sure. Go ahead."

Emma crossed her arms in front of her waist, hugging herself as if cold. Her pacing brought her back to the doctor and she stopped in front of her, never looking at her seat, her actions announcing she was in charge right now.

"What's your name?" Dr. Levy asked.

"Emmaline."

"Hello, Emmaline. I'm Irit and I'm helping Emma. Do you know Emma?"

Emmaline sat on the empty sofa and produced a fond, caring smile. "Yes, I know Emma. I've been with her for years. I try to protect her from bad things that can hurt her."

"How old are you, Emmaline?"

"Thirty-one."

"Well, Emma is lucky to have you." She took a chance. "Could I talk with her now?"

Emma slumped and remained motionless. Irit Levy got up to stand in front of her. Emma looked confused and a little bit dazed as she focused her eyes.

"I just met Emmaline," Dr. Levy said to Emma. "She's a caretaker part who came forward when you began to be agitated. That's a new part for you, yes?"

"Yes. Now there's Julia, Ralph, Christine, and . . ." she shuddered, ". . . Sam." Emma thrust her right hand toward the doctor, her large sleeve cuff falling aside, revealing the bandage on the inside of her wrist.

"See this. Sam came last night when I was getting ready for bed. His whole purpose was to hurt me. He cut my wrist with a razor blade."

"Yes, I can see it. It looks like Sam is left handed. That's a definite departure from any of the other alters, right?"

"As far as I know. And now Emmaline makes five alters. How many more can there be?" Her eyes swam in tears.

Gentle, lest Emma got more upset and Emmaline came back, Dr. Levy said, "That's what we'll find out under hypnosis. We'll do that at your Wednesday appointment." She put her hand on Emma's shoulder and turned to face her. "Try not to worry too much. We've already made progress." She guided her to the door and opened it to note Javier's anxious face as he sat waiting in the teal wingback chair. "Ready to go get your mom, Miss Emma?"

"Oh, yes, Javier!"

CHAPTER ELEVEN

They didn't have to wait long. Once through the gates of Tantamount Studios, Javier parked the limo in the lot to the left, across from the gift shop where one could buy CDs and DVDs of movies made by the studio. He and Emma watched a small group of people emerge from the little theatre on the right that was a showcase for student films and other short works. Their attention was soon trained on Anita as she hopped off the bench seat of the open cart that brought people from the back of the lot where the filming occurred.

"Hey, sweetie! How did it go with Dr. Levy? I hope she got something accomplished." Anita slid into the back seat with Emma as Javier held the door. She tossed the black bag to the floor at her feet and slipped off her heels, rubbing the bottoms of her feet across its surface.

Subdued, Emma responded, "Another part came out. Her name is Emmaline and she's thirty-one. I think she's been with me the longest. Dr. Levy says Emmaline thinks she's there to take care of me." She turned her wrist over and looked down at the bandage. She gave a sigh of resignation. "Looks like she failed with what Sam did."

"Let me look at it, Emma." Anita took her daughter's hand and examined the bandage. "It's not too bad a cut, is it?"

"No, it bled some but stopped when I bandaged it."

"It's a good thing that Emmaline is with you, right? She's a *good* part. I suppose we need for all of them to come out so the doctor can turn them all into just you. Even Sam."

"I guess." She caught Javier's eye in the rearview mirror. He dipped his head to the right, in Anita's direction.

"I hope you had a good day, Mom."

The chauffeur grinned and gave one quick nod of his head.

"Yeah, I did. Filming went great. I may not have to kill Curt, after all." She gave her tinkling, silver bell laugh. Emma joined in, her deeper laugh soaring over her mom's.

Tuesday morning brought an early call for Anita. She instructed the girls the night before to set their alarms as she wouldn't be there to wake them for their second day of school at home. She got ready and peeked in on each one before rushing out the door to the waiting car and driver.

Zelda Bass rang the doorbell. She rang it again. Presently it was pulled open and Emma greeted her with toothbrush in hand. "Sorry. I'm not quite ready. I don't know about Susie. Haven't seen her." She said this around the foamy toothpaste that threatened to drip from her mouth with every word. "I guess Madonna is doing laundry and didn't hear you ring."

Ms. Bass took a moment to assess the situation. "Yes. Do finish dressing and find Susie. Class begins in . . ." She checked her watch. "Five minutes."

Sitting at her desk and looking at her computer screen, Emma looked up when Susie appeared about ten minutes after the start of class.

"You're late, Susie. Do you want to tell me why?" The teacher stood with back straight, tapping a pen in the palm of her left hand with her right.

"I must have fallen back to sleep when I turned my alarm off." Susie shrugged as she got a bottle of fresh orange juice from the fridge.

"Please hurry and take your seat so we can get today's lessons started," Ms. Bass directed, as Susie sauntered toward her chair at the table, tilting the bottle high and guzzling the juice.

Following the curriculum's math requirements, Ms. Bass directed: "We're going to start lessons today with our math texts." She walked behind Susie and looked at her still dark computer screen. "Start it up and go to the LAUSD.org page. That's the Los Angeles County Unified School district's webpage. You'll find the information there, Susie, for seventh grade math requirements. We will use their guidelines. You will start at the beginning. A refresher course you might say."

"But, I've already done that," Susie began.

"Yes, you have. It'll be a breeze for you to do the adding and subtracting and the multiplying and dividing. When you get to the algebra section, you can stop. You're being introduced to algebra and we'll need to go more slowly as you learn its components."

Zelda moved to stand behind Emma, whose computer was on and the website already on the screen.

"Good, Emma. I appreciate the initiative you've shown. Now, you start at the beginning like Susie, but yours will be equations. Later we'll move into geometry and statistics." She moved back to her desk and pulled up the website for herself.

Their teacher had them work that way for another two and a half hours, asking and answering questions, as both girls made steady progress. Susie managed to hold her sulks and sighs to only a few.

"It's time for lunch girls. Let's see what we have today," Ms. Bass announced into the quiet of the classroom. She stood and stretched. The girls went in different directions, Emma to the bathroom Susie and she shared, and Susie to the guest bath inside the entrance area of the home.

They returned to find Madonna had again prepared a healthy meal set at the high bar for them. Chicken Divan steamed aromatically and fresh mixed berries sat in small clear glass bowls releasing and mingling their juices at all three place settings. Lemonade in tall glasses waited for each diner. They ate together, all seeming to be in a fine mood. Near the end of the meal, the teacher's mood changed.

I know I have to put a stop to the girls being late for class and taking it for granted it will be acceptable because they are in their own home. She cleared her throat. "Girls, look at me. We need to get something straight." She gazed at both girls' puzzled faces.

"Honesty is the best policy, so I'm just going to tell you like it is. And how it's going to be." She took a deep breath that lifted the bosom the girls didn't even know she possessed. "Here's the deal: I like you two and it would be easy to be your friend. But, by being your friend, I lose my place of authority as your teacher. You two must understand that I will tell you what to do. I'll help you understand how to do it. But then, you will do it. No sliding.

No cajoling me into letting you skate by without doing an assignment or by my allowing you to go lie down because you're at home and you think you are exhausted."

Again, she looked each girl in her eyes. Susie flushed and averted hers, suddenly finding the play of light and shadows thrown on the wall by the rays of sunshine beaming in to be most interesting.

"Do you get where I'm coming from, Susie?"

Susie smiled at the change from formal words to the informal. "Yes, I gotcha."

A smile tugged at the teacher's lips as she resumed. "I will be a strict teacher and you will be my students, just as if I were one of the nuns at the Catholic school you attended. I'll be polite. I won't ask more of you than the curriculum requires. Unless," she gave a quick smile, "you are super smart and need more challenging material." Her eyes searched their faces. "Does that sound about right to you?"

I thought it would probably be like that, so it's not surprising," the practical Emma said.

"Well, darn," Susie stated, scowling. "Not what I hoped for, but yes, it sounds about right." She looked outside at the pool, not catching her teacher's eye. "I'm sorry I was a jerk this morning. I didn't think we had to be so strict about time." She dropped her eyes to look down at Ms. Bass's shoes, not quite daring to look at her. "I really did go back to sleep after I turned off the alarm. I'll try not to do that again."

"Good. I'm glad we've got that behind us."

"Please don't tell Mom about this morning," Susie implored. "Let her think we were both ready for our classes. She's got enough to worry about." Her voice trailed off and her eyes sought Emma's help.

"That's true. She does have a lot of things on her mind and she doesn't need to add us to the list," Emma agreed.

"As long as you demonstrate that you understand what I require of you, and you are attentive to time and responsibilities, I see no reason to disturb her over this infraction."

Susie threw an appraising look at her teacher and raised her hand.

"Susie? Did you have something to add?"

"Yes, I do. Do you always use such big words?"

Ms. Bass shot a questioning look at Susie before her stern face dissolved and she laughed aloud. "Susie, you certainly are a tension breaker!" Still emitting little giggles, she added, "And yes, I do use big words, as you call them, because that's how we learn. If you don't know the word, either ask me what it means or look it up. You can figure out how it's spelled—or something approximate." She rose from her stool. "Let's get back to our studies."

And that's what they did until three o'clock when the session ended. Ms. Bass gathered her things and put them in the black bag, said goodbye, and went out the door to the car that was awaiting her. The girls couldn't see who was in it. That left a lot of speculation.

The next afternoon when classes were over for the day, Emma rode with Javier to her appointment with Dr. Levy. Javier took a seat in the small lobby and pulled out a racing car magazine to pass the time. Emma took her seat, hardly having time to settle before Mindy appeared. Emma watched Javier's reaction to the beautiful young woman. He didn't disappoint her. She tried suppressing a grin as his eyes lit up and he almost did a complete double-take to make sure the lovely creature was real. She wanted to laugh out loud but she liked him too much to embarrass him.

Mindy opened the door to the doctor's office and in her well-modulated voice announced, "Emma's here."

Dr. Levy rose from her desk and invited her patient in. The room they entered for the hypnotism session was one Emma had not seen before. It was a little smaller than their living room at home. And just as nice. Her eyes were immediately drawn to the one window and she noticed the blinds were closed. A table lamp sat on both ends of the couch dispensing softly glowing light from their azure shades. The room, decorated in calming shades of blue and white, beckoned Emma to come in, sit, and relax.

"Would you like to take a seat on the couch, Emma?" Dr. Levy asked, indicating the eight-foot ivory sofa with soft, tufted back and rolled arms. "If you're comfortable enough and you'd like to do so, you can stretch out on it. You can use one of the pillows for support."

Emma eyed the four throw pillows, all in various shades of light blue. *I could relax on this couch forever.* "Okay. I think I'll just sit for now." She sat at one end. "Oh, this *is* comfortable. Thanks!"

Dr. Levy sat across from Emma in a wingback in the lightest shade of cobalt. "Let's talk a bit first." She crossed her legs, leaned toward Emma, and steepled her fingers under her chin.

"Remember I met Emmaline when you were last here and she said she was thirty-one. Can you tell me what other alters have come forward and have been seen by members of your family?"

Oh, boy, here we go. Emma took a deep breath and plunged in. "Well, I don't think any more have come since last time."

"If you know the ages, tell me that too."

"Let's see . . ." She thought for a few seconds. "Julia says she's six. And then there's Ralph. He came next. He's sup-posed to be thirteen. Worst of all is Sam. He's eighteen. Mom and Dad also saw him. Then there's Christine. She walked out of the store with a pair of UGGs. We're pretty sure that's who that was. And the last one is Emmaline."

Looking up from her notes, Dr. Levy confirmed: Julia is six years old; Ralph is thirteen; Sam is eighteen; and Emmaline is thirty-one?" At Emma's nod, she asked, "How old is Christine?"

"Susie asked her that one day at Target when she was playing with the music CDs." Emma paused, choosing her words. "She must like to take things. Oh, and she curses a lot. She said she was sixteen."

Dr. Levy wrote on her notepad.

"Oh, I've got a question," Emma said. "Why do I have boys? It seems since I'm a girl, I'd only have girls."

"We should find that out as we progress, Emma. And we *will* progress." She nodded her head with certainty. "And I can tell you without question that almost all who have DID have both male and female alters. So, see—while you are definitely special, you're not all that different."

Emma's voice registered hope with her whispered, "Is that a good thing?"

"That's a very good thing!" Dr. Levy straightened in her seat before launching into an explanation of why they were in that particular room and why it was different from the others in her office suite. Her voice was soothing as she told Emma what was needed for a successful hypnotism was a quiet, pleasant room that was understated, yet comfortable, with neither outside nor inside stimulation, to set the mood for hypnotism. Thus, there was no loud music playing, no glaring lights, no food or drink or other distractions. This was to be their time together just the two of them, but, from this setting, she hoped to elicit information from one or more of the alters hidden within Emma.

"Are you ready to give it a go, Emma?"

"Yes, please."

Speaking in a low, soft voice, Dr. Levy began her pre-ferred method of hypnosis.

"Let my words wash over you and envelop you in a safe cocoon. Everything here is calm, peaceful, and safe. Let yourself relax deeply into the sofa as your muscles lose their tightness. Your eyes may begin to feel heavy. Go with the feeling. Listen to my voice." She drawled her words so nothing was rushed; everything was said slowly and softly.

"Take slow, deliberate breaths. Now take a deep, deep breath. Draw the air into your lungs. Fill them." She saw that Emma did this, her bosom lifting with a mighty breath. "Now empty your lungs. Don't rush."

Emma did as directed.

"Do it again. Breathe in. Now, breathe out slowly. Good." She tapped the end of her pen against a round gold brooch on the left lapel of her cropped gray suit jacket. "Focus your eyes on this gold pin on my lapel. Continue to look at it. But, while you're looking at it, if you find you want to close your eyes, you may do so."

Emma set her gaze on the lapel brooch.

"I want you to relax your entire body." Her voice came even slower as she told Emma, "Start with your toes. Then your feet." She paused so Emma could concentrate.

"Now your ankles. Feel them puddle. Move up to your calves and think of those muscles loosening and lying completely still." Another pause while she watched Emma.

"Now your thighs. Feel those inner thigh muscles loosen and lengthen. Good. Now you want to relax your tight shoulders. Think of them loose and slumped. Release them. Let them relax. That's right."

In an even slower cadence, the doctor instructed, "Set loose your tight back muscles. Think of your right shoul-der blade. It yearns to be loose. Think of your left shoulder blade. Feel the muscles in both lighten and loosen. Loosen that tense spine. From your bottom all the way up to the back of your head, have every muscle supporting each vertebra let go until your back is like a wet noodle with no support from anything."

Emma's shoulders slumped, her elbows doing little to support her arms at her sides.

"You're relaxing fully. Think of your neck, how weary it is from holding up your head. Feel your head droop as you imagine no tight muscles anywhere in your neck. Now, think of your face. Your cheeks and forehead. Let them go slack. No smile, no frown, nothing at all."

She could see Emma's transformation as she sat with legs loose and splayed, having slid down in the sofa until her buttocks were at the edge of the seat. Her head drooped forward onto her chest. Her breathing was slow and steady. She was no longer looking at the lapel pin. Her eyes were closed.

"You can feel a heavy relaxed feeling that continues to come over you. It will get stronger and stronger. Let it envelop you. My voice and my words are putting you faster and deeper into an utterly calm and peaceful relaxed state."

Emma appeared almost comatose. She was nearly there.

"Picture yourself at the end of a hallway and there are five steps leading down. Take that first step and feel yourself becoming calmer." She paused.

"Take the second step and you're even more relaxed." Another pause.

"Take the third step. You feel like your body is light as air." She watched Emma's face.

"Take the fourth step. Your body feels like it could float away." Emma's body sagged.

"Take the fifth step. You feel yourself sinking down, down, down. You're completely safe. Farther down. Deeper. Deeper." Her voice was soft and lulling. "Deeper still. Very, very deep." Emma didn't move.

"You're way under. You're fully relaxed. You have no desire to be anywhere else. You just want to float in your safe state of relaxation." Emma had her eyes closed and her head drooped even more. She was motionless. Her dark lashes fanned out on her cheeks and she appeared to be sleeping. But she wasn't asleep; she was far under her realm of consciousness. Her subconscious was revealed and ready for Dr. Levy to explore.

Dr. Levy asked her first question. "Can you tell me how you are feeling right now?"

Instead of Emma's voice, the response came from one she'd heard before. "I'm a little worried about what you're doing to Emma. She will be okay, won't she?"

"Hello, Emmaline. Yes, Emma will be fine. This isn't hurting her. I want to talk with you, if that's all right. I would like your ideas on how we can keep her safe."

"Well, that's what I'm here for. I keep her safe. I'm like a conscience. When she attempts to do something unsafe, I come forward and warn her not to. I wish I could've been with her always, even from the beginning."

Dr. Levy sucked in her bottom lip. Her top teeth formed a white barrier for the pencil she tapped against it. "When did you come to Emma?"

"When she was five. It was after the first time she was abused."

"And you've been with her all this time?"

"Well, yes! I couldn't abandon her. She needs me."

"Thank you so much for your diligence, Emmaline."

"You're welcome." Emma's body wriggled a bit as Emmaline receded into nothingness and took her place inside Emma.

"Emma?" Dr. Levy said to the person sitting before her. No response. So, Dr. Levy tried another tactic. Without mentioning a name, she told her, "I'm going to count from one to five. When we get to five, you will awake and feel fully alert and completely refreshed."

Leaning forward in her seat, she began to count, "One, two, three, four . . . five." At five, Emma's eyes opened. She took a deep breath and offered a tentative grin.

"Did it go all right?"

"Everything's fine. We've had a successful hypnosis session. I didn't learn much from Emmaline, the alter who came forth today, but it's a good start."

"Can we go on?"

"No. That's all for today. Your session time is up. We'll try again on Friday." She rose and offered Emma her hand to help her from her seat. When Emma exited the doctor's office, a very relieved looking chauffeur got to his feet.

"Everything good, Miss Emma?"

"It's all good, Javier." The driver's smile answered Emma's own.

CHAPTER TWELVE

I n the next several weeks, the everyday lives of the
Montford family settled into a routine. Anita worked on
her problems with Curt by agreeing with everything he
said, taking his directing advice to heart, and vowing to
keep her role at all costs. She decided to make their relationship even more personal by inviting him to a dinner
party at her home. He arrived a few minutes late and
rang the bell.

Anita answered the door. "Hello, Curt. Please come in."

He walked past her into the foyer where the lights were
set to medium and soft music played from the whole-
house stereo system. There was no sound of guests. No
laughter, no noise.

"Am I the first to arrive? Or am I the only guest?" he
asked, narrowing his eyes.

"It seems now that you will be dining with just me and
my two teen daughters." She fudged it a bit, thinking
surely Susie would behave as if she were older than
twelve.

Curt frowned and looked away.

Anita hurried to drop the names of a couple who were
her good friends, and who also happened to be important
stars by Hollywood standards. She told Curt they'd had
to cancel at the last minute. He accepted the explanation
with a nod and stalked on in to the living area to be
met with its cool shades of beige and sage green. An oil
painting of the two Montford daughters hung at one end,

the artist's rendition of the original photograph done in pastels, soft and a bit out of focus.

"So, these are your daughters?"

"Yes. The older is Emma and the younger is Susie."

"Cute."

Curt was unaware he was there so he could meet her girls, the cause of her hectic life and schedule. Anita had instructed them to act grownup and to be charming. They came together from the back of the house to meet Curt.

"Good evening. I'm Emma." She smiled and held out her hand. Curt shook it without enthusiasm.

"So pleased to have you, I'm Susie." Curt released Emma's hand and took Susie's small hand for one quick shake.

Anita motioned to the long sage couch. "Please have a seat on the couch—or wherever you like. I'll get us something to drink."

She poured drinks for everyone, including the girls, who had fizzy punch drinks in tall glasses. They attempted small talk about what interested girls of their age, Susie admitting to peer pressure. "Yes, it's true. We have to wear the latest fad to be accepted anywhere these days."

This turned into Curt talking about teen movie stars. "The Fanning girls are the best to hit Hollywood in a long time. Dakota's been acting since she was about four."

"Oh, yes! I love her. She is awesome in the Twilight movies," Susie got in before Curt continued as if she hadn't spoken.

"And Elle Fanning is following in Dakota's footsteps. She may even surpass her." He continued until Madonna appeared to announce dinner was served. She'd prepared a perfect standing prime rib roast, crisp and brown on the outside, juicy and dark pink inside. Anita was gratified to see Curt's eyes light up when he saw the enticing entrée.

Curt was polite, but it was obvious that he was out of his comfort zone. He listened to Anita explain about the girls being homeschooled and the special care Emma now required because of medical issues. Anita had discussed this with Emma earlier so she was onboard with Curt knowing her mother had to miss some of the filming schedule to deal with her medical problems.

It was fortunate Curt didn't ask too many questions. He had the power to embarrass all of them. It was sometimes hard for Anita to talk as she held her breath for fear Emma or Susie might say the wrong thing to him.

Once dinner was over, the girls went to their rooms and Anita and Curt took their wine outside, under the few stars they could see, to talk by the pool. Anita told him of her trials: facing everything alone since Jenkins was gone most of the time; her need to be with her girls; the home-schooling where no one was at their happiest; and saying only that Emma, being a teen and misbehaving, caused her to take both girls out of the parochial school. He was attentive, listening with eyes glinting from the lights of the city and the faint image of the moon. By the time she'd finished, the stars were hidden by the haze that swept in and was present most Los Angeles nights.

"I don't want you to think I'm whining, Curt. My job means a lot to me. And I know I've pushed the envelope in the past when I had to attend to my family, but I hope you now have a better understanding of what has been happening." She gazed at him with eyes large and dark in the dimming light.

Curt sat back in his chair, his right knee up and bent so his foot braced on the edge of the chair's seat, left leg stretched toward the pool. His right wrist lay atop his right knee with his hand and fingers loosely dangling. He appeared the picture of ease as he, cocking his head and listening to her, watched her from hooded eyes. Anita knew that was a ruse. His tightly coiled body could be as dangerous with its tongue as a rattlesnake, and he could strike as quickly. She waited for his response, hardly daring to breathe.

Curt slid his knee down and put his foot to the patio floor, rising slowly until he stood. He leaned his head back and seemed to study the stars. Whirling to face her, he curtly asked, "Is that it?"

"Yes," Anita replied, remembering to be assertive and not aggressive.

"In that case, I appreciate you telling me." He extended a hand to help her from her chair. Grasping it, Anita stood facing him.

"I understand it's hard without your husband's help. When is he coming home?"

"In a few days. But, he's never home long. He's always off somewhere on the other side of the world."

"Oh?" He studied her face for a few moments and then pulled her to him. "Maybe we can make the most of our time together." His eyes gleamed as the pool reflected light into them. Then his mouth was on hers.

Oh, my God! This has to stop right now. "Curt, please don't," she said, extricating herself from his arms. She stepped back, turning her palm out, placing it against his chest. "We can't do this." Her insides were jumping in dread. *What will he do now?*

Curt looked at her a long time, biting his lower lip and nodding with deliberate slowness.

"I see. Then you didn't lure me here with your body and your tale of woe?"

"Just my tale of woe. I need this role, Curt. I *want* this role. And I want to work with you peacefully. Can we do that?" Her voice registered quiet sincerity.

"Perhaps we can. We'll see. Thank you for dinner." Curt picked up his wine glass and walked back into the house.

He set the glass on the table and moved toward the entry door. Anita followed him. She opened the door still holding her glass.

Curt nodded to the glass in her hand and said, "You better finish your wine. You'll probably need it." He walked through the door to his car, a light golden-brown Audi convertible with matching top. He said nothing further as he backed out the drive and into the winding street, heading down Vermont Avenue to the lights of Los Feliz Boulevard.

Susie stood watching. *I'm so glad my room faces the pool.* She'd never been gladder for that than tonight. She wasn't spying on her mom but happened to be looking out as that man her mom invited to dinner kissed her. It didn't look like her mom wanted him to do that. In fact, he left in a couple of minutes and *he* didn't look happy. She knew her mom wouldn't bother her or Emma with it, but she wanted to know what was going on. *Maybe if I tell Dad, he'll beat that guy to mush and Mom won't have to worry about him anymore.* She went to sleep while planning how and how much to tell her dad.

Anita opened the door to the refrigerator and took out a white wine, a crisp French Sauvignon Blanc. She took a fresh white wine goblet from the rack hung above the bar, its thin crystal showering the room with iridescent rainbows from the soft overhead lighting. She poured half a glass of the luscious wine and set the bottle down on the counter. Raising her glass for a sip, she decided it wasn't enough and added more, draining the bottle's contents to half. *Hmmm, won't take long to finish off the whole thing.* She took the bottle with her to the patio and set it on the table by the chair she'd recently vacated. She walked along the periphery of the pool listening to the night sounds of the city. Pausing, she stared down into the pool's blue depths lit by the pool's lights. *What am I going to do about Curt?*

Running her hand through her hair, she lifted the mass away from her neck and let the cool night air refresh her. Sitting, she balanced the wine glass on the arm of her chair, one hand on it so it couldn't fall, and tried to work out what she would do. As the night deepened and turned into morning, she found she'd consumed but a little of the wine in her glass. She didn't want it or need it now.

That weekend Jenkins came home. Landing at LAX at noon on Saturday, he knew customs would be busy with long lines. The flights from Beijing were always huge planes carrying hundreds of passengers so he knew it would be a while before he could get to the waiting car and Javier could take him home. He gazed around him at the Chinese nationals, many of whom were older ladies in the traditional Chinese dress of pants and colorful button-up, tunic-style tops with beautiful designs of meandering rivers, limestone mountains like those along the Li River, and trees looking like large bonsai. The younger ladies were gorgeously dressed in the latest western attire, many wearing jeans and high heels. Numbers of businessmen wore new designer suits, their wealth evident by the material and cut.

Time passed like a parade of sloths. Finally, he cleared customs and hurried to the curb. Whipping out his cell phone, he dialed Javier, who was to arrive on time and circle until he received the call.

"Come get me, Javier. I'm ready to go home."

After holding Anita tightly, savoring her arms, her kisses, the feel of her, and her signature fragrance, Jenkins was ready to see his girls.

"Where are Emma and Susie?" he asked, looking around the spacious entry.

"You know I save our first moments for just us." Anita smiled and ran her fingers along his brow, pushing the hair back. "The girls know that, so they wait for me to tell them when to come out." She winked. "I'll bet they don't want to see, as they say, 'that mushy stuff' between anybody as old as we are. Love is for the young, didn't you know?"

Chuckling, Jenkins added, "Quite right. Especially when it's their parents, I would think."

Anita walked down the hallway to the girls' bedrooms, stopping at the first. Susie's.

"Come out, girls. Your dad's home."

She stepped back as the door sprang open. Susie and Emma bolted out of the room and headed at a brisk walk for the foyer where their dad still stood, luggage on the floor beside his feet.

Susie beat Emma and rushed into Jenkins' arms first. "It's about time you came home, Dad! I missed you."

Emma was a second behind her. She slid an arm around his waist, saying, "I'm so glad you're home. Now we can all work together again to fix me."

Jenkins held his girls and the restrained Englishman inside him faded somewhat as he cleared his throat and blinked his eyes. "I'm glad I'm home too. I missed my girls."

During the next several weeks, Jenkins refused all offers to return overseas. He did minimal work with phone calls, emails, and faxes. Anita went to work every day she was to film and, without remark, did everything director Curt asked. She left quickly when the filming was finished, making sure there was no opportunity for the two to be alone together. After wrestling with her decision, she chose not to tell Jenkins of Curt's pass at her and his insinuation. Thus, the two had ample time to discuss the problems and be pro-active in trying to help Emma. It paid off. Sifting through the dregs of their memories, they pulled forth a time they could identify as a possible lead in trying to dissect Emma's DID.

"There was one unsettling time when Emma was five, and Susie was three years of age, when Emma became quiet and withdrawn." Jenkins brought it up as a possible clue.

He continued, "Do you remember how we worried at first when she didn't want to go outside to play in the garden? It was when she was five, I think."

"Right. It was. We cajoled and enticed her with her favorite toys, placing them far into the back of the yard under the big eucalyptus trees. We'd stand there and call her name, offer her favorite doll alongside a new one, the latest to hit the market. But, it did no good."

"That's true. Emma didn't budge. Instead, she stood without speaking, with those huge eyes staring at the dolls." He bowed his head in thought.

"Yes, and when I brought out Susie and let her play among the toys as an enticement, Emma turned away." Anita put her hand up to her forehead as if she could pull the memories from there. She looked into Jenkins' face. "I remember us discussing that strange behavior and agreed Emma had been avoiding contact with Susie. Although we had some doubt, we reached the conclusion that her behavior *must* be due to jealousy of her younger sister."

"That's correct," Jenkins agreed. "To offset this, we gave her special attention and lots of loving care. I think it was

. . . what? Within a couple of months or so that she began to change? You'd remember better than I since I was often away. But didn't she get better then?"

"As I recall," Anita answered, "Emma began to slowly return to her usual self, although she was more subdued — as she is today, as a matter of fact." Her eyes widened as if she was just now realizing how those early days still applied to Emma's behavior today.

She added, "When she was more outgoing, and I remember she had to work up to it over several years, we were satisfied everything was going to be fine again, so we put the matter to rest."

"However," Jenkins inserted, "When Emma began school in the fall, she did poorly in kindergarten. She should have been well-prepared since the nanny we employed for both watching after the girls and for instructing Emma in the basic preparations for entering kindergarten truly did an exemplary job."

"Yes. But Emma continued to under-achieve that year and it was suggested that she repeat kindergarten. Her social skills were among those in which she was lacking, as well as being inattentive in class. Oh, and there was little to no classroom participation from her."

"I know we agreed for her to repeat kindergarten and she did much better that second time," Jenkins said. "There has to be a silver lining somewhere." He smiled and raised the wine bottle, offering a refill of Anita's wine glass.

"Yes, please, Monty." Anita frowned, trying to remember Emma's second year of kindergarten. A sudden thought hit her. "Maybe it was because of Susie."

"Susie? How so?"

"She entered kindergarten when Emma started first grade. That meant that even though they are two years apart in age, they were only one year apart in school.

Emma seemed to need Susie then. She wasn't avoiding her anymore." She hung her head and shaking it, said, "You know, everything seemed almost problem-free, and the struggles Emma experienced seemed to be lessening. And we let it go." She hid her face in her hands, "It makes me so sad that we did."

"We aren't all-knowing, Anita. There was nothing to make us think it would go further. Who knows? That may have had nothing to do with her problem, what Dr. Levy now thinks is DID."

Jenkins and Anita talked night after night while their daughters slept. They lay in bed with bodies close, working to find how the information they were re-discovering might be of use to Dr. Levy.

"I don't want Emma to think we're talking behind her back," Anita said. "I want her to know we're working *with* her."

"I'm certain Dr. Levy will see to that."

CHAPTER THIRTEEN

Emma continued to see Dr. Levy on a regular twice-a-week basis through the end of that year. Thanksgiving and Christmas came and went with the family observing Emma quietly. The Montfords hoped, with calmness surrounding Emma, the alters within her could be kept at bay. No one wanted to see them come forth and take over Emma's thoughts, actions, and feelings. Worst of all, Emma was devastated each time she returned to herself and found out what her body did and what words came from her mouth.

Dr. Levy was successful with Emma's treatment with hypnotism. Emma, a willing patient, was well suited to hypnosis. Thus, Dr. Levy was able to talk with another alter only she witnessed. It occurred the Monday following Thanksgiving of that second year.

Deep in a hypnotic state, Emma was answering Dr. Levy's questions when her voice became that of a heavily southern-accented young woman. The voice tone suggested an older teen or someone in perhaps her twenties.

"I declare! What on earth was that cook thinkin'? That stuff she called stuffin' wasn't fit for hogs. Stuffin'! Hah! Anybody with a grain of sense knows it's called dressin'.

And it's made with biscuits and cornbread. Not that light bread stuff."

When the new voice started, Emma's head jerked up and she looked right at Dr. Levy before looking around the room. Dr. Levy let her finish her rant about the stuffing, getting a feel for the alter's sex, age, and personality. Now, she remarked, "Yes, it's a shame about the dressin'. Could you tell me who you are?"

Emma's eyes looked at her as if she was a bit slow. "I'm Christine. What's the matter with you? You know me."

"I do beg your pardon, Christine. Would you tell me again how old you are?"

"I'm sixteen. I'll be seventeen on my next birthday."

"And when is that?" Irit looked intently at Emma's face, waiting for Christine's response.

"You expect me to tell you everything?" With a haughty and defiant look conveyed by the tilt of her head and a curl of her lip, Christine disappeared.

"Are you there, Christine?" Dr. Levy waited for her response.

There was none, so she began the procedure to wake Emma from the trance.

Always curious to discover what she'd done during hypnosis, Emma stretched her loose limbs and asked, "What happened? What did I do?"

"Christine talked to me today. She's very indignant over the stuffing you had for Thanksgiving instead of having cornbread dressing. She *is* sixteen and didn't curse at all." The therapist laughed. Emma laughed with her.

Lessons with Ms. Bass continued in the Montford home. The three who met weekdays seemed content with their arrangement. Ms. Bass soon discovered both girls were quite bright and learning their lessons came easily to them. Emma didn't seem to be stressed at all in the class-room setting. It wasn't without trial, however, as Zelda Bass waited, dreading her eventual "baptism by fire" into Emma's DID world Mrs. Montford forewarned her of.

Valentine's Day was approaching and Ms. Bass gave Susie a reading assignment. As part of the required grade curriculum, the reading, writing about, and discussion of books was on Susie's assignment "must do" list. This day's class work for Susie was to begin reading the wildly popular book by Dan Gutman, *Oh, Valentine, We've Lost our Minds* and write about what she'd read.

"Oh, I can do that. No Prob." Susie made kissing sounds and threw air kisses to Emma.

Emma's assignment was to continue the ninth grade required reading. The book chosen was Lewis Carroll's *Alice in Wonderland*. Once completed, Emma would discuss with her teacher the many aspects of the symbol-ism found in the story. It was quiet in the room with Susie reading, Emma reading, and Ms. Bass working on the computer.

Peace was suddenly shattered by, "Fuck! I ain't reading this shit!"

Zelda jumped as if stung by a bee. She stared at Emma, whose face bore a sneer and the voice coming from her was male, sounding several years older than boys Emma's age. "Here's what I think of this crap!" Emma's mouth said while her arm hurled the book across the room to slam against the glass of the sliding door. The book fell to the floor, pages splayed out and the spine broken.

"Emma!" Ms. Bass seemed unable to stop herself from exclaiming.

Susie stared at Emma, her happy Valentine mood dis-placed by dismay.

Leaping up from the computer chair, Emma's body whirled as her head jerked from side to side, first looking at Zelda, then turning to Susie. "This idiot," she thrust her hands out and looked at them, indicating herself, "loves this shit. But I hate it. It's stupid. A grinning cat. A broad ordering 'Off with her head.' My ass!" Emma's voice deepened with every sentence.

Ms. Bass rose from her chair. "Emma, you must get control of yourself. I think . . ." She was cut off by a roar.

"I am not Emma!" The veins stood out from Emma's neck. Breathing hard, the deep voice continued, yelling, "That silly bitch hasn't got a clue about me. One day, I'm going to beat the hell out of her and then I'll be in charge."

"That makes no sense, Emma . . ." Zelda Bass started, when she was interrupted by Susie.

"Ms. Bass, just be quiet, please. You're not helping the situation." She dismissed Zelda by turning to Emma.

"Sam? Are you Sam?"

"Hell, yes, I'm Sam. Who'd you think I was?"

"Sam, please go away for now. I'd love to talk with you later, but now is not a good time."

"Will we talk about getting rid of Miss Perfect?"

"Absolutely."

"Okay. But, I'm going to hold you to your promise." He gave Susie a level-eyed stare that she knew to be a threat.

Emma collapsed into her computer chair and gazed almost unseeing at Susie. Susie gazed back. She asked, "Are you all right, Emma?"

Her body shaking, Ms. Bass jumped in before Emma could respond. "That's the first time I've ever seen anything like this." She turned her wide eyes toward Susie. "She's done this before?"

"Yes. Now let me see how Emma is doing, please."

Emma looked up at Susie standing beside her. Her eyes went to Ms. Bass with a jerk of her head, taking in the teacher's face and body language. The questioning look on her face disappeared as one of resignation took over.

"Who was it, Susie?" Emma asked just above a whisper. "Was it Sam?"

"Well, yeah," Susie returned the whisper, "but he can't do anything, so don't worry about it. He just didn't like the Cheshire Cat or the Red Queen."

"I'll have plenty to tell Dr. Levy when I see her next time." Emma sighed, and with emotion playing across her face, she looked unhappy and alone. She slid down in her chair with slumped shoulders, her body seeming to melt into place like hot cheese.

Anita received a phone call at work from Zelda Bass. She told her that yes, she knew they'd shared with her about Emma's earlier "emotional acting out." But, it wasn't until today that she'd seen evidence of it. It frightened her. What if Emma became violent?

Anita was quick to appease her fears. "Tell you what, I should be able to leave the lot early today, so if you don't mind waiting a short while after the classes end, I'll be glad to talk further with you about this."

"Oh, I'd like that very much."

Zelda returned from the bathroom where she'd gone to make the call to Anita and asked the girls to draw something they'd studied in class today while she reined in her galloping thoughts and waited to talk with their mom. She planned to be seated in the library and waiting for Mrs. Montford when she entered the front door.

"Yeah, Emma. Draw the Cheshire Cat," Susie teased.

"I might just do that, smarty pants."

Anita placed her hand on Zelda's arm, hoping to ease her discomfort and fear. The two women sat side by side on the coral covered sofa. She thought about what she should say regarding Emma's behavior, if anything at all. She raked her fingers through her heavy curls in frustration. She didn't know what or how much to tell this young woman who was helping mold her girls to be good students.

"I can't tell you exactly what is happening with Emma or why someone else seems to take over her body. She *is* having therapy, and her therapist thinks it might be DID."

"What in the world is that? I know you spoke of it before, but Emma has seemed so normal that I forgot about it."

Anita said, "I hoped you might have familiarized yourself with it by now. It stands for Dissociative Identity Disorder. Please look it up so you know what it is. You can find it on Google."

"And you think Emma truly has that?" Stopping only for a deep breath, she exhaled and said, "That sounds really scary. God, yes, I have to find out about it!"

"It's something like multiple personalities all caught up inside Emma."

"Dear God, no!" Zelda put her face in her hands as if trying to erase any thought of what that might be like.

"I *do* know I'd like for you to stay on as the girls' teacher. You're doing a fine job and they are learn-ing well."

Zelda frowned and hesitated in answering.

"Will you do that for the girls? Will you stay?" Anita's voice, though urgent, was now barely above a whisper.

Zelda straightened her back and sat erect. "I don't know, Mrs. Montford. I've always thought Emma to be a sweet, well-behaved girl—for a teenager." Now, she looked away, her gaze fastening on the rows of books on dark wooden shelves lining two walls of the room, which was decorated with masculine looking pieces. The artwork portrayed shipwrecks and hunting scenes. No sweet idyllic ladies sitting gracefully in lush gardens decorated these walls. "Her behavior frightened me." She turned her head and attention back to Anita. "No, it didn't simply frighten me; it almost scared me to death. If Susie hadn't been there to take charge of the situation, I don't know what I would've done. I would *never* have expected this, and I can't say that I can ever handle it happening again."

"Zelda, listen to me, please. I think having Emma forced to get used to another teacher, perhaps one she doesn't like nearly as much as you, would be a detriment to her progress." She continued with her plea, "Won't you agree to just stay for a trial period of, oh, maybe two weeks, and then if it happens again you won't be so afraid because you know she will come out of it and be the Emma you know. She won't stay the person she becomes at those times. Underneath, she's our Emma."

Zelda sat like a rabbit ready to bolt, her body tense with indecision. She opened her mouth to speak, but closed it. She tried again, and not making it, sat in silence, her body all but thrumming.

Dejected, Anita deflated like a rubber tire, leaning back against the sofa.

In a sudden movement, Zelda raised her right hand and slapped her thigh. "I'm not a coward. So, okay, I'll continue for now . . ." she promised haltingly, pausing for several seconds while Anita waited, trying to antici-pate what the coming words would be, ". . . and see how it goes."

Anita dispelled with a whoosh the breath she'd been holding deep in her lungs. "Thank you, Zelda. Thank you so much from both Mr. Montford and myself. Oh, and from the girls, of course." Smiling now, she added, "They think you're pretty cool, as Susie puts it."

Zelda Bass attempted a half-hearted smile. "I think they're pretty cool too. At least I did. I hope I will again."

PART 2:
CHAPTER FOURTEEN

The Montford family settled into an almost comfortable routine that carried them through the next couple of years. Each family member adjusted to the life he or she lived. Anita had different roles offered her now that she could no longer play the fresh-faced innocent ingénue. Jenkins relished his time at home and only accepted assignments out of the country when they piqued his interest or offered an outrageous monetary enticement. With a few hitches that had to be addressed, and were taken care of with expediency, they discovered their lives were working out better than any one of them dared to hope. When Emma's alters appeared in the classroom, Zelda, with Susie's help, was able to control whomever it might be. It was fortunate that an occurrence was rare.

Jenkins worked from home as much as possible. The telephone lines and cell phone towers hummed with calls to and from foreign countries and dignitaries as he continued his work seeing to the business of the United States. His fax machine regurgitated reams of paper, giving him a headache each time it belched forth, bringing him yet again, a problem he must solve. His fingers flew across his keyboard, leaving black trails of words on his computer screen. He wondered if he might wear out his software as he prepared one spreadsheet after another. All in all, Jenkins Montford was an extremely busy man, but he was pleased to be doing his exciting and sometimes volatile and dangerous job from the familiar workspace in his own home.

He rarely lost patience with an argumentative client, but it did happen, most often with China and Russia. At those times he would affect an icy calmness that brooked no further challenge. Upon conclusion, he laid his phone aside and then would emit a mighty roar of triumph tinged with frustration. Usually, Jenkins would include a few colorful words, which succinctly established his stance on the matter.

Anita Montford was delighted to have her husband home so much of the time. His work kept him busy, thus unavailable to her a good portion of the days, but he did find opportunities to run errands and help with the girls' appointments and such. What she liked best about it was Jenkins was there to share her bed. She always slept more soundly when he held her body close to his.

Her work was more fulfilling and she was more sought after than ever with the recognition she received from her Best Actress nomination for *Where We Began*. She was filming that movie when the DID problems began with Emma. It was the movie she was appearing in when she encountered the harassment from Curt, the assistant director. That hassle was put to rest after Susie told her dad.

"Mom was just trying to be nice to him since he'd yelled at her for not being there those first two days," Susie told Jenkins. "But he grabbed her and kissed her, and she broke away from him. He left right after that."

"The sodding bastard!" Jenkins said. His face turned dark red with fury. "Is no one safe in this dog's dinner of a world?" He drove his right fist into his left palm. "I'll see to Mr. Curt!"

"Whoa, Dad. What are you gonna do to him?"

"I'm not certain. I'll have to see."

Jenkins paid him a visit at the film site. After that, Curt suddenly became exceptionally courteous and professional with Anita. Jenkins refused to discuss with his wife the meeting with Curt, telling her only that she need not worry about further harassment. Curt would not be bothering her or causing her problems. Not now, and not in the future.

Following the county's school calendar, Ms. Zelda Bass reported to work at the Montford home every school day. Although this was the same Ms. Bass who first came to instruct Susie and Emma more than two years before, one might scoff at the thought. This Zelda Bass, unlike when she first appeared in a long skirt and fringed shawl fashioned from a round table-topper, was now quite fashionable. Her salary from the Montfords was generous and Mrs. Montford's advice on where and what to buy was helpful in what she chose. It greatly improved her dating opportunities, too.

Susie had quite different ideas. Zelda listened and then made sure not to follow those suggestions. Emma's recommendations were more in line with her mother's. Like dozens of times before, Zelda marveled at how different the girls were, yet so alike. She enjoyed the whole

Montford family but truly loved teaching the girls, even though she had to prepare two extensive lesson plans for each day. Both girls continued to ace their studies and keeping them interested in learning kept Zelda on her toes.

Susie was nearing the end of her ninth grade. She had, on several occasions over the past two and a half years, broached the subject to her parents of returning to public school. It wasn't that she didn't like Ms. Bass. She adored her. It wasn't that she wanted to be away from Emma. She knew she was needed to be there for Emma's support and she was still the one with whom she shared everything. When she examined her motives closely, she knew why she brought up the subject with her parents. She needed a better outlet for seeing her friends. And for them seeing her. Especially the several new cute boys her girlfriends told her about. Her body was changing and to her horror, she'd grown boobs that rivaled Emma's. To her further dismay, she found herself thinking about boys, a lot.

Anita and Jenkins took their daughter's request seriously, knowing she'd never have brought it up if it wasn't bothering her. They talked together and with Susie. Then they talked with Emma and Susie together. Their decision was she would continue her studies at home with Emma, but there would be all sorts of opportunities to enjoy boy and girl events, and she would be allowed to see a movie or go to sporting events with boys near her age. Especially now that she'd just turned fifteen and was leaving her tomboy image behind.

Susie's fun-loving nature had not waned. She was just as much fun—and just as mischievous—as before. Her friends loved to be with her. For those boy/girl events, she demanded that Emma join in. No matter, Emma wasn't around when Susie was with a new male friend. This was something she could have for herself, and not have to share with Emma. She wasn't sure how she felt about it, yet. She would never abandon her sister for any boy. Still . . .

Emma, while not exactly enjoying her sessions with Dr. Levy, looked forward to them. A good working relationship continued between the two. Dr. Levy was always polite and welcoming and made Emma feel that she genuinely cared about her. On the one hand, she appreciated the attention she received during their conversations before the hypnosis began, or on those occasions when she wasn't hypnotized at all. On the other hand, she would be so relieved when their time together was no longer needed. That would mean she was integrated, that all alters had joined into just one. And then that would be her. Emma. No one else living inside her. No more voices arguing in her head. No more time lost when she had no idea what happened. No wondering how she had a possession that she'd not had before. Where did it come from? How did it get in her room? No. This part of it she would not miss.

Now only a few days away from her seventeenth birthday and almost having completed the eleventh grade, she was eager to become 'everyday Emma' and be like the other girls her age. She played it down with Susie, but she was just as interested in having a boyfriend as Susie was. Wouldn't it be super to double-date! And, wasn't it amazing how Susie had changed her mind about boys after she grew boobs?

CHAPTER FIFTEEN

Susie leaned against the frame as she stood in the open doorway to her bedroom. She looked down at her sandaled feet, crossed with one knee bent. Her hands in the pockets of her khaki jeans added to her appearance of nonchalance. She was having a conversation with Ralph, Emma's thirteen-year-old male alter. While she had aged, Ralph had not. Now he was imploring her to do something she knew she shouldn't do.

She watched Ralph wink at her, an exaggerated closing of the right eye with his mouth open and skewed to the right. He closed it but couldn't hide the incongruous pink lipstick Emma wore.

"Oh, come on now, Susie. You know you're my special girl. Just do this for me." He lowered his brows and the blue eyes twinkled with a mixture of mirth and flirtation. "I wouldn't ask if it wasn't something I really want to do."

"But what if we get caught? What if something happens to us while we're gone?"

"We won't get caught!" Equal doses of excitement and exasperation shot his voice up to a near squeak. "I am *dying* for an In-N-Out burger, and who's gonna' take me if you won't?" He set his hands on his hips and jerked first one knee high, put that foot down, and then the other knee flashed high before his foot hit the floor simulating an Irish jig. He danced around Susie saying, "Come on, girl. It's gonna' be all good. Please, please, please!"

Susie simply could not stay angry with Ralph, so she gave in to the laugh bubbling up within her. Laughing at the lengths he would go in order to get her to drive to the nearby In-N-Out Burger off Los Feliz, she said, "Okay, already. Boy, you're pushing it. But, if Mom does find out, *you* are going to take *all* the blame."

"Sure. That's fine! *We'll* be fine!" Ralph slung his arm around Susie's shoulders and guided her to her mom's BMW sports car parked beside the drive. She wished her mom had driven it today instead of Javier taking her, then, the car wouldn't be there for Ralph to insist she take him for a burger.

Ralph unlocked the car door and handed Susie the keys he'd taken from the key hook holder on the wall in the kitchen.

"Hurry up, Susie," he urged, sliding into the passenger front bucket seat.

Susie slipped behind the steering wheel, a fire starting in the pit of her stomach, sending fingers of flame to her head, which was telling her, "No. No. No." She tried to ignore it as she took in the sunny day. A slight breeze gently tugged at the eucalyptus trees' leaves and waved the tall spears of the red Oleanders bordering the drive. She hoped nothing would go wrong as she pulled out of the circular, tan brick driveway and started down the hill to Los Feliz Boulevard.

An elderly woman Susie had seen in the neighborhood walked along the sidewalk carrying her poodle against her shoulder as if she carried a baby. Her left arm supported its back and her right palm held its bottom. Something, perhaps a squirrel or a chipmunk, seized the dog's attention and it scrambled from the woman's grasp, back legs pistoning. It landed on its front paws and, immediately following, its back legs dropped to the pavement. The poodle was a white blur of fluff and determination as it sped into the street in pursuit of its prey.

Susie's brain registered the dog jumping from the woman's arms and the dash into the street. Her next thought was accompanied by an involuntary shriek as the car's front right wheel hit a bump. "Ahhh," she cried as the car slowed. She looked around wildly, seeing the woman head into the street. "Oh, my God, Emma! Damn! I think I hit that little dog!" She slammed the brake pedal so hard the car stopped abruptly and the front end dipped.

In the seat beside her, Ralph yelled, "Emma's not here. You know that!" He was flung forward against the seat belt. "What in the hell are you doing?"

"Well Emma damned well better be here," Susie screamed back at her passenger. "Somebody's got to help me with that old lady. She looks like she's gonna have a heart attack or something. Emma, I need you to help me. Come back."

Ralph slid down in the seat and crossed his arms in front of his chest, his lips pouting and pink with lip gloss.

"Oh, for God's sake, Emma!" Susie hissed. She threw open the car door, swung out of it in one move and raced behind the car. She stopped, tripping over her own feet and almost falling. She put a hand on the trunk of the car to steady herself. Dropping to her knees by the elderly woman, Susie saw her eyes filled and tears running down her cheeks. The woman held the poodle's body in her arms as she bent over, crying and crooning. Susie flinched each time she heard her say, "My baby. Oh, my baby."

"I'm so sorry. She ran into the street so fast I . . . I . . . I just couldn't stop in time. She was there before I knew it."

"So *you* ran over my baby?" She turned a tear-filled stare on Susie.

A new voice joined the scene. "It was an accident, ma'am." Emma knelt on the other side of the woman with her hand on her shoulder. "No one could have known your baby was going to jump down and run into the street. Not even you could have expected it."

She now had the woman's attention and she slipped her hand beneath the dog's body and lifted it from her. "Let me help you with her."

Emma looked at Susie and then at the BMW, her frowning face transmitting her disapproval of whatever happened to cause this situation. It looked like she thought it was a bad situation for both girls.

"Susie will help you up and then we'll take your baby home." Emma leaned down to look in her face and gave her a reassuring smile. "Would you tell me her name?"

With her tears wetting her wrinkled cheeks, causing small rivulets to divide and change course, she answered, "Phoebe. Her name is Phoebe." Tears dripped from her chin as she looked from Emma to Phoebe. "Oh, my poor baby."

Susie recovered from the shock of Emma being there instead of Ralph. She wanted to yell, "It was Ralph's fault. He's the one who wanted me to drive the car." Instead, she pursed her lips with the corners turned down. "I'm so sorry, ma'am," she repeated. "Please give me your hand and let me help you stand up."

With Emma still carrying the dog, the woman led the way into her fenced yard, the white wooden planks and posts struggling under the weight of masses of heady, fragrant pink roses. Much like in their own yard, the green lawn sported spots of color. The orange Birds of Paradise with their deep blue markings made quite a showing.

Susie shook off her foggy feeling and announced she'd better get the car out of the middle of the street and they were fortunate no one had rounded a curve and plowed into it. She hurried to start the engine and move the car to the woman's driveway. While she did that, Emma and the woman climbed the steps to the porch and stood watching her.

"Have you lived here long?" Emma asked, making conversation to cover her anxiety.

"For many, many years. I own this house and my son and daughter-in-law live here with me. It's the house I raised my son in. Do you think we might call my son and ask him to come home to help me with this?"

"Yes. I have a phone in my bag. Tell me the number and I'll call."

Susie joined them on the porch. "Uhhh, you better use mine," she said, handing Emma the smart phone from her Khakis' pocket. Emma looked at her as if asking, "What's going on?" then, in a rush, she got it. She didn't have her cell phone, or her bag, because she wasn't herself when they left home. Whoever she'd been, there would've been no cell phone. So far as she knew, none of the alters used a cell, or any other type of phone or tablet.

Emma snatched the phone from Susie and, with a sweet smile, asked, "What's your son's number?" She handed the dog's body to its owner who held it against her bosom as if it was the most natural thing in this world to do.

It took several attempts, but at last she was certain the number she gave Emma was the correct one. She spoke into the phone, explaining the situation as best she could remember. "It happened so fast. I'm sorry I'm not good at remembering. Hurry home." She handed the phone back to Emma. "He wants to talk with you two when he gets here."

Susie drew a deep breath. She wished the pavement would open up, perhaps like one of those famous sinkholes that swallow houses and cars and roads, and maybe she and the BMW could sink down into nothingness. She did not relish the thought, much less the action, of what would occur when her mom and dad found out about this. And they would. The woman's son would make sure of that. It could be bad. Real bad.

She had one hope. She would have to rat out Emma and say Ralph made her do it. But, then Dr. Levy would have her come in with Emma and talk about Ralph. Oh, the dilemma. The decisions about what to reveal made her head hurt. She wondered if she should tell the truth, or just lie about how things went down. She wished she hadn't given in to Ralph's pleas.

The house's owner sat down in a patio chair near the end of the porch and laid the dog in her lap. She pointed her bony, deformed first finger in the direction of a two-seater swing that hung by chains from the porch's sky blue ceiling. Green vines climbed over and through a lattice behind the swing. They had frilly flowers in shades of purple and white. There was a red one too. The flowers were so beautiful Susie just gaped at them. She was almost glad there was a reason to be at this house.

"Ma'am, what kind of flowers are these behind the swing?" she asked. "I've never seen any flower as pretty as this one." She pointed to a large purple one with a yellow heart and white, thread-like tendrils forming a circle atop the purple.

"Why, that's a Passiflora, better known as a passion flower. It *is* lovely, isn't it?"

Susie drew her mouth to one side and squinted at the flower. "Why's it called a passion flower?"

"It's said the white filaments surrounding the center look like the crown of thorns Christ wore when he was crucified. That was called the Passion of Christ." She aimed her hand toward the vines, sweeping from one side to the end of the other. "So, there you have it; a lesson on flowers." Her lips and right cheek moved in a wistful half-smile. "And a most unlikely one, too."

"Could you tell us your name, please? I'm Emma Montford and this is my sister, Susie."

"Eleanor. I'm Eleanor Anderson. My son is Samuel Anderson. He's been on the daytime soap opera 'Nights Long and Dark' since it started years ago." She looked both girls up and down, nodding her head. "Yes, you two are Anita Montford's girls. I see the resemblance. She always was a pretty thing."

"Thanks, Ms. Eleanor. Mom would like that." Emma nodded at the lifeless dog. "Where would you like me to lay Phoebe? Or would you like to continue to hold her?"

"Oh, yes. I very much want to keep holding her. Until I have to let her go." She sniffed and rubbed her right eye.

At that precise moment Samuel swung into the driveway behind the BMW. He opened his car door, letting it swing out as far as its hinges would allow. Bounding from it, he was on the porch in a few strides.

"Okay, Mom. What's this all about?" His handsome face with its fierce dark eyes scowled at both Emma, who stood by his mother, and at Susie, who tensely sat on the edge of the swing. "Are these the girls who ran over Phoebe? Who was driving?" His narrowed eyes searched both faces. Neither girl spoke.

"Well, yes, they are the ones in the car that hit Phoebe. But, it was an accident. It was not their fault." Ms. Eleanor stood and handed Phoebe's body to an unsuspecting Samuel. He almost dropped her in his surprise.

Ms. Eleanor continued. "Phoebe jumped out of my arms and ran away from me, the naughty girl. She was chasing something. At least she thought she was. She ran right out into the road and right under the wheels of the car." She turned her eyes on the girls. "There's nothing they could do to avoid her, even though they were going slow on this winding road." She motioned to the road, the curves forming a perfect "S" in a number of places.

"What are you saying, Mom?"

"I'm saying it was nobody's fault. I'm sorry to have bothered you. You go on back to work and my two new friends and I will take care of little Phoebe." She glanced at both girls. "You will help me dig a plot in the garden out back and bury her, won't you?"

"Sure!" Susie jumped off the swing, setting it swinging from side to side. She backed into it and the swing slowly swayed to a stop.

"Perhaps before you go you could show us where a spade is so we can dig the grave for Phoebe," Emma suggested.

Susie dug a Phoebe-sized hole and wrapped the little dog in what looked to her like a baby blanket. Ms. Eleanor knelt and placed her in the grave, patting the blanket into place. She stood and said, "Goodbye, my little one. You were a good companion to me. I'll miss you." Her voice hitched at the end as she added, "Lord, take care of my baby."

Emma reached for Ms. Eleanor's hand and clasped it with both of hers. She held the frail, knobby fingers as she directed her voice to the small grave. "Phoebe, Ms. Eleanor loved you very much and I'm sure she will remember you always."

The gray head drooped and Eleanor took her hand from Emma to swipe her eyes. "Thank you, Emma."

Susie thought it a bit much to pray about her going to heaven, but since Emma played along with it, she did as well. "Bye, Phoebe. I'm sorry I hit you with the car." She paused for a moment, feeling she needed to say more.

Inspiration hit. "And I know you'll be happy in doggie heaven."

Soon Emma shoveled dirt over Phoebe. Ms. Eleanor flinched with the first few spadesful and then stood staring down, lost in her thoughts.

Emma tamped down the mound of dirt and looked around at the manicured gardens. "Flowers would be nice."

"Oh, that'd be so cool! Can we pick some to put on top of her, Ms. Eleanor?" In earnest, Susie picked up the blue-veined hand and drew it to her breast. Ms. Eleanor squeezed Susie's fingers and nodded her permission before withdrawing her hand and clearing her throat of the clog preventing her from talking. Smiling through her tears, she made a shooing motion, sending them in search of flowers.

Emma chose roses and Susie headed straight for the passion flowers. Once the fresh-dug mound was obscured by flowers, Susie said they needed to go home.

"Goodbye, Ms. Eleanor," Emma said.

"Oh, call me Eleanor. You two young ladies have acted like real adults. So drop the Ms." Emma gave her a sweet smile.

"Okay, *Eleanor*." Susie promised, grinning at her emphasis of the name, "We'll be back to visit soon."

Looking both ways, Susie made sure no car was coming as she backed the BMW out of the driveway and headed back up the road to their home. She didn't know if Samuel would tell her parents she was driving when they hit his mother's dog. She figured she shouldn't blame Emma. But, if she said Emma was driving, it might have a different outcome. Right now, she had no idea what she would say.

Looking ahead at the road, Susie told Emma, "I know it wasn't *you*. I know it was Ralph that talked me into taking

Mom's car, but I'm telling you: I am *not* taking you—or any of your parts—anywhere *ever again* until I'm legal and can drive without having to steal Mom's car. You got that?" She parked the BMW in its spot and turned to Emma, waves of earnest anger almost radiating from her body.

Emma dropped her eyes to her fidgeting hands. She raised them again to Susie's. "Yes. I got it. Are we going to tell Mom?"

"I guess we have to." Susie was surprised when the words left her mouth. Until then, she had no idea what she would say.

The girls knelt in front of the car to check for damage. Again kneeling, one on each side of the car, they checked for tire damage. There was no damage anywhere. After all, Phoebe had been a small dog. Knowing they had escaped without a horrific situation occurring, the sisters went inside their home to wait for their mother's arrival. Both were afraid of the punishment for their actions. What would their mom say and do to her reckless children? And would she tell their dad?

After hearing both girls' versions of taking the car and the following incidents, their mother said, "I think you've learned a valuable lesson with your actions today. You know it was wrong to take the car. You caused someone to lose something she loved. You caused unnecessary worry to her son. And you better hope he doesn't report this to the authorities. You could still get into real trouble over this if he does."

"I sure hope he . . ." Susie began.

Anita put her hands on her hips and glared at her daughters. "I'm talking now." She took a deep breath and let it out in a whoosh. "I'll call her and apologize for my girls' behavior." She shot another look at each one. "You two will visit her and do any chores she might want you to do until I tell you you've done enough."

Anita let her hands drop from her hips and sat on a stool facing them across the high dining bar. "You will not take my car, or drive any other car, until you have your licenses. No matter *who* asks you."

"Yes, Mom," Emma said, her voice soft.

"Well geeze, Mom," Susie wailed. Her mom's face darkened and a rare frown creased her forehead.

"Okay, Mom." In a flash, Susie did a one-eighty. She sang out, "No problem. I'm not driving until I'm old enough. I promise." She put on a sincere face for her mom. Turning, she narrowed her eyes at Emma as if reminding her of what she'd said, and meant, earlier. She was not driving anybody anywhere until she got her license.

Anita nodded her head as she chewed on her lower lip, appearing to consider her children and their promises. "Go to your rooms and each of you write an apology note to Eleanor."

Watching them slink toward their rooms, Anita wondered what she was going to do with her girls. She hoped if they could ever get Emma's alters all together into one, and if Susie would just behave, she might survive with her sanity intact.

She checked for the phone number for Eleanor on her computer using reverse lookup by address. Luck was with her because it was listed with the address she queried. *Fat chance of anyone finding my address this way.*

She made the call of apology and thumbed off her cell phone. *What a sweet lady she is. If only she knew the hell we're going through, she wouldn't think so highly of my girls.*

The girls did follow through on their promise to their mom. For the next several months they dropped in on Eleanor, sometimes for nothing more than a visit, but often it was to help her with a gardening project or to check on Squiggles, the beautiful and loving King Charles Spaniel who was a spectacular replacement for Phoebe and made Eleanor's world whole again.

CHAPTER SIXTEEN

It sometimes seems promises are made to be broken. A few weeks after hitting the dog, Susie was home alone since Javier had taken Emma to her appointment with Dr. Levy. He was to drop her off and run some errands for Anita before going back to pick her up.

"Wow! Would you look at this one!" Susie said, letting her breath out in a rush. She held her mom's latest acquisition, a gown to wear to this year's Academy Awards. Snooping in her mom's closet, she had pulled it from its hanger, the better to admire its silken pleats. The gown was slit low between the breasts, all the way to the tiny waist which had a slim silver belt. The silvery material flowed like mercury between her palms. "This is the most gorgeous thing I've ever seen. Mom will look like a million dollars in it. It is way lit!" She held it against her chest and wished for the day she might wear something as elegantly beautiful.

She gave it one last longing look and was rehanging it when her cell phone rang. It played the tune to the old 1960s hit "Oh, Susie, Darling" so she knew it was from Emma.

She answered with "Why are you calling me . . ." when a hysterical Emma blurted, "Susie, come get me! Now, please. Just come now! I need you. I need you now!"

Susie's heart almost stopped. She heard Emma's panic and the skin on her arms rose in goose bumps. "I'll be right there, Emma. Hang on!" She thumbed off her phone and dashed to the kitchen where the BMW's extra set of keys hung. She raced to the car without stopping to tell Madonna anything, started the car and flew out of the driveway. She realized she was being careless but didn't care. She needed to get to Emma. Now!

The car careened to a stop on the wide entry sidewalk in front of Dr. Levy's office. She would've stopped in the middle of Wilshire Boulevard if she'd had to. She fled the car and found Emma just inside the building's foyer.

"Ohhh, Susie," she cried, tears running down her cheeks, her nose red and stuffy, her eyes wide with fear. "Thank God you came!" She threw herself into Susie's arms.

The elevator doors opened and Dr. Levy rushed out. "Emma!" she exclaimed. "Dear, it's all right. Come back and let's talk."

Emma shook her head almost violently. "No! I want to go home with Susie. I'm not staying here. I'm scared!"

Susie fiercely held on to Emma. "I'm taking her home now, Dr. Levy. We'll talk to you later." She turned around, taking Emma, who had a death grip around her neck, with her. At the car, she said gently, "Emma, you have to let go now so you can get in. And I have to go to the other side so I can drive us home." She pried Emma's hands loose and helped her into the front seat.

Emma continued to sob as Susie took the drive a bit slower going home. The almost five o'clock traffic was horrible. Susie wondered how she'd gotten there amid the rushing, lane-hopping cars all around her. Everything about the drive there was a blur.

Susie reached over and took Emma's cold hand. "We'll be home soon, Emma, and then you can tell me what happened."

"Oh, Susie, I was so scared. It was horrible! Sam came. He . . . he threatened to kill me."

Javier found Emma gone when he went to retrieve her and asked Dr. Levy what happened. She could only give the short explanation that Emma had called Susie to come get her. He straight away headed for the Tantamount Studios to get Mrs. Montford, calling to inform her he was on the way there. It was fortunate that she had no further scenes this late in the day and, indeed, had been ready to call Javier to come for her after picking up Emma. Now she was home. Emma was still crying, and she was furious.

"What?" Anita exploded. "You're telling me that woman called Sam forth and he said he was going to kill you?"

"I suppose she was making headway with you and your alters, Emma, but I've never trusted her," Anita ranted. "She's too smug, acting like she knows how to handle everything that comes her way." Anita threw up her hands and spat out, "It sure looks like she can't handle Sam!"

Susie ventured into the maelstrom. "I'm sorry that I drove the BMW, Mom. I know you made me promise not to, but this was a real emergency."

At that moment, Jenkins walked through the door, having been alerted during a meeting nearby by Anita as Javier drove her home.

"Damned right, it was!" He reached for Susie, saying, "You're not in trouble for this, Susie. You did, in fact, do the right thing." He allowed Susie to leave his grasp as he enveloped Emma. "Let's all sit down and talk this through. I want to know exactly what happened, Emma, if you can recall it."

Sniffling and trying to control her breathing, Emma explained she had notebooks that she wrote in to keep track of everything happening to her that she could remember. She knew she'd had different parts write in the book because not only was the handwriting different, but the subject matter was not written by her. Fresh tears appeared as she said, "This time Sam wrote in it. He . . . he said he was . . ." She took a hard swallow, trying to stifle her sobs. "He said he was going to k-kill me. And he wrote it in blood." Emma collapsed in her mother's arms, her body shaking as she pressed her face against Anita's bosom.

"In blood?" burst out an incredulous Anita. "Where did the blood come from?"

Jenkins sat on the other side of Emma. Now he took her right wrist in his hand, turned it palm up and pointed to the marks across the delicate blue vein there that pulsed steady and quick. "I'd say it came from right here."

Emma hung her head. "I didn't want to tell you. This is the second time Sam's cut me."

"What did you say, Emma?" Jenkin's voice held a note of alarm. "Did you just say this has happened before?"

Emma nodded, still looking down.

"Look at me, Emma." It was a demand from her father and brooked no argument. Emma raised her eyes to her father's.

"You have to tell us these things, Emma! When was the first time?" Anita shrieked. Her body language announced she was barely holding it together.

"I know when it was. It was the first day of school with Zelda." Susie answered for Emma. "Right, Emma?"

Forced now to give a truthful answer, Emma said. "Yes."

"Why didn't you tell us?" Anita asked with her voice rising even higher.

Emma appeared miserable as she tried to placate her volatile mother. "I hoped it wouldn't happen again, and it hasn't until now. And because I knew it would upset everyone, I decided not to say anything. I'm sorry to worry you."

"Baby, it's not about us. Don't keep something like this from us. Never again, Emma!"

"Okay, Mom," Emma promised in a wee voice, retreating into her misery.

"She's not going back there!" Anita vowed.

"She has to, my love. Dr. Levy has all the notes and can document what progress has been made . . ."

"Progress? Hah!" Anita injected.

"Yes, progress. *And* she knows about each of the alters. We know she can draw them forth under hypnosis. So, Emma has to go back to her. We can't start over with a new doctor and lose the ground we've already made." Jenkins tilted his wife's chin up so she could meet his eyes. "Okay?"

Still fuming, Anita tightened her lips into a line, but she did concede with a nod. Jenkins touched those tight lips with his and Anita's body lost some of its tension. "Oh, Monty, will this never end?"

Dr. Levy called that evening asking to see the four of them. Jenkins took the call and said they would be there. Anita refused. "You go with the girls, Monty. You can tell me the excuses she comes up with."

Fearing the loss of the Montford family when she felt they'd experienced a huge breakthrough in Emma's treatment with the threats from Sam, Irit Levy called in an associate to help explain what was happening with Emma. She thought two people on the same page would be easier to accept than just her interpretations. Dr. Shirin Weintraub joined her in the session Jenkins Montford had agreed to attend with his two daughters.

After introducing Dr. Weintraub, Dr. Levy asked, "Was Mrs. Montford unable to come today?"

Jenkins replied bluntly, "She won't be joining our session today. She's very angry and she may not return."

"I'm sorry she feels so strongly about it." Irit wasn't surprised. She knew Anita didn't trust her and she felt much the same about her. "Let's get started now with Dr. Weintraub."

The five took seats and the new doctor addressed Emma. "Are you experiencing anything different? Either physical or emotional?"

Emma gazed at the ceiling as if she might search it and find answers there. "I have more headaches now. And they're getting worse."

"Are you hearing voices that seem to come from inside your head?"

Leveling her gaze at the doctor, Emma replied, "Yes. I often hear several voices at once. And they give me massive headaches."

Dr. Weintraub turned to Dr. Levy. "The alters are talking together. That's a good sign." Turning back to the Montfords, she said, "This is a step toward integration where all the parts become one again."

"And that would be me?" Emma asked.

"That's right."

Susie thrust her fist above her head. "Yes! All right, then!"

Dr. Weintraub smiled and continued. "How is your social life, Emma?"

Squirming deeper into her seat, Emma sat erect. She met Susie's eyes. "Not as good as I would like. I'd like to be normal and have a real boyfriend. Susie and I sometimes double-date, and while I think Eric likes me, all he's done is kiss me." She flashed a look at her father. "Sorry, Dad."

Looking again at the doctor and avoiding her father's stare, she went on. "But, if I was normal, I think he would've tried to touch me inappropriately by now. Susie's practically having to fight off Sean every time we go out. He's all over her."

"Really?" Jenkins uttered in his clipped native British accent. They all ignored him.

Dr. Levy spoke. "Susie, what is your opinion of what Emma's just revealed?"

Susie reached over and took Emma's hand. She tugged upward until it lay against her heart. "I'm going to tell them what I think, so here's the real deal, Emma." Her eyes sought Dr. Levy's.

Irit Levy leaned forward, attention fastened on Susie. "Yes, go ahead, please."

Susie flipped her head to one side. "Okay. Here goes. I think Emma is being silly. I think Eric isn't — uh — *mauling* her because he respects her too much. He's gentle with her, always holding her hand and leaning over to kiss her . . ."

Emma gasped. "You watch us?"

"Oh, yeah," Susie said, "Sean and I can see you kissing. We can see what goes on in the front seat. That is, when I'm not slapping his hands." She slid her hands down her jeans-clad thighs, and leaned in, warming to her story. "I can tell Eric likes you. He wouldn't ask you out if he didn't. He's just a nicer guy with better manners than Sean."

Jenkins joined the conversation. "Emma, it's true I'm your father and, quite naturally, I would think you to be beautiful. The fact is you are. All of our friends tell us again and again what an outstanding beauty you've become. And I know you to be a gentle lady. Were we in Britain, you might well be a candidate for Prince Harry's bride." He smiled. "A bit young for him, but still a likely candidate."

Blushing from her neck to her light blonde hairline, Emma ducked her head, "Oh, Dad. Now you're embarrassing me." She looked up. "But, thanks, anyway."

"He's right," Dr. Levy agreed. She glanced at the wall clock. "It's time for our session to be over for the day. You will be making another appointment, yes?"

"Yes," Jenkins said. "And thank you to both of you for today. At least we're talking about what's important to my daughter. I hope it has allayed some of her fears."

Emma appeared thoughtful as they started home. "What's up, Emma?" Susie asked.

"I was thinking about all we discussed today. I wouldn't mind the headaches and all the voices in my head if I could just get back to being only me."

"Have faith. It will happen, Emma," Jenkins said. "Now, who'd like a frozen yogurt?"

Susie was doing her usual when out with Sean. He had her pinned to the corner of the backseat in the Ford Explorer and they were lip-locked together. After Eric picked up Emma and Susie at their home, he'd swung by the condos on Hillhurst Avenue just south of Los Feliz Boulevard to get Sean. He drove them up Mulholland Drive, careful on the winding road, as they climbed high above the city. He'd parked the Explorer and they looked down on the city lights twinkling far below. Then Sean pounced.

In the front seat, Eric looked meaningfully at Emma, jerking his head to indicate the two wrapped together in the back seat. When he leaned toward her for a soft kiss, she turned toward him, leaned over the gearshift and cup holders and put her arms around his neck. She scooted as close as the compartment holding the CDs would allow. Their lips met in a kiss unlike any they'd shared at this point. Emma held nothing back, kissing him in ways she'd never done before. Their breathing grew loud and labored, and as if commanded, Eric caressed her breast through the material of her blouse and bra. Emma required no padding in her bras as she had a large bosom, and her nipple hardened in Eric's hand. They both moaned.

"Get a room!" came from Sean in the back seat. He laughed while Susie felt a spear of fear. *Oh, no! She can't switch now! I've got to do something.*

She shook Eric's shoulder. "Eric, we have to go home right now. I forgot about something I have to do for Dad. He'll ground me forever if I don't get it done by . . ." She rose to check the clock on the dashboard, knocking Eric's hand away from Emma as if by accident. ". . . Oh, hell, it's after nine and I've got to get it to him before he goes to bed."

Emma looked over her shoulder and gave Susie a dirty look, mouthing, "Stop it. Be quiet!"

"So, Eric, crank her up and let's go!" Susie ignored Emma.

Startled at the frantic note in Susie's voice, Eric did as ordered. He got the car going and headed back toward home. Emma leaned against the car door with her arms across her chest, the perfect picture of a pissed off person. It was quiet in the car. Even Sean took his side of the back seat and other than stealing quick glimpses of Susie as she watched Emma, he looked at the houses glide by as Eric kept to the 30 mile per hour speed limit.

As they entered their foyer, a puzzled Emma asked, "Why did the boys bring us home so early?"

"I got scared, Emma. I have no idea what you were doing back there. You were letting . . ." She shook her head. "No, you were *encouraging* Eric to feel you up."

"Oh." Emma's eyes went round, as they tended to do when she heard or learned of something that was hard to take in. "I was *not!*"

"Whatever." Susie looked at her without even the ghost of a smile. She left Emma and went to her room.

CHAPTER SEVENTEEN

The girl lolled on the sofa with her blonde head leaning against the top of the cushion supporting her back. "What's this crap?" She looked down at her bosom neatly buttoned into a tailored white blouse. "I don't dress like this. This is the kind of stuff that girl Emma dresses in."

"Could you tell me your name, please?" The psychiatrist sat without moving as she watched the girl sit up straight on the sofa and look down at her clothing.

"It's Angelique, of course."

"What kind of clothing do you prefer, Angelique?" Dr. Levy asked.

"Sexy things. Not these!" Putting her palms almost together, she threw her hands down, indicating the simple shirt and tan slacks. "You know. The kind that gets the boys' attention. I'd never get any real action if I wore something like this when I go out at night."

"Would you share with me the things you do when you go out?"

Angelique looked at Dr. Levy from the corner of her eye while her devilish grin grew larger. "No, I don't think so. You probably wouldn't like it." She must have seen something in Irit Levy's face, some hint of disapproval, perhaps, because she slyly added, "I will tell you it's a hell of a lot of fun. The guys fight to see who gets my attention." She licked her lips, her pink tongue gliding around the circle of her mouth.

"So, you see a lot of guys each time you go?"

"Sure. Why wouldn't I? It's exciting every time to choose which one I'll sleep with that evening. Oops!" Angelique covered her mouth with her right hand as if surprised she'd revealed something secret about herself while she was being coy with the doctor.

Dr. Levy might have wondered if she was having sex or just pretending. She asked another question. "Does Emma's family know about your evening escapades?"

"Of course not. I'm too smart for that."

"Not even Susie?"

"Oh, please." Angelique drawled her answer, dismissing the question. She could have thought Dr. Levy would ask a question she didn't want to answer, for Angelique faded and, while Dr. Levy waited for more revelations, they didn't come.

The doctor now said, "When I count backwards from five, you will wake up. Five, four, three, two, one."

Emma roused and looked around, her eyes landing on the clock. "Oh, it's time for me to go. But first, please tell me what happened today."

Looking thoughtful, the doctor rose and walked over to the rheostat on the wall beside the sofa. Located just above the lamp, she adjusted it so the light blue shade glowed almost white. "I think we need a little more light."

Emma asked, "Why? Did something different happen? Did another part come out?"

Levy took a seat by Emma on the sofa. She placed her hand on Emma's right forearm as she said low and soft, "Yes, I met a new alter today. Her name is Angelique." She bit her bottom lip, likely unaware she was doing it as she thought of what to say.

Hesitating over her words, Emma at last asked, "Is that a good thing—or is it bad?"

The words rose to her mouth and flew out. "Are you on birth control, Emma?"

Emma furrowed her brow and her mouth twisted in distaste. "No! I don't have any reason to use birth control." Her expression turned fearful. "Do I *need* to be on birth control?"

"I think you might. Angelique intimated she was sexually active."

"Oh, my God, no!" Emma dropped her face into her hands. Raising it, wet now with her tears, she asked, "What should I do?"

"Well, the first thing would be to tell your parents. They can decide if you should see a gynecologist who can tell if there has been sexual activity. If so, then you'll need to address it in whatever way everyone thinks best."

Dr. Levy opened the door for Emma and watched her back as she walked away, her head down and shoulders slumped. She returned to her file drawer and pulled Emma's. She added the notes from the day's session, which included, "I met Emma's newest alter today. Angelique is seventeen, Emma's own age. She is different from all the other parts. I think she most likely is slipping out of the Montford home at night and is actively seeking sex. Emma was upset to know this. I suggested she discuss with the family and have a check up to see if she's had sex, and to determine if she is sexually active now."

Emma parked her midnight blue Prius on the concrete parking area by the Montford's driveway. She knew she needed to talk with her mom about birth control and what she'd found out about Angelique, but she needed to talk to Susie first.

She entered the house calling out "Susie? Are you here? Where are you, Susie?" She found her in the laundry room digging through a mound of her soiled laundry Madonna hadn't yet washed.

"I have something serious I need to talk about with you." Her eyes filled and she looked down, scraping the toe of her sneakers against the red-clay tiled floor.

They sat by the pool, chairs drawn together so they were facing. Their knees almost touched. Their hands did. Two blonde heads, one almost platinum and the other a darker gold, leaned together. Emma told Susie everything she'd learned that day in therapy.

When finished, she ventured, "Do you think I've been sneaking out at night to see boys?" Her voice was shaky. "Have you seen me or found any evidence I've done that?"

"Well . . ."

Agitated, Emma fired, "You've got to tell me, Susie! I have to know."

"Okay, I haven't caught you sneaking out at night, although I'm pretty sure you do. *And* I think Angelique came out last night with Eric."

"Oh, no, she didn't!" Emma wailed, her voice dripping with the pain that spread to her clinched fists.

"Well, Eric was finally all over you, touching your breasts and kissing like crazy. And you not only let him, but you started it."

"Then it wasn't me! Dammit, Susie, I don't remember any of this."

"All right. But it still happened. Eric thinks it was you."

Silence from Emma prompted Susie to continue. "We need to tell Mom so you can get checked out by an OB-GYN."

"No. I'm going to make an appointment with our family doctor, Dr. Lee, and let him see what he can find. And I want you to go with me. I'll ask him not to say anything to Mom because what we find out will determine what we tell her."

Oh, Shit. I am so tired of this. Susie's frown said it all.

Emma finished her gynecological exam and was sitting dressed on the exam table while Susie sat in a chair.

Dr. Lee cleared his throat. "Emma, presently there is semen in your vagina. That would indicate it's almost certain you've had sex within the last 48 to 72 hours. I will run a pregnancy test, but I don't think you are pregnant."

Appearing stunned, Emma sat unmoving, her eyes vacant, seeing nothing.

Susie asked, "Is there more? Anything else we should know?"

The doctor looked down and swallowed. His Adam's apple moved with the contracting of his throat. He studied the grey and white tile on the floor before lifting his eyes to Susie and then to Emma. "I found some old scarring, most noticeably, a healed tear through the vulva on one side of the vaginal entrance and a healed contusion of some size on the inner vulva on the other side."

Emma responded to this with a gasp.

"Holy cow!" Susie gasped loudly and shot a puzzled glance at Emma.

"This indicates old trauma that had to have occurred years ago. I'd say perhaps ten or so. No damage was incurred with the latest sexual acts." Again he looked from one girl to the other. "Is this something you need to report? I'm required to report suspected sexual abuse and I'd bet my license that this earlier sex where you were injured was, without doubt, abuse."

Her face registering alarm and fear, Emma spoke in a ragged whisper. "Thank you, Dr. Lee. You do what you have to do."

The doctor still stood, tapping his report papers against his thigh, consternation emanating from him as he contemplated Emma. His professionalism battling with his compassion, he asked, "Do you not remember what happened all those years ago?"

Emma shook her head, eyes cast down.

His voice rising with his next question, he asked, "You don't remember the sex that just happened, either?"

"No, but I *will* tell my mom and dad and let them help me figure out what must have happened to me."

Turning his gaze from Emma to Susie and back again, he asked, "You *are* seeing someone for help about this forgetting problem, aren't you?"

By this time, Susie was on edge, her defense of her sister uppermost in her mind. "Of course she is! She just hasn't worked out yet with her doctor what she's gonna do. But she is gonna talk to Mom and Dad."

Dr. Lee moved away from the counter he'd leaned against and patted Emma's back. "That's a good idea. I hope you can get it all taken care of. This is a horrible thing to have happen to you. Good luck in getting to the bottom of it."

Emma asked Susie to drive home since she was shaken to her core. This was another emergency time when the two thought it necessary to break Susie's promise to their mom. They discussed possibilities and could come up with no prospects who might have abused Emma. At home, they sat together in Emma's room planning how and when to engage their parents in the conversation that was imperative they have. They decided to tell them at the end of the night's dinner that there was something of great importance they needed to talk about. Both parents were free for the evening so they would have plenty of time.

"I just hope I can get through it without falling apart," Emma said. Her voice was shaky, matching her trembling mouth and hands.

Emma put on her brave front and explained to Anita and Jenkins about the new part, Angelique, who emerged at her last therapy session. She related Dr. Levy's suggestion of being checked out for sexual activity. Here she bogged down, hanging her head, her curtain of hair making it impossible to meet her parents' eyes.

Anita sprang from her chair. "We've got to make an appointment right away. We have to know!"

"Damned right, we do," Jenkins added. "What else can you tell us, Emma?"

Emma opened and closed her mouth, cleared her throat, and tried again. Nothing. She flipped her hair out of her face and looked at Susie.

Jenkins eyes followed these actions. "Do you know anything about this, Susie?"

"Well, Dad, I'll tell you if Emma wants me to." Her eyes questioned Emma, who nodded with her mouth closed in a tight line.

As Susie told them about the appointment with Dr. Lee and his findings, Emma grew more agitated, seeming to draw into herself, becoming almost physically smaller. Both parents had volatile reactions with Anita wringing her hands and bursting into tears, and Jenkins explosive, "I'll be god damned!"

Emma sat up straight and, looking at the other three, she smiled. In an older voice, both quiet and gentle, she said. "Everything will be all right. Don't worry. I'll take care of it."

Susie was uncertain if she'd met Emmaline in the past, if this stressful time was indicative of when she appeared. This would've been a logical thing for Emma to say, if she hadn't been so upset, but Susie knew with the voice change, it was not Emma speaking. Softly, Susie asked, "Emmaline?"

"Yes. I'm right here. My presence helps calm things down."

Anita, recovering from her initial anger and horror, and recognizing what was happening, said, "Thank you, Emmaline." *Good Lord, I'm talking to her as if she's real.*

Emma roused. "I think I can talk about it now. After all this time of wondering why I can't remember a good portion of my elementary school years, I know now . . ." she stood and faced her parents, ". . . it's because I was abused at that time. I had to have been, or I wouldn't have had the scarring that proves it."

Fury shading his every word, Jenkins replied, "We're going to figure out how it happened, Emma, and then we're going to nab the bastard who did it!"

"Yes, we damned sure are!" Anita vowed. She put her fingers to her temples and massaged the headache that grew there. "But, for now, I think we're all emotionally exhausted. Jenkins, let's go to our bedroom and talk about this. You girls can do that if you want, or just have private time for yourselves. But, we *are* going to figure this out." She hugged Emma, holding her tight for a few seconds, then turned to Susie, enfolding her into the three-way hug.

Anita and Jenkins undressed and prepared for bed. Their bodies were in the place meant for sleep, but sleep would not be on their agenda for several hours. They spent hours turning over every leaf that had fallen from their family tree of four since Emma was a small child. They talked and ranted and searched their memories.

At last Anita said, "I think I may have it, Monty! Remember that time when we were puzzled by Emma being so quiet and withdrawn? And then when we were talking about that and when we took Emma outside to play, remember how she didn't like it back by the pool?"

"Yes. Now it's coming back to me. We talked about this before but didn't know how to address the particular situation. She didn't want to go anywhere near the shrubbery behind the pool. And she wouldn't play with Susie out there." He hit himself between the eyebrows with the heel of his hand. "I'm an idiot! I should've thought of that and put it together. Since no one else was around, it had to have been one of the gardeners who molested her."

"Molested her, my ass! It was rape and abuse of an innocent child." Anita threw herself onto Jenkins' chest, her body quivering with growing rage. "Why didn't we pay more attention to what was going on?" she wailed. "Why didn't we follow through?"

She sat up, her gown slipping unnoticed off her shoulders, and glared at Jenkins as she stumbled through her words. "We're terrible parents, Monty. We failed to protect our daughter.

I can't bear to think what pain and misery she went through, and she must have wondered why we didn't help her. And it must have gone on for a couple of years at least. How could we have been so stupid and blind that we didn't notice?" She came to a halt with, "Oh, my God, Monty! I think I'm going to have to have therapy. This guilt is going to kill me!"

"Take it easy, my love. Now is not the time to blame ourselves." He took her face between his palms and forced her to concentrate on his words. "Now we have to decide what to do about finding the gardener, or God forbid, *gardeners*, who did this. We have to be proactive in talking to Emma both with and without Dr. Levy present. We saw Emmaline tonight. We may see others who will help Emma remember the events of that time. She obviously suppressed it completely."

His hands dropped from Anita's face as he looked at the clock. "Damn, it's almost three o'clock already. If we can calm ourselves, we *may* get some sleep tonight."

"Not yet, Monty. We need to make a plan to keep Angelique from taking over Emma and sneaking out at night. She *can't* go out anymore because who knows what will happen to her. At the very least, she'll either get pregnant or contract some kind of sexual disease. Maybe even, God forbid, AIDS!"

Jenkins stared at his reflection in the big dresser mirror. It showed a big man, bare-chested and wearing briefs. It didn't show the turmoil inside his head. He snapped the fingers of his right hand, raising it shoulder high. "Susie! She'll have to watch Emma. They can either sleep together in her room or Emma's."

Daring to let herself get excited, Anita's voice rose as she added, "Yes, and they need to rig up some system that lets Susie know when Emma moves, or rather Angelique, decides to try sneaking out."

"Right."

"So, we'll tell them about it in the morning." Anita yawned and stretched. "I do feel better. Maybe I *will* sleep."

"We're making progress, my love." Jenkins kissed his wife and they settled into the big California King with its extra length providing room for Jenkins' long form. He held her curves against him as they drifted into sleep . . . relief now permitting it.

Over waffles and bacon, the Montford family discussed their plans. Anita and Jenkins took turns telling their girls what they believed happened all those years ago and their solution to keep Angelique from wandering.

"Oh, we already thought of that," Susie said around a mouthful of waffle dripping syrup down her chin. "Emma's staying in my room and sleeping with me every night." She swallowed, gulped some milk, and continued." She . . ." she tossed a look at Emma ". . . agreed to let me use a rope to tie us together. It's long enough to turn over and get comfy, but if she needs to go to the bathroom, I go with her."

"And vice versa," Emma contributed. "The rope will be tied around one of my wrists and around one of Susie's, and each end will have a lock."

"I'll have the key and Emma can't get to it, so she can't get out of the rope." She grinned at Emma. "I got you now, girl!"

Jenkins nodded while thinking it over. "Impressive." He beamed at his daughters. "You two are pretty smart. I'm learning how smart you are and how hard you're working on getting Emma back to just her."

"Oh, one more thing—just in case," Anita cautioned. All eyes looked to her. "Call Dr. Lee and get a prescription for birth control pills. Again, just in case."

CHAPTER EIGHTEEN

Tying the two together at their wrists seemed to
work well. They had to coordinate a number of
things. Emma had to exchange one of Susie's
pillows for her favorite. They had to go to bed at the same
time, although the length of the rope allowed one to place
a pillow or two behind her back should she wish to read
or attend to emails on her tablet after the other settled
in to sleep. Both girls admitted it was inconvenient and
not as comfortable as they hoped, but it was working. If
Angelique had returned at all, her presence hadn't been
evident. They agreed if this much togetherness didn't
break their friendship, it would make them even closer.
Neither girl was prepared for the trouble which reared its
ugly, dangerous head before a month was up.

They lay tethered together with Susie on the right side
of the bed nearest the door. Emma lay on her right side
on the left side of the bed with her roped right wrist supporting her head on the pillow. She faced Susie, who lay
on her left side, hands tucked together and resting on her
pillow in front of her sleeping face, her breathing deep and
gentle, little puffs of air escaping her lips.

Emma hoped Susie wouldn't start snoring. Her consternation over the real possibility that Susie might do that caused her even more anxiety.

Susie's breathing was a steady in and out as she headed for deep sleep. The kind of slumber where dreams are born. Susie inhaled a deep lungful of air. To Emma, it sounded like "Schchaaa." Susie held it for a couple of seconds. "Kuuuhhhh," was the sound her fluttering lips made when she exhaled. "Schchaaa-kuuuhhh," it came again. And again.

"Damn! Would ya stop makin' that friggin' noise?" Christine sat up as she addressed Susie, glaring at her in the feeble glow of the night light plugged into the wall socket by the bathroom door.

"Schhhaaaa-kuuhhh," was Susie's answer as she lay unmoving.

"What the hell? I done told ya to shut the fuck up!" The words came out of Emma's mouth through a nasty sneer placed there by Christine. "I'm not tellin' ya agin. I'll slap ya silly if I hear another snore outta ya."

Susie woke to see Emma looming over her, her face pressed close to hers, almost touching her pillow. "Whoa! What's the problem? You're scaring me."

In the next moment she realized it was not Emma, but another part whose voice was raised by her threats. Remembering Dr. Levy's descriptions of the different alters, this one sounded a lot like the southern girl.

"Christine?"

"Shit, yes. Who in the hell did you think it was?" Anger dripped from each drawn-out word.

"How should I know? I was asleep," Susie fired back.

"Well, ya better quit that Goddamn snorin'."

"If I do, will you be happy?" Susie asked. Her jumpy insides, together with her heart and brain, hoped Christine would be happy and Emma would return.

"I guess. Anythin' would be better than listenin' to that godforsaken noise."

Emma returned, dropping back to her pillow. Susie could tell it was Emma lying beside her, eyes closed as if she was listening to music—or voices in her head. She stayed quiet, giving Emma the time she needed to sort through what happened and who she was, if she could recover that information.

Susie waited. Emma lay without moving, her face distorted in obvious pain. Soon she put her hands to her face, covering her eyes. She moved them to her temples and massaged in circles, paying no mind to the fine blonde hairs she pulled with each arc. Several long minutes passed before she spoke.

"I have the mother of all headaches, Susie. There are all these voices in my head talking at once. It's making me crazy."

"What are they saying?"

"Christine is yammering on about you snoring and how she'd like to choke you so you couldn't bother her like that again." She stopped massaging her temples and moved her right hand to the top of her head where she dug her hand into the thick strands and raked her scalp with her long, red-painted nails. "And Emmaline is telling her to cool it and everything is going to be okay."

Susie's mind registered the red nails. "Where'd you get your red fingernails done, Emma?"

With her right palm on her forehead, her left hand rested on her stomach. She opened her eyes and looked at the vermillion polish tipping the fingers of her left hand as she held it in front of her face, turning it to all sides.

"I don't have any idea." She sucked in breath and let it out a bit at a time, thinking as hard as her headache would permit. "Maybe it was Christine, but it was probably Angelique."

"Is there anything else you care to tell me?"

"Not now. I just need for it to be calm and quiet so maybe the voices will hush and my headache will go away."

Emma's headache continued the next day, sometimes sharp severe pain and other times a low pulsing was all she felt. She saw Dr. Levy that afternoon and they began hypnosis right away. Dr. Levy made a note about the red fingernails, seeing Emma's nails painted vermillion for the first time.

Sitting primly on Dr. Levy's couch in the dimly lit room used for hypnotism, Emmaline appeared first and told how difficult it was to keep some of the others in line, particularly Sam and Angelique. "Sam is very volatile and says he's going to hurt Emma. Angelique is a narcissist and wants what she wants and says Emma doesn't matter to her, nor does anyone else. It's hard trying to talk sense to them."

Dr. Levy saw Emmaline disappear as Emma's body hopped up and then sat down again with her legs bent at the knees and under her body so that she sat on them. She bounced a couple of times, jiggling her upper body, and she wore a delighted, childish expression.

"Hello, Julia," Levy said. "How are you today?"

In a perfect imitation of a happy six-year-old girl's voice, she sang out, "I'm fine." She bounced again and said, "This is fun. Your sofa is so soft."

The therapist heard even the slight lisp Julia enunciated with her words that contained an "S." Only the words *fun* and *you* didn't have the "sss" sound.

"Why are you here today, Julia?"

Looking crestfallen, as if she feared she wasn't welcome, Julia replied, "I just wanted to say 'Hi' and to get away from the others for a while." Her head drooped and her shoulders slumped. "They're all shouting and being bad and talking about stuff I didn't want to hear."

"Even Emmaline?"

"No, Emmaline is telling bad ole' Sam to behave. But," she said, as if sharing a confidence, "He's getting nicer. He's not mad *all* the time now."

"That's great, Julia. Thanks for visiting me today." Emma's body lost the little girl playfulness and she stood up, smoothed down her denim skirt, and sat back down with her knees crossed, and body relaxed, waiting with eyes closed.

"Five, four, three, two, one." Emma woke on "one" and yawned. Her eyes met Dr. Levy's and she asked, "What's going on inside me today?"

"I'm optimistic we are making progress. It seems everyone was talking today except Ralph. He may not have been needed in the conversation. I know an hour sometimes just isn't enough for them to work out a problem, but they seemed to be trying. We'll have to see how it works."

"Yes, but what happened?"

Dr. Levy dropped her head toward her shoulder, regarding Emma while she thought. "First Emmaline talked with me and said everyone seemed to want to talk at the same time. That's why you were having such a bad headache. Is it better now?"

"Yes. It's better but not quite gone."

"It appears things are calming, somewhat. Anyway, Angelique and Sam were being obstinate, and Julia was getting frustrated by the arguing. So, when Emmaline receded, Julia came. What a happy, delightful little one she is."

Emma spread her lips in a tight line. "I'm glad *somebody* is."

"Julia did say Sam was acting calmer."

"Thank God! Maybe he'll disappear."

"That's our goal, Emma. To make all of them disappear. It *will* happen," Dr. Levy reassured her.

CHAPTER NINETEEN

ZELDA

In the four years Zelda Bass had homeschooled the Montford girls, she'd experienced changes in her own life. Many times she'd thought of throwing in the towel and walking away. What kept her there was the achingly clear need the family had of her. She respected Jenkins and Anita Montford for their determined efforts to see Emma through her illness, giving their constant support, until she was whole again. Zelda didn't have to feign her fondness for either girl. She'd never seen two girls so different in personalities who were best friends and loved each other without question. She had noticed, however, that Susie sometimes wasn't as patient with Emma as she had been when she began teaching them. Although it was sometimes a challenge just to get through the day's classes when an alter stepped in for Emma, she was unsurprised when it happened now.

She believed she had witnessed all the other parts that Emma carried within her. It was often scary, because Sam had the presence and power to frighten anyone when he came forth. He was always angry and menacing, but it was directed at Emma. He was never at a loss for foul, threatening words which thundered off Emma's tongue. He had been all talk, however. Other than the occasional push so Emma would hit her head or trip over something in her path that she knew was there, he hadn't harmed anyone. So far.

Christine was another part she was unsure how to deal with. Sweet at times, she had the uncanny talent to hurl insults—barbs that really hurt, interspersed with curse words worthy of a sailor. And all was delivered in the smoothest honey-suckle-of-the-south accent imaginable. Even with growing up in Montgomery, Alabama, Zelda had never heard such a syrupy southern drawl as that used by Christine.

When Emmaline appeared, it was almost a relief, because she brought further calmness if things in the classroom were going well. If not, her presence and soothing words of assurance were just what was needed. Emma, at those times, appeared wiser than her years and work done as Emmaline was of the highest quality.

Julia was a delight. Of course, she couldn't contribute to the work either Susie or Emma was engaged in, but she could bring joy and happiness. In her little girl's high, piping voice, she always spoke of pleasant things and begged Zelda and Susie to play with her. Or read a book. Or put together a puzzle. After her first visit, Zelda asked Susie to procure some things to have on hand for when Julia visited.

Ralph the Flirt, as Zelda came to think of him, didn't come as often as he had before. A definite disruption to the classroom, at least he was fun. He was so in love with Susie and spoke to her in terms of endearment, being as manly as he could be, considering he possessed only a thirteen-year-old boy's bag of tricks. Emma's body would present at the end of the day a bruised knee where Ralph had performed some outrageous trick to impress Susie and took a fall during its execution. Zelda thought she might actually have enjoyed Ralph's visits if it hadn't been so incongruous to watch Emma's body play out his plans.

And then Angelique joined the others later in Emma's ongoing hosting. She was new to the group, having developed only recently. Zelda thought she was the part of Emma who yearned for a normal teenaged girl's desire for a boyfriend of her own. That included the desire to experiment with kissing and touching and to have the freedom to come and go as most seventeen-year-old girls are allowed to do today. Then it went too far.

Zelda was informed by the Montfords about Emma sneaking out of the house at night for sexual trysts with who-knows-what boys, and their subsequent answer of how to keep her home and safe. When Zelda looked at the angelic-featured Emma, it was difficult to envision her playing the wanton high school girl out looking for sex. She'd talked with Angelique once, and the coy voice and cunning attitude, plus what she knew Angelique to be up to, bore no resemblance to the Emma who sat in her classroom most of the time.

The Montfords were now almost like family to her. She spent a third of her time with them five days a week as she followed the school calendar. When the girls were off from school, she was, as well.

Nearing the end of her second year of teaching in the Montford home, she'd accepted her insistent fiancée's proposal and planned a wedding back home in Alabama. Having grown fond of both girls, she would've liked for both Emma and Susie to be bridal attendants. She spoke with Anita. Zelda was disappointed when Anita said they couldn't do it, but she understood how an alter's visit had the potential to create havoc with her wedding day. Susie was distressed and cried bitter tears and Emma said she felt horrible about being the reason they couldn't do it. But, she did get married the day she'd planned, and in these two years she'd been very happy in her marriage. Her husband realized it was a regular job, as if she was teaching in a high school, and kept out of it by making the most non-committal sounds he could when Zelda spoke of her job to him.

Now she was in her fifth year of teaching in the Montford home. It was almost Christmas, which meant the first semester of Emma's twelfth grade was almost over, the second semester officially beginning in January. Emma would be graduating in June at the end of the second semester. Then her job with them would be over, for while Emma, of necessity, had to be homeschooled through her graduation, Susie did not have to follow. Finally, Susie would be free to go back to rejoin her friends in public school, or back to parochial school should she choose to, rendering an end to Zelda's job.

Deep inside her soul where her conscience lay, Zelda was pleased for Susie. She'd kept her opinion to herself for these almost five years, but had marveled at Susie's selfless ability to always put Emma first, giving up a once-expected life of the average teenager to be a care-taker for Emma. In essence, Zelda thought, Susie had lost herself along the way. She hoped with fervor that Susie could find herself again and experience her life without always having to look out for Emma or to run interference for the alters. She wanted Susie's last year of high school to be what Susie wanted it to be.

Emma shared with her that she faithfully took her birth control pills in the event Angelique wanted some action during the day when she wasn't tethered to Susie. Susie had also told her she hid the key to the specially made rope with locks on either end beneath her mattress in a spot directly below where her pillow lay. No way had

Emma, or Angelique, been able to ferret it out without awakening Susie. So, as far as she or any of the Montford family could tell, Angelique had been afforded no opportunity to give away her body. Enough time had passed since Angelique's night time outings until Anita confided that the family felt confident in releasing Emma from Susie's guard. She said Emma had not heard Angelique in her head for some time and, therefore, they all took that as a positive sign of Emma's coming integration where she would become whole again. Zelda was relieved and happy for the family. All was good . . . for a time.

CHAPTER TWENTY

The family was uncertain whether Emma/Angelique had succeeded in making a run for it during the night when everyone was asleep. So, they didn't know what to think when Emma returned from a full day away from the house one Saturday in February with Christmas red lips and nails. Her face was heavily made up with darkened lashes and brows, a matte finish with powder, and turquoise eyeshadow as dense as the deep pink rouge on her cheeks.

She entered the house as her family sat down on the stools for dinner, with a luscious looking dish of lasagna steaming with a savory smell in the middle of the table. Emma dropped her bags, several bearing a trendy teens' shop logo, on the sofa in the rec room, sailing happily past her gawking family.

Returning to take her place at her stool, Emma closed her eyes and sniffed deeply. "Ahhh, that smells divine!"

She *sounded* like Emma, so Susie released the breath she'd been holding and belted out, "What on earth did you do to your face, Emma?"

Anita jumped in with, "Good Lord! I don't wear that much makeup when I'm filming!" and Jenkins asked in a calm, conversational tone, "Where did you have your makeup done, Emma?"

Emma looked up from her plate where she was ladling a sizeable portion of lasagna onto it. "What? Is there something wrong with my makeup?"

She looked from one to the other, trying to keep a straight face. She couldn't do it. First a smile tugged at the corners of her lips, then her eyes crinkled, and then she began to laugh loudly, dipping her head and her shoulders shaking.

Incredulous looks were fired at her as her laughter began to wind down. "I'm sorry. I shouldn't have upset you that way. I really wasn't thinking, but . . ." she giggled again, ". . . you should've seen your faces!"

"Emma . . . !" Jenkins warned.

"Okay. Here's what happened. I got stopped by the makeup counter by one of those mannequin-looking girls with all that perfect makeup that hides their zits. She asked me if she could do mine for me. So, she did. She kept applying more and more thick foundation."

"I'll say she did," Susie snorted, but Emma continued as if Susie hadn't spoken.

"I realize she got carried away with all of it, but I . . ." she emphasized the "I" so they would all know that she was aware it was her and not one of the alters who allowed it to happen, ". . . let her do it. And then when I left, I forgot about it as I did the rest of my shopping." She giggled again as each member of her family still sat with a disapproving expression affixed to their faces. "Then I figured out why I was getting all those weird looks everywhere I went. So, I decided to see what all of you would say.

"You're *teasing* us, Emma!" her mom crowed. "I can hardly believe my solemn daughter has a sense of humor."

Jenkins spoke slowly, seeming to be awed by Emma's revelation, "Excellent, Emma! Now, here is real evidence to suggest you are being integrated into one being. We would've expected one of your alters, but we got *you!*"

Emma swept into the rec room classroom three or four minutes past the 8:30 A.M. start time. "We've got Justin Bieber tickets!" she shrieked.

Zelda jerked her head up and leveled a stare at the cause of the noisy intrusion.

Susie shot out of her seat, crying out, "No way!" Her joviality was quick to fade as the joy drained from her face. She regarded Emma seriously, tilting her head and examining her with concerned curiosity.

"Is that you, Emma?"

Emma snorted, "Yes, for Pete's sake, Susie. Of course, it's me."

"Well, you *sounded* like you, but you sure didn't *act* like you."

Zelda interrupted them. "Perhaps you'd like to tell us what's going on, Emma."

Acknowledging her teacher with a nod and a 'sorry', Emma divulged what she knew about the source of her excitement. "I just got off the phone with Eric." Her voice rose again as she explained. "He scored four tickets for the Justin Bieber show at the Staples Center on the twentieth of March. He asked me to go with him, and is asking Sean and you. We're supposed to meet some other friends there."

"Oooo, I am *so* excited!" Susie gushed. "I can't believe he was able to get four tickets. I thought they were already sold out."

"They are. I think his dad got them through his work or something like that."

"Excellent!"

Zelda again spoke while trying not to dismantle their exuberant happiness. "That's wonderful news. I know y'all will have a fantastic time. But, take your seats, please, and we'll start our classes for the day."

Both girls lost their happy looks as they tried to dampen their excitement and put on their classroom faces. Seeing this, Zelda added, "You know the more we hurry, the sooner the twentieth of March will get here."

The girls caught each other's eyes and giggled. Things were back to normal.

Midafternoon on Sunday, March 20, 2016, Eric and Sean arrived to collect Emma and Susie for what they thought to be the event of the year—an evening with Justin Bieber bustin' his moves on stage, singing his songs straight to each of them, and occasionally crooning a love song while he strummed his guitar. What they hoped would not happen was a repeat of his 2013 tour where he threw up off stage—and on. Had it happened in Los Angeles, they would not have seen it anyway, as Anita had no interest in taking the girls to see the boy wonder from Canada. It was a given that had their dad been home, he would not have taken them, either.

They talked and laughed and the boys teased the girls about being "Beliebers" as the Bieber fans were called, while heading into downtown Los Angeles to find parking near the Staples Center, the large arena for sports and entertainment.

Emma gasped and threw a sharp look at Eric. "Did you think to reserve valet parking?"

"Oh, God! I didn't think about parking," Sean admitted.

Eric played them off with a slap to his forehead, as if he had forgotten to reserve parking. Susie saw his grin in the rearview mirror and added another slap to the back of his head. "Don't scare me like that, boy," she threatened. "We'd scalp your ticket and buy parking with what we'd get for it!"

They were still blocks away from the Center when the sidewalks came alive. They seemed to be crawling with people like the moving walkways in the airports as they funneled "Beliebers" toward the entrance. It was a good move on Eric's part that he'd made reservations for the car to be parked. He only had to circle a stretch of blocks twice before he pulled up at his appointed time to where he was to leave the car for valet parking in whatever space in whatever lot the company was using.

Once inside, they found their seats, pretty decent ones at that. They all got huge sodas and consumed them during the opening acts featuring Post Malone and Moxie Raia. They got in the mood for the evening with the two relatively unknowns. And then The Bieber was onstage!

Midway through his first set, Emma put her hand on Susie's thigh, shaking it hard to get her attention. Susie thrust her arms in the air and her body continued dancing in place, undulating to the music's beat. Emma shook harder. Susie dragged her eyes from Bieber's dancing moves to see what Emma could possibly want. She saw that Emma was firmly cupping her crotch with her right hand and it looked like she was doing the pee-pee dance. Amid the deafening noise, Susie heard Julia's unmistakable childish voice say, "I've got to pee. Will you take me?"

Susie's happiness vanished in an instant.

Eric, on the other side of Emma, shouted, "Everything okay?"

Susie shouted in return, "No. Emma's feeling nauseous. We're going to the bathroom. Don't worry. We'll be right back." She elbowed Sean and when he took his eyes from the stage, she yelled, "Gotta go. Be back later." She prayed neither boy would see Emma with her hand between her legs while she jerked Julia along behind her as she raced to the women's bathroom.

After Julia peed, she hopped off the seat and reached to the floor where her jeans and pink panties puddled around her sandals. She wriggled into them and pulled the jeans together at the waist. She tugged and stuck her thumb through the button hole. Nothing worked. With a pout of Emma's perfect pink lips, Julia asked, "Can you button me up, please?"

Irritated, Susie wondered how long this would last with Julia demanding her entire attention. She grabbed the two sides of the waistband, yanked them together and slid the button through the hole. Supposing she needed to zip her up, too, she grabbed the zipper. Up it went. "There, you're all done," she sighed through the words.

Julia tugged on Susie's hand. "Let's go," she drew out her demand in a whiney, little girl voice.

Susie shook her head in slow motion as she gazed at Julia, thinking about what she should do next.

As if reading her thoughts, Julia announced, "I want to go outside. I don't like it in here. It smells like doo-doo." She pulled Susie's hand, and not knowing what else to do, Susie followed her out into the corridor. Julia dropped her hand and in a flash ran to the first entry to steps leading down into the arena. She peeked in and then sprinted to the next opening. Again she stopped in the open space and looked around. "Come on," she yelled back to Susie. "Let's look in there from all of these doors." She looked across the arena to the far side. "There's lots more and you can stand here and see right down to the stage. That boy was dancing and talking when I was down there." She pointed back to the first opening. Again, she looked inside. "Oh, now he's singing."

Her steps slow, Susie walked to Julia and took her hand. She pitched her voice low and threatening. "Julia, you *will* be quiet. This is not how you're supposed to behave at a concert. You will hold my hand and we are going to walk around for a bit. You need to calm down right now."

With no warning, Julia burst into tears. A loud wail accompanied the water works.

What's next? I'm so tired of having to deal with this. "Julia, stop crying. Stop it. People are looking at us." They were. Two young men in jeans and sneakers followed them with their eyes until they were forced to either stop and stare or look forward again. They stopped staring and followed their noses forward.

Susie watched as a group of girls emerged from the nearest women's bathroom. They saw the crying teenager and one asked if they needed help. Susie replied they didn't have any tissue, she just needed to get some toilet tissue for her friend. She dashed to the first stall and ripped off a couple of lengths of tissue.

The messy tears mixed with Emma's makeup left tan smears on her cheeks. Julia blew her nose on the second length of paper so Susie took Julia's arm and they went together into the bathroom to get more tissue. As she unrolled more and handed it to Julia, "Here, wipe your face," Susie heard the arena crowd noise swell even louder and expected that the first half of the performance was over. She seethed. *That's just great. I've missed the whole first half.*

Doing a one-eighty, Susie decided she needed to comfort Julia and see if that would bring Emma back. Sternness failed. She knew Eric and Sean would be look-ing for them and expected to see them materialize amid the crowd of many colors at any time. In the growing noise in the corridor, she leaned her forehead against Julia's and reached her arms around her shoulders, pulling her close in a hug. "I'm sorry, Julia. I didn't mean to be a meanie." She offered a smile and at this moment, it was about the best she could do.

A hand on her shoulder brought her around to see the eager face of Sean. "Boy, Susie, you really missed a good one!" Noticing Emma, whose back was against the wall, he asked, "Is Emma better now?"

"I think so. Let me ask her." She hugged Julia again and put her mouth to her ear. "Emma, please come back. I need you."

Emma whispered into Susie's ear on the other side, "What's happening? Why do you have your arms around me? Did I switch to someone else?" Panic entered her voice, "Eric didn't see whoever it was, did he?"

"No." Susie turned back to Sean, letting her arms drop to her sides. "She's not nauseated any longer and says she'll be fine. Where's Eric?"

"He went looking for you in the other direction. He should find us soon. We may as well stay here."

Eric appeared on the other side of the corridor, his height of six-foot-four, coupled with his black hair, made him visible through and above the crowd. His eyes caught Sean's raised arm as they swept the concert-goers and he worked his way over to them.

"Emma! Are you all right?"

"Just fine. I'm looking forward to the last half." She threaded her arm through his and the couple walked through a lull in the corridor traffic and down the stairs to their seats.

"Guess we'll join them," Susie said, steering Sean in the direction Emma and Eric went.

The Justin Bieber Experience during the second half was all they wanted it to be. The four teens left the arena, retrieved Eric's car and chattered about The Bieber's moves and songs all the way to the Montford home.

Susie, only a bit more subdued than usual, said, "I'm really sorry we didn't catch up with Addie and Camille. I haven't talked with either of them in such a long time. It'll be great to maybe go to school with them next year."

"You mean when Emma graduates in a few weeks, you want to give up homeschooling?" Eric asked.

Thinking, *Oh, I do not want Emma spazzing out right now so I'd better cut this conversation off at the knees,* Susie said, "I'm not certain. It may be a possibility. We'll see what Emma does in the fall." She knew things were going along fine and the alters were appearing less and less. And then Emma had to have Julia come along and almost ruin the evening.

Eric parked the Explorer on the concrete slab behind Emma's Prius. They all climbed out and went inside for the Tex-Mex snacks Madonna had prepared for them.

Susie sat on a bar stool and watched the other three dive into the food and take plates full of tacos and fajitas to the rec room. There they sat on the couch and ate their food off the large coffee table made from an ancient door Jenkins had sent to him from his estate in England. A top of heavy glass allowed the intricately carved swirling pattern to show through without it being damaged.

Susie thought about all that happened on this night, understanding fully that Emma couldn't help it. Still she muttered, "But, dammit, can't I at least have an evening out where I don't have to take care of her?"

As she was thinking this, Emma called, "Aren't you going to eat with us?"

Swallowing what she thought of as her 'nasty words', she faked a smile and her hearty reply. "Be right there, if you guys haven't eaten it all."

The next day in Dr. Levy's office, Emma told her about Julia.

Sincerity and compassion gleamed in Irit Levy's dark brown eyes as she addressed Emma. "I know you're quite disappointed that Julia came forth when we haven't seen anything of her in a while. I know, too, that you're hoping to be integrated soon." She leaned back in her chair, holding Emma's gaze. "It seems you aren't ready yet. We'll keep a close watch on any of the alters to see who presents and how often. That will give us a good idea of the progress."

"Yeah, I guess you're right," Emma said, her voice hitching as she struggled to hold back her tears.

"Write down what anybody tells you they've seen, and we'll talk about it next week."

CHAPTER TWENTY-ONE

Jenkins and Anita sat across the desk from their lawyer as he attempted to explain about the statute of limitations in California.

"You mean there's nothing we can do?" Anita could not accept what she was hearing.

"I'm afraid not," Larry Blake confirmed. He shook his head and threw up his right hand. "That's the law."

"Bloody hell!" Jenkins exploded from his chair. He leaned over, directing his anger into his lawyer's face. "That's my daughter we're talking about. Some bastard raped her when she was less than six years old and she's had to deal with multiple personalities ever since. Do you have any idea what that means?"

Larry pushed his chair back from his desk and stood. "Calm down, Jenkins."

"Yes, I'll do that, Larry," Jenkins said, his voice no longer hot with rage. It was now icy cold. He looked down at Anita who sat stunned in her chair. "May I escort you out, my dear?" He offered her his arm, and rising, she took it. They turned their backs and walked out of the office.

They retrieved their car from the building's parking garage and Jenkins pointed it toward the way home. He obeyed traffic signals as if he were a programmed robot. Inside his flinty, set expression, his mind was whirring as if he truly had been programmed.

"Look, Anita!" Jenkins pointed to a sign beside a glass door in an office building with notable established practices. It was neither seedy nor run down, but it did house a private investigative agency. "Let's go see what we can find out from them."

Greeted by a trim and stylish secretary, she got the needed information from them—names, address, phone and credit card numbers—before ushering them into an office bright with sunshine and florescent lights. They sat across the desk from an attractive couple looking to be in their late thirties or perhaps, forties. A couple of wrinkles marched across the woman's brow and the man had touches of grey at his temples. *Who can tell in this land of the beautiful who are often made so by the talented hands of numerous plastic surgeons*, Jenkins thought.

The man rose and held out his hand. "Mac McIntosh. And this is Paula, my wife."

Jenkins shook the offered hand. "Jenkins Montford." He turned to Anita. "My wife, Anita."

"Yes," said Paula McIntosh. "I recognize you from your work in films, Mrs. Montford. I'm pleased to meet you."

Anita smiled. "Thank you. I hope you'll be able to help us."

Mac motioned to the chairs. "Have a seat and let's hear what you need from us."

Thirty minutes sailed by as the Montfords related Emma's DID problems, fielded questions posed by the private detectives, and gave their best guesses as to what happened to their daughter and in what approximate timeframe. They had no proof, but due to Emma's reactions back when she was taken near to the far side of the pool and the property at the back of the lot where the gardeners often trimmed trees and bushes, they felt the perpetrator had to have been one of the gardeners.

"It sounds like it's been at least ten years or more since the abuse happened, so yes, your lawyer is correct. The statute of limitations has run out for trying the perpetrator. That is, if you could actually identify who it was," Paula said.

"What if we could provide the name of the perpetrator? Unless Emma could identify a photo of the guilty one, we'd know only that he'd be among the group of men working for us as gardeners at that time," Anita added. She swallowed as if she had something stuck in her throat that simply would not go down. "We need . . . no, we *have* to know who molested Emma." It was a mother's heartfelt plea.

Jenkins cut in, "We've sorted through records, and while the gardeners we had then have all moved on, we have their social security numbers. Can't you locate them with those?"

"You've got their social security numbers?" Mac asked, grinning. "Not a problem."

"We'll locate the men and see if we can find pictures from ten years ago to go with photos of them today," Paula confirmed.

"Now," said Anita, "I just pray that Emma can identify the right man." She looked through glassy eyes at the detectives. "Or men."

"And," Jenkins emphasized, "we *will* have retribution. One way or another." Again, his voice was icy and his eyes were cold. "Please be in touch as soon as you know something."

With the cooperation of the Montford family and their help, both physical and financial, Zelda had, over the years, participated with the girls in the Los Angeles Homeschooling Network. They took part in educational and recreational field trips and mingled with other homeschooled students throughout the entire Los Angeles county school district. As the years passed, the girls were quite active in social groups springing from the need of the homeschooled students to interact with others of their own age.

As high school graduation approached for Emma, not only was she well-prepared with an outstanding education and proficient in all required areas of study, she was equally adept socially. The homeschool network even offered a prom, similar in every way to the public schools' proms. Eric wasted no time in securing a spot at the prom for Emma and himself at the Millennium Biltmore Hotel in downtown Los Angeles. It was nearly a century old and quite magnificent.

"It has to be the perfect gown, Mom, made just for me," Emma explained, her voice on the edge of a whine as she threw herself on her bed, her back denting the taut coverlet.

"All right, darling," Anita soothed. "I simply thought you might like to wear one of mine since you love them so."

Emma sat up. "No offense, Mom. I just want something so spectacular that it blows all the other gowns out of the water. We need to go shopping."

Anita's white teeth gleamed for a moment as she tugged in her lower lip with her upper front teeth, deep in thought. "Get your bag, baby! We're going downtown to the Fashion District."

"Oh, that is so boss, Mom!" Emma jumped from the bed and grabbed Anita around the waist. "Can Susie go with us?"

"Sure." Definitely out of character for Anita, but signaling her excited mood, she yelled, "Susie!" She was eager to shop with her daughter for her first prom dress. *That's what mothers are supposed to do with their daughters. Another coming-of-age ritual. I'm getting so old.*

Emma increased the pressure of her hug around her mom's waist, eliciting, "You're squeezing me in two, Emma."

Emma dropped her arms and laid her head on her mom's shoulder. "Thanks, Mom. You're the best."

Anita spied a parking spot on the street in the downtown Los Angeles Fashion District. The occupant was pulling out into traffic and as soon as his rear bumper cleared the car before him, Anita zipped into the space. Today there was no Javier. Today Anita was enjoying an outing with her girls.

"Ahhh, I made it!" she exclaimed. Finding a parking spot on the street was luck. Sheer luck. "Come on girls, let's go get a gown!" Excitement radiated off her and it was infectious.

"Right, let's get me a gown," Emma agreed.

"Why don't we start right here with Queen's Clothes? They've got gowns in their window," Susie said.

They entered the store, eyes round in awe to see so many gowns in one place, and in all colors.

"Emma, do you have any idea what you're looking for?" her mom asked.

"No. I'm really not sure."

"What color? Long or short?" her mom, leading the way, threw back to her. "Straight or full skirt?"

"Well, let me just look around and see if anything grabs me." The three each went to a rack and started shuffling through the many gowns that were hung by style, not size or color.

Emma tried on one of the gowns expressly made for the 2016 prom season. It had a royal blue billowing skirt with a silver and pale blue beaded top. "I like this, but it doesn't say, 'I'm the one.'"

Susie suggested, as she forced an exaggerated yawn, "Let's go somewhere else. There's like a billion of these shops and it looks like they all sell gowns."

"Yeah, nothing speaks to me here," Emma agreed.

"Are you sure?" her mom asked. "How about this black and white one?" She held up a gown with a long, black satin skirt and a heavily beaded white strapless top.

"No. I think I like the kind of top that goes around your neck and fastens in the back like a collar."

Susie headed for the door. She had a directory in her hand. "Says here that we can walk just a little way to Twelfth and Maple and Maral Fashions is on the corner. It's huge and it also says they've got like a ton of gowns."

The three women easily found the store and upon entering Emma's eyes lit up. "Oooohhh," she sighed. "This is more like it." The first section had a lot of colorful gowns in scarlet reds, cobalt blues, emerald greens, and sunshine yellows.

"Hey Mom, looks like Microsoft got their windows homepage idea from here," Susie quipped.

"They might have. The colors are right."

The next section had dresses in pale colors of every hue and material. Emma simply walked toward it, Anita and Susie left to follow. They did.

Emma stopped with one foot raised for her next step. She let it drop as she pulled from amid the other gowns one similar to that which adorned a mannequin nearby. She held it to her chest. "Oh, I hope they have my size. This is it. This is the one I want to wear to my senior prom!"

The gown was exquisite. Gold material flowed from the waist downward, sinuously curving at the hips and flaring before touching the floor. The halter top fastened around the neck with a gold bulb button, leaving the shoulders and upper back bare.

"Try it on," Anita and Susie said in unison.

Flipping through the gowns on the rack, Emma found her size. Susie accompanied her to the dressing room where Emma yanked off her T-shirt and capris and stepped into the gown. Susie zipped it and then buttoned the collar at the back of Emma's neck. The two sisters stared at Emma's reflection in the mirror. Emma's lips parted but nothing came out.

Susie swung her head from side to side. With effort, she pulled her eyes from Emma's reflection and opened the door. Emma swept through it with Susie on her heels.

Anita gasped. She brought her hand to her forehead and absent-mindedly brushed her hair back from her face as she stared at her daughter. "Emma, you are stunning! That gown is extraordinary. I don't think I've ever seen anything as beautiful."

Emma grinned, a real one that showed most of her teeth. She turned in a circle, showing all sides of the golden creation, its appliques and beading shimmering in the bright overhead lights.

"Man, Emma, if you walked outside in the sunlight, you *would* knock everybody's socks off," Susie declared.

Anita paid for it and the three hiked back to their car with Emma and Susie carrying the gown in its bag between them, as if it were a body being transported.

CHAPTER TWENTY-TWO

Susie answered Eric's ring at the door. She invited him into the foyer and told him to wait right there and so he had. He knew only that Emma's gown was a golden hue. He'd chosen a midnight blue tux with a golden cummerbund and pocket hanky to match Emma's selection. He looked quite handsome with such an ensemble on his tall frame, Susie thought.

Emma glided to join him, her steps kicking up the gown's hem, from where gold sandals peeked.

"Emma!" barely audible, escaped from his lips on a sigh of wonder. "Emma," Eric repeated, a little louder. "You are . . ." He searched for the right word. ". . . sensational!"

Emma dropped her shining eyes to her hands where she carried a tiny gold-sequined purse. "Thank you, Eric," she said. Again looking at him, she added. "This gown does make me feel special. And you look handsome as can be."

Eric produced a wrist corsage of Cattleya orchids, the fragrant golden yellow blooms heightened in beauty by their purple throats. "I asked the florist what would go best with a gold gown and she recommended these."

Emma slipped her hand inside the elastic wrist band. She examined the corsage and laid her wrist against her waist to get the full effect of the colors against the dress. "It's perfect," she said. "Nothing could've been better."

"Stand still and smile at me," Anita instructed as she aimed her smart phone and snapped several pictures of the couple. "It's time for you to leave now. Have a good time, but be careful," she warned.

Susie watched them go. Eric helped Emma into the Explorer and then backed out of the driveway. "Please, please, let this evening go all right. Let it be just Emma out there with Eric tonight," she prayed in silence.

Awake when Emma arrived home, Susie met her at the door and pulled her inside. Eric bid them goodnight and left after a quick peck to Emma's lips. Susie asked, with her heart in her mouth, "How did it go? Did you have a good time? Did Eric say anything strange happened?"

Emma hugged Susie to her chest with their heads close together. "Everything's good, Susie. Nothing happened. At least Eric was happy and didn't mention anything. Plus, I don't have any lost time I can't account for. So, I think it's all okay."

"Oh, thank God!" Susie said, but her fears were not allayed. She wondered how much of Emma's behavior Eric had witnessed when she wasn't Emma, but some alter. *I suppose I'll have to bring up the subject and just ask him. But, would that be a betrayal of Emma's trust?*

I'd say there were about four hundred people there." Emma slid the gown down her hips and stepped out of it. "We talked to homeschooled kids from all over the area. Eric knew several people I'd not met and we talked to them for a while."

"Well, did you knock them dead in that killer gown?"

"Yes! Everybody loved it. I'm a little surprised no one else had this same one. Some were similar, but nobody's looked as good as mine." She grasped Susie's hand and flitted around the bedroom with her nose turned up, acting regal and royal as she pulled Susie along with her.

"Mahvelous, dahling. Now stand still and I'll take the pins out of your hair."

Minutes later Susie affixed the rope that tied them together and they lay talking in bed. Within minutes Emma's enthusiasm began to fade and she began to fidget. She heaved a deep sigh and wriggled her body.

"What is it, Emma? I know it's something." Susie turned her head toward her. "What do you want to say?"

Another sigh, then Emma pleaded, "I know I'm supposed to stay in because of those times I sneaked out and saw those boys, but Susie, please let me go tonight. I want to meet Eric."

"I can't do that!"

"Listen, Susie. I know I'm not a virgin and I could've gotten pregnant when I was going out and having sex at night. But, Eric doesn't know that. And I've been so careful not to get in a position where we could have sex." She looked into Susie's eyes and seemed to speak from her heart. "We really want to have sex. I think I'm in love with him, but I know I have a long way to go before I can even think about being in love."

"I don't know, Emma," Susie hedged.

"Think about it. It's my senior prom night. Kids are supposed to have sex on their prom night, and all over LA kids are doing it. I want to do it with Eric as if it were my first time. You know I'm still on the pill and he has protection too."

Silence hung in the room.

"Please, Susie," Emma whispered. "I don't remember those other times. I want to remember this. I want it to be special with Eric."

"But what if Sam or Angelique or . . . or *anybody*, comes out? It'll scare Eric to death."

"No one has come forward in a long time. Even Dr. Levy couldn't get anybody but Emmaline to talk to her last time and that was just for a few minutes. She thinks Emmaline will take care of me, anyway, and keep the others under control if some part did decide to cause a problem."

"You know Mom and Dad will ground me until I'm ninety if they find out I let you go."

Another imploring look from Emma and Susie said, "All right. But you have to tell me your plan in case something weird happens. Where are you going to meet Eric?"

Emma leaned on her elbow and planted a kiss on Susie's cheek. "Oh, thank you, Susie. I love you, I love you, I love you." She flopped back on the bed. "Eric reserved a room at the Hollywood Hotel. You know it's not far from here, just down the road on Vermont. He's waiting for my call to tell him I'm coming."

"The Hollywood Hotel! Good God, that's too expensive!"

"Éric got some kind of half-off deal on the internet."

"Look, it's almost 1:30 now. You have to cross your heart and hope to die that you'll be back by 4:30 at the latest. With getting there and back, that'll only give you about two hours together. Can you do that?"

Emma flopped her hand across her chest and made a mark in the shape of an "X."

"Cross my heart and hope to die!"

Susie withdrew the key from beneath her, unlocked the tether, and watched Emma get dressed, pick her purse from the dresser, and ease out the door. She lay down again, knowing she would get no sleep until Emma returned without any problems occurring.

Emma breezed through the hotel lobby to the bank of elevators as if entering at almost two in the morning was an everyday occurrence. She supposed the desk clerk had probably seen so many young couples enter tonight that it was no wonder he paid no attention to her. With only a touch of hesitation, she punched the fourth-floor button and the elevator silently whisked her upward, sighing to a stop and opening its doors at the fourth floor. Emma dashed to room 412 and gave the door a timid knock. No one can hear that, she thought, so she rapped it hard with her knuckles. Eric appeared in cotton lounge pants, and laughing, he took her arm and pulled her inside.

"You're here!"

"Yes. We've actually made it happen," was barely out of her mouth before Eric's mouth covered hers. Drawing apart, he led her toward the bed where she saw he'd already turned back the sheet and spread.

While Eric slipped her long-tailed shirt over her head, Emma told him she could only stay a couple of hours.

"Really? Is that all," he asked, disappointment shadowing his words. He continued pulling off her tights as she danced on one foot and then the other.

"Yes. Susie made me promise to be back by 4:30 in case Mom or Dad woke up early and looked for me."

"Well, let's make the most of what time we have." He slid his blue plaid cotton pants down his legs. He was naked and ready for Emma.

Emma laughed low in her throat, her voice deepening as she ordered, "Get on that bed. I'm going to give you the loving of your life."

Obviously delighted with this new Emma, Eric obeyed, stretching out on his back and easing a now naked Emma into his arms. She kissed him long and passionately, unlike the kisses they'd shared before when parked in the Explorer. These were torrid, full of fire, deep and wet. He appeared turned on and ready as he tried to slide Emma off him.

"No!" she said, leaning on her palms placed on either side of his chest. "I'm in command. Now, let me do what I want."

"Wait! I need to put on the condom." As he reached for the foil square on the side table, Emma snatched it and tore it open with her teeth. Straddling him, she wriggled her bottom across his upper legs and applied the condom. She covered his face with tiny kisses before again catching his mouth with hers.

For an hour the two had sex until their bodies could no longer participate. Collapsing together, they lay catching their breath for a minute or two. Eric gasped out, "My God, Emma. That was fantastic! How did you know to do all those things?"

Emma began to cry, soft little hiccupping sobs.

"Oh, don't cry, Emma. If I hurt you, I'm so sorry." He held her against his chest while hot tears wet the patches of hair spread across its width.

"No," she whispered. "You didn't hurt me." She sat up and touched his face with such tenderness. "I think I'm in love with you, Eric. I'd never have done this otherwise. You know that, don't you?"

"Yes. And like I said when we were planning this, I think I love you, too. I've certainly never felt about any other girl what I'm feeling for you tonight. Emma, you were just amazing.

I don't think I'll ever get enough of you." He grinned. "Wanta go again?"

Emma shook her head and got out of bed on the other side and came to him. "I have to go now if I'm going to get back in time." She leaned down and laid a soft kiss on his lips. She hurried to dress and was tiptoeing out the door within a minute or two.

As she drove home, her thoughts were consumed with guessing what she had done with Eric. Only when he was holding her afterward did she know what was happening. "That's why I cried," she said to herself. "I realized it wasn't *me* who was with Eric. Now what do I do? How can I see him again? He probably thinks I'm a slut."

She eased into the house and to Susie's room. Ripping her clothes off, she grabbed her pajamas from the floor where she'd shed them earlier and crawled over Susie to her spot.

"Emma, what happened?" Susie whispered.

"Tie me up, Susie, and then I'll tell you."

The girls whispered together and cried together for a long time. "I know it was Angelique who was with Eric tonight. I so wanted it to be me."

Susie tenderly patted Emma's arm. *I feel so bad for Emma. That's the saddest thing I've ever heard.*

CHAPTER TWENTY-THREE

How to determine who would be the homeschooled valedictorian and salutatorian for this year's graduating class? That was the big question. It was such a high scoring group this year that many students' grades were well above a 4.0 and some had achieved the same highest number. The committee met and the answer agreed upon was to go by the SAT test scores required of each graduating student, both homeschooled and public school educated. They requested the scores of the entire list of homeschooled students in the Los Angeles area who were eligible to receive their diplomas at this time. The highest possible SAT score was 1600. The highest scores from this year's top two tested students were 1600 and 1580. Somewhere in Los Angeles, a boy whose parents emigrated from Agra, India, and who were now cardiac surgeons in a prestigious Los Angeles practice, received notice he scored the highest on the SAT and would be the valedictorian of his graduating class. That is, if he wanted to attend the communal graduation ceremony provided by the Homeschool Network. It turned out that he did.

Susie retrieved the mail and laid it on the hall table in the foyer where it had been placed for as long as she could remember. A letter from the Homeschool Network lay on top. She was so tempted to open it, but common sense prevailed.

Jenkins was gone for a few days and her mom was filming. Addressed to the parents of Emma Montford, Susie knew she couldn't open it. She'd tried, but never mastered steaming open envelopes.

"Shoot!" she said to her mirrored twin who looked back at her from the mirror above the table. "I guess I better leave this here and not say anything to Emma until Mom sees it. I hope Mom gets home before Emma gets back from seeing Dr. Levy."

Within seconds, Anita opened the door, and Susie hurried to help with her bags. Javier held several which he transferred to Susie.

"Thanks, I think, Javier. See you later."

She shut the door behind her mom before bursting out, "You got a letter from the Homeschool Network. Maybe it's telling us if Emma will be selected to be on the graduation program agenda. Geeze, she has straight A's; she ought to be!"

"Susie, wait. Wait! Just let me put this stuff down and kick off my shoes. Then we'll look at it." Anita looked around. "Emma's not home yet? I didn't see her car."

"Nope. She should be soon. But I'm calling Emma to tell her to come home so we can find out as soon as possible."

Doctor Levy's soothing voice took Emma into a hypnotic state. She was curled into the chair with one leg tucked beneath her and the foot of the other resting on the small stool about six inches from the floor. Her breathing was slow and steady as her eyes closed and her head drooped.

"Who wants to talk with me today?" With eyes searching for even the slightest movement or indication anyone but Emma was there, Levy waited.

"Anyone?" No answer or movement came from Emma.

"Emmaline, are you there?" Nothing.

She furrowed her brow as she asked again for anyone to surface and talk with her. Just as she thought no one would come forward, Emmaline's calm, adult voice issued from Emma's lips. "Hello. This is Emmaline. What is it you want?"

"Hi, Emmaline! It's good to hear you. I'd like for you to tell me what you know of the others. It seems there's been very little activity lately. Can you tell me that?"

"Yes, I can. And I will. I've protected Emma the best I could for all these years since she was just a little girl. Her need was enormous then, and that's why I came to be. That's my job."

"And you've done an exemplary job, Emmaline. I'm sure Emma appreciates you saving her on several occasions, particularly when Sam wanted to hurt her."

"Yes." She sighed. "Sam."

"What is Sam doing these days?"

Emmaline laid Emma's head against the back of the chair and looked toward the ceiling as if seeking inspiration or answers. She snapped her head upright and with eyes narrowed answered, "Oh, he's a clever one, isn't he? He's not been around for a while and I don't know where he is. I like to keep track of everyone but there's not been much talking going on. Maybe some of the others aren't needed any longer."

With one elbow on her crossed knees, Dr. Levy rested her chin on her fist as she thought what to ask or say next. She assessed Emmaline as she asked, "How do you feel about that, Emmaline?"

Emmaline answered, Emma's eyes holding Dr. Levy's. "I think they all should just go. Particularly Sam."

Dr. Levy sat back and dropped her hand from her chin to her lap. "Why Sam?"

Usually serene, Emmaline now leapt to her feet and began to pace back and forth in front of the chair and sofa. "Because he hates Emma and wants her dead so he can be the leader. He wants to be in control of everyone."

She stopped in front of Dr. Levy. "I'm the one in control. I tell them what to do. Not Sam. Me."

"And did you tell them what to do?"

"Well, I told Sam and Christine and Ralph that they weren't needed any further and they should disappear. I also suggested it to Angelique and Julia."

"Have they disappeared? Is that the reason we've not seen them lately?"

"I think so."

"What did they do, Emmaline?"

The rest of the session was devoted to Emmaline talking about the others inside Emma's body and alluding to the reason she came to be Emma's primary caretaker. She finished with, "Emma is no longer threatened by anyone from the outside," and would say no more.

Dr. Levy counted down and woke Emma from her hypnotized state.

"So, what happened?" Emma asked from the corner of the stuffed sofa where Emmaline had sat in the tranquil room in which Dr. Levy held her hypnotisms. "Who did you talk with today?"

The two leaned close together and Levy stopped just short of laying her palm on Emma's knee. "We made excellent progress today, Emma." She talked of Emmaline's appearance and what she'd said. She concluded with, "For the first time, I see real promise of integrating everyone back to just you. That is, when you remember what it was that made you need the others."

Emma drove home thinking about what it might possibly have been that happened to her that was so horrible that her mind couldn't handle it. Tiny flashes of color, green and blue, zipped through her head and then were gone. *Green and blue. What could they mean?* At least they were some kind of hint. If only she could remember . . .

Susie waited for Emma in the living room. Anita sat beside her with the Homeschool Network letter opened in her lap. As soon as Emma opened the door, she was set upon by Susie screeching something about graduation and her mom saying how proud she was of her.

"Wait, what are you talking about? Slow down and tell me again." She backed away, trying to disentangle herself from Susie's arms.

Anita waved the letter in front of Emma's face before sitting in a wingchair of palest coral. Susie dragged Emma to the sofa and plunked her down. "Listen to this, Emma!"

Her clear tones adding importance to the words. Anita read,

> "The Homeschool Network is pleased to inform you that your daughter, Emma Grace Montford, has received the second highest scores of all students taking the SAT in preparation for Graduation 2016, making her eligible to serve as salutatorian of the graduation ceremony for the homeschooled students from the Los Angeles area."

Emma screamed, jumped from the sofa, pulled Susie up, and the two hopped and jumped around the room as if they were little girls.

"What's all this, then?" a deep masculine voice interjected into the shrieking.

"Look, darling." Anita rose and showed the letter to Jenkins. He scanned it in a flash as his frown turned to a grin. He held out his arms and Emma stepped into them.

"I'm exceedingly pleased with your achievement, my dear Emma." Her dad brushed a kiss into the hair beside her ear and turned to catch Anita's eye. "We'll go out tonight to a fine restaurant and celebrate. Let's make reservations and get ready to go."

He again gazed at his daughter. "I'm proud of you Emma."

CHAPTER TWENTY-FOUR

A loud ring came from inside the front right pocket of Jenkins' trousers. It rang again before he could withdraw his cell phone. He checked the number and answered it. "What have you got for me?"

Mac McIntosh said, "We were able to find all the gardeners working for you between eight and twelve years ago, except one. He got bitten by a diamondback out in the canyon off Mulholland. It's hard to survive a rattlesnake bite. He didn't make it."

"Outstanding. Shall we come in to get the pictures? I'd rather have them as soon as possible so we can ask our daughter about them. Her seeing them is paramount in getting her to remember."

"Sure, just come pick them up from Abby, my secretary. You can settle up then. The current addresses for all the men are included with the photos. If you need us further, just come back and we'll talk."

"Thanks, Mac. I'll do that." Jenkins punched the off button and laid the phone down. He needed to think about what he would do with the information. And, he needed to talk with Anita as soon as she got home. Together they would plan how to show Emma the pictures in hopes her reaction would trigger memories of who abused her. *I hope it won't cause her pain that will bring forth one of her alters.*

Emma's head drooped and her body relaxed like a rag doll as Dr. Levy put her into a deep hypnotic state. A few minutes earlier, Emma had hurried into her office filled with anxiety and agitation and begged to be hypnotized. She said Angelique had ruined her night with Eric after the prom and she wanted Dr. Levy to get her to come forth and find out what happened. She remembered nothing of the evening until after the sex was finished.

"I wish to talk with Angelique, please," the therapist requested. For a span of seconds, nothing happened. Then from her spot on the end of the sofa, Emma's right hand raised and her middle finger shot up, giving the ages old sign meaning, among others, "Fuck you!"

"Angelique, we're not playing games. I need to talk with you. Only you can give me the answers to my questions. Will you please come and at least listen to me?"

Emma's body jerked up straight with her head held high. "So, you only want to talk with *me*?" came from Emma's mouth in the sexy drawl Angelique alone spoke. "Well, bring 'em on!"

She leaned forward, her body loose as she dangled her hands between her jeans-clad legs. "I'm all ears. Whatcha want me to say?"

"Tell me about Emma's prom night with Eric. I'd like to know what you did. I want to know about anything you participated in."

"Ooooo." Her body shook with little shivers. "I love having sex! So I did it. Emma knows nothing about how to have sex. It would've been a disaster if I hadn't been the one with her boyfriend."

"Why? Were you protecting both her and her boyfriend?"

"Well, sure." Angelique stared straight into Dr. Levy's eyes with Emma's. "He didn't know what to do, but he's a big boy and he could've hurt Emma. He couldn't hurt me." She stood and walked around behind the sofa, trailing her fingertips across its back. "Besides, I knew what I was doing."

"How did you learn these things?"

In a husky voice, just above a whisper, and dripping with sexual connotation, Angelique confided, "He had the best sex he'll ever have. There's no one better than me. I learned that when I met up with guys a few months back. They *loved* me and would fight each time to see who I would sleep with." She walked back around the sofa, arranged the end pillow, and flopped down. "I got really good at it. So, I decided to give Eric a thrill. Emma ought to realize I did it for her."

"Will you do it again?"

"Maybe not. She's got to work out for herself how to get good at it." She gave a conspiratorial wink and smiled at the therapist. With that, Emma's body relaxed and her head fell toward her chest. Angelique was gone.

As soon as she was released from the hypnotic state, Emma asked, "Did she come? Did she tell you anything?"

The therapist related all that Angelique said, also adding her own interpretation. "It's possible we've seen the last of Angelique. She came to have sex with Eric because you didn't know how to do it, as she says, and she didn't want it to hurt you."

Emma jerked her head up, amazement evident in her widened eyes and raised eyebrows. "Really?"

"Yes. We're getting closer, Emma. Oh, you won't be integrated tomorrow or next month, but it will happen."

"I've made a reservation for just the two of us tonight at Café La Boheme."

"Why, darling, that's so thoughtful!" Anita dropped her purse and the red and white canvas bag in which she carried everything else. She kicked off her heels, sending one flying. It landed in the large container holding a tall decorative ficus tree that commanded a spot in front of the slim window by the door. She looked at it and shrugged before standing on tiptoe to place her arms around Jenkins' neck, lifting her lips to his. A quick but passionately deep kiss later, she asked, "What's the occasion?"

"We deserve a night out together, don't you think?"

"Well, of course."

He dropped his hands from her waist and patted her bottom with his right hand, his left turning her toward their bedroom. She picked up her purse and shoe and plucked her other heel from among the ficus roots. Jenkins took the canvas bag and they headed down the wide hallway. Inside their bedroom he told her about the detective's call. He reached into the top drawer of his large cherry wood desk and brought out the photos of the gardeners they once knew by face and name.

He said, as he handed them to Anita, "I've booked one of the side booths in the back. It's quiet in the Café so we can talk and make plans. Plus," he smiled for the first time since her arrival, "they have excellent food."

Anita took the photos and flipped through them. "It makes me furious to think one of these guys is responsible for everything Emma's been through . . . and for all the misery the whole family has experienced."

"He'll get paid back in spades," Jenkins said, his teeth clinched and his mouth now an angry line.

"It's nice to see you, Ms. Montford," the professional, but still somewhat star-struck, young waiter said, as he placed large opened menus in front of Anita and Jenkins. After a short discussion, Jenkins ordered the Mediterranean sea bass for Anita and the Australian rack of lamb for himself. They declined wine, opting for water and coffee. Clear heads were needed for the plans they would make tonight.

When the waiter returned with their food, he found the two with their heads together examining several photos spread across the table. He placed the plates as close to the diners as space permitted. Each acknowledged him with a quick nod and then resumed talking while handling the photos with care.

Reading through the materials the private investigators gave him, they discovered two men were still nearby, living in older apartment buildings south of them. One was located off Vermont and one on Commonwealth. "Let's hope it's one of these two so we can just get it over with," Jenkins murmured.

Anita gasped. "What do you mean, Monty? What are you going to do when we find him?"

Jenkins looked at his wife a long time, saying nothing, the low light reflecting the anger in his eyes. "I'm not sure, my love," he finally said, his voice gentle. "If the police won't prosecute him . . ." he threw his hands up, "I will see that he's punished. He can't just get away with doing that to our daughter."

"Or to our family," Anita spat, her lovely face twisted with anger. "We've all suffered because of that psychopath. He'd have to be crazy. No one should get pleasure in such an unnatural way with a little girl." Anita's body shook with revulsion. She clasped her elbows as if trying to get warm. "It's just sick!"

They took bites of their food, hardly tasting the excellent entrees, and continued to whisper together. By the time the waiter brought coffee, they had a plan.

All four Montfords sat in Irit Levy's waiting room. Soon Mindy escorted them to Dr. Levy's office. Her warm smile and calm demeanor was a definite contrast to that of the Montfords, who seemed to thrum and vibrate as they waited.

"Take seats, everyone, won't you?" Irit Levy pointed to the four chairs making a half-circle around the front side of her desk. She faced them, leaned her hips against her desk's edge and crossed her ankles, one foot atop the other.

"I understand you asked for this family meeting because you have some information that might help Emma remember what trauma she experienced in the past. Yes?"

"That's correct." Jenkins nodded his head and looked at his small family. "We felt we should all be together here with you when we shared it with Emma."

"Emma, is that all right with you?" Levy asked.

"Well, sure. I just want to know what happened and figure this out. Why I'm like this with all these different parts that you can see and I can't."

"Okay then. We'll get started." She glanced at Anita. "I'm glad you could join us, Mrs. Montford."

Anita flushed, but did not reply. Maybe with guilt. Perhaps with anger. Jenkins, looking at his wife's face, couldn't be certain. Then he handed the sheaf of photos to the therapist. The first slim stack contained photos of each of the men taken around the time of employment by the Montfords. Mac and Paula McIntosh had done a fine job of securing photos of the men both then and present day. None of the men had seemingly aged a great deal in the approximate ten years that had passed. The second set he handed her when she'd examined the first. Emma had yet to see them.

Emma watched the photos in Levy's hands as her therapist looked through them. Those strange flickers of greens and blues again flitted across her memory. "I'm getting flashes of greens and blues again!"

"What do you think it means, Emma?" Irit Levy moved to Emma and looked down at her client. Her stare was focused only on Emma's eyes as she strained to remember.

"I'm concentrating so hard. It looks like big blurs of greens now. I *was* going to say that maybe it's something with the pool because it has blue and green tiles and is painted blue all the way around it. But, that wouldn't explain the big blobs of green."

"Trees," Anita whispered to Jenkins. "Remember, she wouldn't go into the trees at the back of the yard."

Dr. Levy appeared to be wrestling with some issue. Her left arm lay across her upper stomach, supported at the elbow by her right hand. She raised that left arm and tapped her chin with the fingers of her left hand, deep in thought.

She spread her arms, palms turned out as she admitted, "I'm not a hundred percent certain that what I'm going to say is the correct way to find out what Emma can pull from her memory, but I'd like to try." She dipped her head in the direction of Mr. and Mrs. Montford. "With your permission, of course."

"Anything," Jenkins was quick to affirm. "As long as Emma is okay."

Emma sat big-eyed while Levy considered what to do. Her demeanor changed to one of urgency and she asked Emma to take the empty seat in front of her desk. She sat behind it in her chair. As if dealing cards, Dr. Levy laid out the photos of the gardeners from the past, taken when they were working. They all wore sun hats and dark blue shirts. Some had a hoe or a large pairs of clippers in their hands.

For a moment, Emma gazed at Dr. Levy, wondering what she was doing. Then her eyes dropped to the photos spread before her. She said nothing, but picked up the first and scrutinized it. All four of the other people in the room held their breath.

"What am I looking for?"

"You'll know," Levy said, gambling on her recognizing the abuser.

Emma picked up the second picture. She frowned and began to squirm uncomfortably in her seat. She laid it down.

She picked up the third, blinked several times, and laid her forehead in her left palm. Without looking up, she groaned. "The blue and green colors are swimming in circles in my head. And, ow, my head really hurts."

Dr. Levy leaned across the desk, turning her head to look up at Emma's face as she raised it from her palm. Her voice urgent, she implored, "Emma, tell me what you see. What you remember. What are the blue and green colors?"

With her eyes now closed, Emma whispered, "I see trees and bushes. And a man. A big man in a blue shirt. He's pulling me by my hand. I don't want to go!" Her voice rose as she remembered more of what happened. "He made me."

Tears spilled down Emma's cheeks. Susie shot up from her chair, her intent evident in her actions and the look on her face. She was *going* to Emma. She was stopped, however, as though she'd hit an invisible wall, by Dr. Levy's arm slicing viciously down and a violent shaking of her head. She mouthed "No!" and Susie sat back down.

In her low and calm professional therapist voice, she asked Emma, "Can you tell me more about what the man did, Emma?" Jubilant that it was *Emma* talking and not one of the alters, she wanted to keep it that way, making sure to address her always by her name.

"He hurt me." Her voice rose in anger as she said, "He *raped* me! My God, that's what happened." Her voice dropped a notch as she again said, in what sounded like disbelief, "That son-of-a-bitch gardener raped me. No wonder I'm so messed up . . ." Her voice trailed off as she picked up the photo of the third man and carefully looked it over, her mouth twisted in distaste.

"This is the man."

"Are you sure, honey?" Anita ventured.

His voice quiet with a steely timber to it they'd not heard before, Jenkins asked, "Are you completely sure, Emma?"

"Look again," Dr. Levy urged.

Emma picked up the first two photos she'd looked at, looked them up and down, and set them aside. "It's not either of these."

She skipped the third photo and examined the next four, turning the photos this way and that to catch every nuance of light. "No. I'm certain. It's not any one of these four, either." She laid the photos down and picked up the third one again. It took no more than a few seconds before she threw it down on the table. "Yes. I have no doubt about it. *This* is the man!"

CHAPTER TWENTY-FIVE

The homeschooling network was hosting an expo where classes and fun activities were held over the course of a four-day weekend to acquaint those interested in their programs with the materials and with each other. The graduating class was featured on the last day. Today was day four and the day of Emma's graduation.

"What are you gonna do about Eric? He keeps calling me to ask what's going on with you. You gotta talk to him." Susie turned her back to Emma. "Zip me, please. I can't get this danged zipper to work."

Emma laid aside the dress she held and tackled Susie's zipper. "It was caught. Now it zips right up." She picked up her dress and stuck her arms in the armholes and spoke while it slithered down her body. "I've texted Eric and told him I was really busy getting ready for graduation and I'd meet him there."

Busily combing her golden hair Susie whispered, "I meant about the sex." Then continued, "It seems to me that graduation night is every bit as important as prom night. Don't you think he'll want to do it again tonight?"

She looked in the mirror at her sister getting dressed behind her.

"Well, Dr. Levy thinks Angelique may be gone, along with most of the parts, by the way. So, Eric won't get what he's expecting. If I do decide to have sex with him, he'll know something is different."

Susie turned around, and tapping the comb against her thigh, she asked what had been on her mind ever since Emma's prom night. "Do you love Eric?"

"I think so."

"Then you have to tell him."

Emma wailed, "Oh, Susie, I can't tell him about what Angelique did."

Susie reached out and gently touched Emma's face. Her eyes were luminous with feeling as she advised, "No, don't tell about the other guys. Simply tell him about the DID. If you truly love him, he needs to know what you've been going through. He also needs to know that it's almost over. He *especially* needs to know . . ." She turned Emma's head so she had to look at her, ". . . he especially needs to know," she repeated, "that it was you, not Angelique, in bed with him. He'll get creeped out, otherwise."

"But, what can I say?"

"Hell, make something up. Use your imagination, Emma!" Susie giggled. "But, I think you're gonna have to read some sexual technique books, or go online . . ." She deepened her voice and wiggled her eyebrows. ". . . and find something like 'The Ten Best Sex Tips to Please Your Lover.' Maybe really watch some porn movies so you can do whatever it was that Angelique did."

Emma's face registered horror, her mouth open, her brows making hills across her forehead.

"Uhhh," Susie considered, "you might not be ready for that. But, I guess, for now, just be yourself and see what happens. Who knows? You might be every bit as good as Angelique."

There was a knock at the door. Anita opened it and stepped into Emma's room. "How's it going in here? About ready? We'll need to leave soon."

"Almost," Susie answered.

Emma said, "Mom, I sure wish I had some relatives going to my graduation. It seems like everyone will have grandparents there."

Anita held Emma close before dropping her hands to capture her chin. "I'm so sorry, sweetie. I miss your grandma and grandpa every day. Even though I know it was an accident, it's hard to forgive that damned motor-cyclist that cut through the lanes and caused the accident that killed them."

Sniffling a bit, Emma said, "At least I remember them, even though I was a little kid then. It's too bad Dad's parents were old when they had him and that he was an only child."

"Yeah," Susie chimed in, "they never even got to see us. I wish they hadn't died before we were born."

"Me too," Anita said, turning back to Emma. "We'll just have to cheer louder for you when you give your speech to make up for not having other relatives there."

Jenkins drove his small family to the Sheraton Fairplex on Harbor Boulevard in Garden Grove where this year's expo was being held. Handsome in his tailored suit, he received a number of compliments from the three ladies in his life, ending with Susie's, "I hope I find a man to love me who is as good-looking as you, Dad. Sean's got a long way to go!"

"Susie, you are an imp," her dad responded as he parked the car, his wide grin proving his pleasure.

Emma got out of the mid-size SUV and reached behind the back seats for her rented cap and gown, refusing Susie's help.

"Good grief, Emma. I won't drop them."

"Susie, this is *my* day. I'm taking no chances!" She began walking toward the entrance.

"I'll stick my fingers in my ears so I can't hear your speech."

"You do, and I'll break those fingers."

"Girls, behave. You must act like ladies today," Jenkins warned from behind them as he held Anita's hand. They walked so close together that their hands were hidden by the billowing skirt of Anita's sage green sundress, which almost seemed alive as green-painted dragonflies flapped gossamer wings across its fabric.

They met Zelda and her husband just inside the door. Hugs were exchanged by the women and girls and handshakes by the men. Holding Emma at arm's length with her hands on her shoulders, her teacher said, "I'm so proud of you, Emma. You worked hard and earned the honor of being salutatorian." She laughed, and those around them looked their way. "You make *me* look good. So, I thank *you!*"

As salutatorian of her graduating class, Emma spoke second on the program, behind the opening remarks of the Homeschool Network president. She approached the stage with confident steps, cleared her throat, and looked at her audience. She spoke directly into the microphone.

"Good afternoon to each of you assembled here today. You came to share in the joy and the sense of accomplishment we graduates of the homeschool network are feeling. I assure you, we are feeling *fine!*" She paused while the audience laughed. A great tension breaker, suggested by her mom, was what she had needed to progress with her speech without feeling nervous. It worked. She continued her speech with praise for the network, a special recognition of her teacher, and what her future interests were, given the state of the world's economy, terroristic activities, and opportunities available.

"But, we, *this* class of graduates, will create new opportunities. *We* are the future." She paused and looked into the eyes of her fellow graduates. "And we *will* deliver!"

Smiling, she returned to her seat as applause rang out around the room.

While the rest of the graduation agenda proceeded, Emma stole glances at Eric sitting in the row behind her and often caught him watching her. When their eyes met, a current ran through her body, speeding her pulse and altering her breathing. She decided she did want to be with him after the ceremony was over.

Emma received congratulations from her parents, Zelda and her husband, and a number of other students and parents whom she had gotten to know through the homeschooling network.

"Thanks, everybody. Now I want to congratulate my boyfriend!"

She approached the group surrounding Eric, his height making it impossible to miss. Her lips were framed in the suggestion of a smile as she said, "Hi, Eric. Congratulations. We did it. We're finally finished with high school!"

Eric looked down at her with eyes slightly hooded. "Yes. We made it. Congratulations on your speech. You did a good job with it." He turned back to his parents who watched the interplay between their son and his professed girlfriend with apparent interest. "Are we ready to go?"

Stricken, Emma managed, "Are you going somewhere?"

"Yes, the family, including . . ." His hand swept the group around him. ". . . my cousins and their parents, are going out to eat."

Watching the play of emotions on Emma's face, he added, "Perhaps I'll call you sometime."

Emma gathered her wits and her nerve and replied, "Of course. I'd like that." She drifted away, trying not to run.

Her mom and dad talked about their daughter's accomplishments as Jenkins took a longer route home, managing to catch almost every red light on the way.

"What happened?" Susie whispered as they sat in the backseat of the SUV.

"Later," Emma hissed through jaws compressed hard enough she feared they would break.

Emma noted the excess of cars lining the narrow streets of her neighborhood, even near her house, and assumed someone was having a party. *That's nice. Eric's having a party, too. I will not cry, I will not cry.*

Her dad parked the car and all four piled out, Emma with her folded gown and tasseled cap in her hands. He opened the front door and stood aside for his ladies to enter what, now at five o'clock, was a dimmed foyer and living room. Emma was the last. So caught up in her thoughts, she didn't notice anything until the room erupted with cries of "Surprise!" and "Congratulations!" all around her.

Emma stopped in her tracks and let her gown and hat trail from her fingers. Her face was a mask of astonishment, which soon turned to delight. Madonna stood at the entrance to the kitchen beaming at her as the aromas of different kinds of foods wafted under her nose. Standing packed into the parts of the house she could see was an amazing assortment of people invited by her parents to this party in her honor. She saw a number of her closest friends from the homeschool network and some of their parents. Some of her friends she'd had since childhood, with whom she and Susie used to regularly play, and several of her mom's associates, who were either movie or television notables, were also there.

Touched, she blinked back tears and, with her chin trembling, stammered, "Thank you *so* much, Mom and Dad. This is so . . ." She had to stop as she searched for the right word. ". . . so, oh, I don't know . . . but it's wonderful!" She wound down and looked again at Madonna.

"Did you prepare all of this?" she asked, gesturing into the kitchen where dishes of food covered the counters. She went to their cook with arms outstretched. Madonna met her and the two exchanged hugs. "Thanks, Madonna. This is magnificent. And it smells so good. Boy, I'm starving!"

Her face and chest flushed, Madonna replied, "It's my pleasure to do this for you, Miss Emma."

The party continued with full plates emptying and the guests spilling out beside the pool. Many of the teen girls took turns in the various bathrooms to change into their swim suits. The boys stripped off their slacks, shirts, and ties, revealing their swim trunks beneath. Emma and Susie soon emerged from Susie's room with their suits on. The younger of the Hollywood stars of both the big and little screens joined them. Emma spoke to each kid in the pool, thanking them for helping make the night one of the best of her life. "It means the world to me," she finished.

Water splashed high from the deep end of the pool and Emma turned to see what caused it. She was astonished to see Eric rise from the depths, his dark hair dripping into his eyes before he jerked his head, slinging his hair and ridding himself of the majority of the rivulets cascading down his face.

"Eric!" It was out of her mouth before she had time to think. "You came!"

He stroked toward her and Emma met him mid-way. Eric whispered, "I don't know what's going on with you, Emma. I tried to stay mad and stay away." His open face hid nothing as he lowered it to hers. "But, I just couldn't."

Toward midnight the guests began to leave, after six hours of fun, food, and frolicking in the pool. The lit tennis court had entertained its share, as well.

Javier came on his day off to congratulate Emma, to enjoy the festivities, and now to offer his help. He and Madonna moved through the few kids still hanging about the pool and cleaned up the area. Very little of the chocolate, coconut-filled congratulatory cake was left, and the non-alcoholic drinks for the teens and snacks provided later in the evening, were close to being depleted as well.

Jenkins flipped the outside lights off and on, and off and on again. "It's been a great day and I'm more than proud of Emma," he declared, before once more flipping the light switch off, where he left it. "But, I'm tired," he added, "and it's time for me to go to bed." The kids laughed and began to make their exits. All except Eric. He remained with Susie by the pool, which now was lit by the moon and stars, and the dull lights of LA shining through the smog.

Emma stood with her mother at the front entry and said goodbye to every guest upon leaving and thanked them for coming. She pointed to the wrapped packages spread about the surfaces in the entry and living area, and true to the sweet nature they knew her to possess, she thanked them for her gifts.

Anita shut the door for the last time and sat on the sage sofa. She bent over and unbuckled her espadrilles, green to match her sundress, and slipped them off. Wiggling her toes, she declared, "I hate to admit it, but I just can't wear heels all afternoon and night anymore."

"Don't say that, Mom. You'll be young always."

Anita caressed her daughter's cheek and pushed back the damp hair that threatened to curl over her forehead.

Emma said, "Thanks for the party, Mom. Tell Dad for me, please. It really was great!"

Anita stood to go to her bedroom. "By the way, Mom, Eric is still here. He's outside with Susie. We're going to have a long talk. I don't know how much I'll tell him, yet, but I really, really like him and I think he feels the same about me."

"Take as long as you need, sweetie. You're old enough to make your own decisions, and this is one you have to make yourself." Anita held her for a brief hug and then was gone, her bare feet leaving footprints in the plush carpet of the living room — carpet that had seen many feet on its surface this night — and her espadrilles dangling from her right hand.

Emma slipped through the opening in the sliding glass door and joined Susie and Eric poolside. At once, Susie rose from her chaise lounge, yawning with her mouth stretched wide. "I'm tired, and sleepy, too. I'm going in now."

At the glass door, she turned back and looked straight at her sister. "I'll be in bed, if you need me."

Emma nodded, and lowered herself into the chaise lounge Susie vacated. She turned so she faced Eric. She looked down, swallowed the lump that felt as if it had grown to the size of a baseball, and lifted her eyes to him. "Eric, there is so much I need to tell you."

CHAPTER TWENTY-SIX

Sometime in the wee hours, as Emma told her tale to Eric, he reached over and took her hand.

Emma started with the definition of the disorder. Next, she described how one person could have any number of others living inside her, or him, and how these parts acted independently so the person didn't know about them.

Eric narrowed his eyes. *Why is she telling me this weird shit?*

As Emma continued talking about that DID stuff, he could wait no longer. He had to ask her. "What in the hell are you talking about, Emma?" His voice rose with a fear he didn't yet understand.

She lowered her voice further so she would be sure he'd heard her correctly, as she answered, "*I* have DID, Eric."

"What? You? *You* have this shit?"

"Yes." Her voice trembled as she told him she'd had the problem since before eighth grade.

"Is that why you had to be homeschooled? Because of this . . ." his voice faltered, ". . . this, uh, stuff?"

"Yes. I couldn't go back to St. Michael's."

"Did they throw you out?" Incredulous, his voice grew louder.

"Uh-huh. And then Mom took Susie out, too, and we started school at home."

"What did you do that was so bad they threw you out of school?" Eric's eyes gleamed in the faint light.

"Among other things, I was told I called my teacher a bitch."

Eric sat without speaking, as if trying to absorb what she was saying, and have it make sense. At last he spoke. "How many parts were inside you?" Immediately following, uncertainty hit with a frozen shot straight to his heart. His demeanor that of a wild man, gesticulating broadly with his long arms, he screeched in a deep baritone, "Are they still there? They're still there, aren't they?"

Tears slipped down Emma's cheeks and dripped from her chin. She shook her head. "No. My therapist thinks they've all been integrated back in to just me. She thinks it's all over."

Eric reached for her hand and engulfed it in his. "Have I ever seen any of the parts?"

"I'm not sure. But, I don't think so."

Eric held her hand tighter. Having trouble forming his next question, which he so obviously wanted to ask, he squirmed higher in his chaise as his mouth opened and closed. He glanced at the sky in hopes of finding inspiration from its milky depths as the city lights dimmed. Heaving a huge sigh, he turned his gaze on Emma and blurted, "Was it you with me on prom night, or one of your parts?"

"Oh, Eric," Emma whispered. "It was me."

Jubilation spread across Eric's face along with his grin. "Oh, thank God!" He turned his body toward Emma, swung his legs off the chaise, and stood up. He reached down and gathered Emma into his arms as if she weighed nothing.

"Oh, my God, Emma! Sex with you was amazing. You know it was my first time and I didn't quite know what to expect. It was your first time, too, wasn't it?" Not waiting for her answer, he continued, "How did you know how to do all those things?"

God, I'm glad I'd thought about this and have an answer prepared! As "off the cuff" as she could make it sound, Emma replied, "Susie and I found this sexy DVD tape Mom and Dad got from somewhere. It was probably porn. We watched it. It showed a lot of ways to do it. So, I just thought about what the girls did on that tape. But, the truth is, I really wanted to do those things with you, Eric."

She lifted her face to his and his head blotted out all light as his mouth captured hers in a kiss that started gently before rapidly escalating.

Lifting his head, he hugged her close and whispered in her ear, "I love you, Emma. You're *my* girl."

"I love you, too, Eric." Emma's insides danced with excitement. She had successfully hidden the full truth. Eric need never know. *I will get a book on what women do to please their men and I'll memorize it!*

For the past week, Susie and Emma had been free of the confining rope that tethered them together each night and Emma had been allowed to return to her own room. Tonight Susie was sleeping alone. She tried to stay awake, but the long day took its toll on her just as it did her parents.

She awoke as soon as Emma slid into bed beside her, sleep forgotten. "What happened? What did Eric do?"

"He loves me, Susie! He really loves me," she whispered. "And I had to come tell you!"

"Did you tell him everything?"

"Most of it," Emma hedged. "I told him it was me having sex with him the night of the prom." She turned facing Susie. "Oh, Susie, that made him so happy. I can never tell him any different now."

"I see no reason why you should have to." Susie giggled. "You're going to learn how to give great sex! You think maybe we *do* need to watch some porn movies?"

"Why you?" Emma snickered. "You don't need to know how to do it yet."

"I will soon. After all, *I'll* have a senior prom next year!"

Emma applied to both The University of Southern California and The University of California at Los Angeles. Both campuses were within driving distance of her home in Los Feliz. She loved the football program and the film and theatre departments at USC, but her schooling desires, and her heart, lay with UCLA.

She continued to see Dr. Levy during the integration process. She had the deepest hope that no parts would appear, which would mean a setback in her achieving complete integration.

Dr. Levy said, "Tell me about your school plans, Emma. Will you be attending university or one of the local colleges in the fall?"

Emma's face lit. "Oh, Doctor Levy," she burst out, "I've been accepted to both USC *and* UCLA!"

"Excellent! Which will you attend?"

Shaking her head in what might have been contemplation, Emma tightened her lips. "UCLA. I had to choose, so I finally chose UCLA. It's in a little better section of the city and it offers so many things I'm interested in learning. But, it was a hard choice." She looked at her doctor, who was nodding her head in agreement.

"I know you'll have all the common core class requirements for the first two years, but you'll need to declare a major and minor to work toward after that. Have you thought of what discipline you want?"

Losing her smile, Emma looked down at her hands, which now lay palm down on her thighs, arms stiff, as if bracing herself.

"Emma?" Dr. Levy prodded, bending her face low so she could see into Emma's.

In her typical low-key way, Emma answered, her voice solemn. "I want to do research to try to find out why, and how . . ." she looked up, ". . . DID alters come to be."

Dr. Levy raised her eyebrows. "Go on."

"I know they are *supposed* to come to help, but . . ." She stopped and gathered her thoughts. "But, *where* do they come from? I mean how are they made? *What* are they composed of? Ectoplasm, is it? Are they like ghosts that have no real substance?"

"You mean, how does the mind make them?"

"Yes. But more."

Dr. Levy studied her for what seemed to Emma at least a couple of minutes. In reality, it was perhaps thirty seconds. In a quiet, yet urgent voice, she said, "I wish you luck, Emma. This has been a mystery since the beginning of time, ever since the first person experienced voices in her head. The medical community, as of yet, cannot understand or explain it. Finally, someone in your generation will probably figure it out." She gave Emma a gentle smile. "Perhaps you'll find the answer to unlock the mystery."

Sean was back from his visit to see family in Virginia. Madonna opened the door at his ring and told him he'd find Miss Susie at the pool.

Susie leaned back in a chaise with an open book propped on her bent knees. Still preferring to hold a book in her hands and read the real deal, she shunned her iPad and Nook tablet. She'd found it almost impossible to see the screens in LA's bright sunshine.

She turned a page, the huge poolside umbrella partially blocking the sun as well as Sean's approach. On soft-soled sandals, he crept behind her and plucked the book from her loose hold.

"Wha . . . ?" she started. And then she saw the boy who made her toes tingle. His sun-brightened brown hair needed cutting, his shorts were low-slung on his hips, and that to-die-for grin that lifted one side of his upper lip was in place, and he was right there beside her.

"Sean!" she greeted him, as she scrambled from the chaise and launched herself at him. He braced for the tornado and caught her tight against the length of his body, laughing down at her glowing face.

"In the flesh. Or what's left of it." He looked down at his thin frame. "My grandma is the worst cook in the world. You wouldn't believe what she tried to make me eat." He scrunched up his nose and closed his eyes. "Grits. Collard greens. Who eats that stuff?"

"Not me," Susie answered, the cheerfulness in her voice contagious. "But, my mom would. If somebody would cook it for her, that is." She giggled. "Is your grandma coming to visit any time soon?"

Sean kicked off his sandals and stripped his shirt over his head in one fluid motion. He grabbed Susie's forearm and jumped into the pool. They surfaced with mouths together, water dripping down their faces. It was obvious neither cared.

Susie planned, since her second year of homeschooling, to return to a neighborhood school once Emma was better. She had nothing against Zelda Bass. The teacher had been a terrific instructor for the almost five years she'd come to the Montford home and taught both her and Emma a curriculum that the Homeschool Network sanctioned, as well as the Los Angeles Unified School District. Soon after Emma began preparing for her studies for her senior year of high school, it was time for her to make her decision known, and to act on it.

Thinking back, she remembered how she wasn't sure if she would return to St. Michael's or enroll in a public high school. Several of her friends from childhood, and from her years at St. Michael's, were attending Marshall High, the designated public school for her area. It was a good school, and she preferred to go there. And now, with her relationship with Sean soaring to a whole new level, she wanted to be there with him.

She recalled how she and Emma had sat in Carl's Jr. risking their dinner Madonna was preparing at home as they devoured hamburgers and slurped chocolate milkshakes. Their one concession to saving even a tiny amount of room for their evening meal was they were splitting an order of fries.

"I think I've made up my mind about what to do about school after you graduate this year, Emma." Susie selected a fry and dragged it through a puddle of ketchup that sat wet and glistening on her burger's paper wrapper.

"What? Aren't you staying with Zelda?" Emma used their teacher's first name as she and Susie always did in private.

"No . . ." Susie drew out the word, at last raising her eyes to meet Emma's. "I want to go to public school. I'm gonna go to Marshall."

Emma leaned against the booth's high seatback and crossed her arms across her chest. "Are you sure? You've never been to public school. You've been pretty sheltered from what goes on there."

"Anything's gotta be better than that Catholic school with the nuns bossing you around." Susie chuckled and chomped a big mouthful from her burger. Talking around the food in her bulging cheeks, she added. "Sean loves going to Marshall. You've heard him. He's said many times that he enjoys the sports, all the school activities, and just being with other kids."

Susie swallowed and dropped her eyes to the fries lying by her burger. Instead, she chose to take a big draw on her shake. "I think I'd like to give Marshall's a try."

Emma's smile was slow in coming, but brilliant when it did. "Don't worry, Susie." She reached across the table and took Susie's left hand in her right palm, twisting the ring Sean had placed on Susie's finger, aligning it so the sapphire setting sat on top of her finger with a deep blue glow radiating from its heart.

"I understand, Susie. I really do."

Despite her fun-loving personality, which at times may have led an outsider to think she had no merit as a student, and her many duties overseeing Emma and her different alters, Susie still maintained an above 4.0 average. Qualifying for Advanced Placement (AP) classes at Marshall as a senior required her to apply for those classes before the fall of her junior year, while Emma was still having daily classes with her at home as a senior.

"Makes no sense to me, but that's what the website says. I guess it takes a while to line up the kids with just the perfect teacher and material."

"I suppose," her mom said. "I'll ask Zelda to see what's needed and make sure they get the right materials. You go ahead and fill out the registration online."

"Here it is the summer before my senior year of high school," Susie, mused. "Emma's already graduated and ready to go to UCLA the same time I start my senior year at Marshall." She wrapped her arms across her breasts and clasped the opposite shoulders, giving herself a delicious hug. "I can't wait!"

"Tell me about Marshall." Susie sat in Sean's lap as he lounged with legs stretched out on a chaise by the pool. They were alone except for Madonna, who was baking something that smelled delicious in the kitchen just beyond the door to the pool.

As Sean was being his usual 'let's see how far I can get' self, Susie tried to divert his attention from her bosom that was mostly exposed in her spiffy new thong bikini. "Mmmm. Do you smell that?"

"Yeah," Sean said, his voice muffled. "Smells like ginger cookies to me."

Now, with Sean nipping at her bikini top, she wasn't so sure she should have ignored Emma's warning, "That top is pretty revealing, don't you think?" The design of the red and green bird of paradise flowers brought the eye to the middle of her chest. Just what she'd wanted.

She pushed Sean's face away. "Come on, Sean. Stop it!" She smiled to lessen the harshness of her words. "I really want you to tell me all about Marshall."

"Okay, get up so I can concentrate."

Susie stood and then sat down in the chaise beside Sean's.

"All right. Well, you know John Marshall was a chief justice of the Supreme Court, so it makes sense, at least to some," he grinned, "that our mascot is . . ." He stopped, his grin widening. "Are you ready for this?" He continued at Susie's mesmerized nod. ". . . Johnny Barrister."

He wrinkled his nose at Susie's gasp, and said, "Yeah, me too. Wouldn't it have been boss to have our athletic teams called The Stallions, or The Warriors, or something that sounds fierce? I don't think any team is the least bit intimidated by playing a bunch of lawyers."

"Sounds pretty pitiful." Susie turned down the corners of her mouth. "Oh, and the colors? Don't tell me they're pink and blue."

"Almost. They're two different shades of blue."

"Oh, my God! What am I getting myself into?"

Sean shot up from his seat and grasped Susie's arm. "Into a year of school with me, you lucky girl!" Jumping, he sailed through the two or three feet into the water, pulling Susie with him. They surfaced with faces alight with smiles.

Sean laughed down into Susie's dripping face, his own rivulets cascading into hers. "Ah, girl, I'm so glad you'll be with me this year." He hugged her close and laid his chin atop her head. "You know what?"

"Unh-uh. What?"

"I think I love you, Susie." Wonder and amazement lifted his words. They flew straight to Susie's heart.

Sean leaned back, keeping his lower body tight against Susie. "Anybody home other than Madonna?" He wiggled his eyebrows and jerked his head toward the glass doors and entrance into the house.

A grin split the bottom of Susie's face. "No."

"You want to go inside to your room?"

"No." She shook her head and pushed Sean away. Still grinning, she suggested, "You go on home, Sean, and cool down. I've got stuff to do." She rolled her eyes at him. "Looks like you do, too."

CHAPTER TWENTY-SEVEN

Jenkins checked his mobile phone screen. The call was from Mac McIntosh. Eager, he punched the answer button and in his deep baritone, boomed, "What have you got for me, Mac?"

On the other end of the line, Paula McIntosh's calm voice answered. "Mr. Montford, we have that information you requested. We have the name and address of the man your daughter identified as her molester. Just come by and pick up the packet, unless, of course, you want us to either fax or email the contents to you. Or we could send it by courier."

"That's bloody terrific!" Jenkins felt a rush of adrenalin flood his body. "No, I'll be pleased to stop by and pick it up. Thank you so much." He was excited now and ready for action. That bastard gardener, whom they had aided by employing him, would pay for harming his daughter. And this man, Jack Fairfax, with whom Mac had arranged for him to meet, would see that the perverted, sadistic son-of-a-bitch would pay big time.

Should I call Anita on set to share the news? He checked his watch. *No, perhaps not.* They were filming some pretty intense scenes on the soundstage today and for certain he didn't want to interrupt those. Anita would never forgive him—even though this was something they had eagerly awaited. He punched Mr. Fairfax's number into his cell phone.

With packet in hand, Jenkins knocked on the office door of Huntsman Enterprises. The location was past its heyday when the area around the intersection of Vermont and Melrose was a much sought-after spot. The small stand-alone office building did nothing to stand out from those around it.

"Come on in," a voice called from inside.

Jenkins opened the door and entered. "Mr. Fairfax?"

"Who wants to know?" A burly man dressed in khakis and a blue striped pullover rose from behind a desk, the top of which was covered with a variety of scattered papers. "Are you Montford?"

"Yes. Mr. Fairfax, I presume?"

"You got that right. Come on over here and take a seat. Let's hear what you've got to say." He swept a newspaper to the floor so Jenkins could have a seat in the one guest chair the office boasted. Jenkins sat.

Fairfax returned to his seat, leaned back in it and clasped his hands across his stomach, his lean six-pack clearly visible. "Now, what can I do you for?"

Confused, Jenkins repeated, "Do me for?"

Fairfax laughed, showing remarkably even white teeth. "I'm just funning with you. What can I do *for* you?" He raised his right hand to scratch a spot in his thinning brown hair, while Jenkins marveled at how his biceps bunched and re-bunched as he scratched.

Now, here's the man I want to hire to do some serious damage. Jenkins had no doubt that this apparently funny man had a deadly serious side.

"I don't know if Mac McIntosh told you anything about my case . . ."

"No," Jack Fairfax interrupted, "I don't discuss my cases with anyone except the client. So, tell me what it is you need." Before he could start, Fairfax asked, "Where you from, anyway? You from England?"

"Well, yes."

"That's good. Thought you sounded British. I like the Brits. They're good allies to have."

Jenkins nodded and began to tell him the story of his little girl being raped by an employee, who had been checked out before hiring him. As he talked, *the enforcer*, as Jenkins had come to think of him, asked questions.

"Emma's age?"

"Five or six." And, no, he didn't know how long it went on because the gardener was employed by them for several years.

"What happened with Emma as she aged?"

Jenkins told him of her emotional and mental problems caused by the abuse.

"Son-of-a-bitch!" the enforcer spat. "You got his name and address?"

Jenkins slid the packet across the desk. "Mac McIntosh's firm did the investigating for me. Emma identified him from a picture, and they found him. I guess we're lucky he's still around. He lives right off Commonwealth."

Fairfax opened the packet and withdrew the pictures. There were pictures of the rapist in his gardener's uniform of years back, including the one Emma had identified, and there were others taken present day by McIntosh's people. There were photos ranging from him entering and leaving his apartment to those taken while tailing him. Holding the pictures, Fairfax tilted back his chair and sorted through them, examining each one.

"What you want me to do?" His voice was low and menacing.

"Whatever you can do short of killing him. I want him to hurt. To hurt so bad until he begs you to kill him." Jenkins surprised himself with the vehemence of his words. But he meant them. It felt good just to say them aloud.

He bent his head, looking down as he continued, "I couldn't help her then because I didn't know. It makes me feel like I failed as a father. A father is supposed to protect his children. I wasn't able to. So now I want him to feel every moment of the trauma my little girl endured."

Jack Fairfax laid a big hand with enlarged knuckles, that must have seen many fights, on Jenkins' shoulder. "I'll get the bastard. Don't you worry about that."

He walked with Jenkins to the door and opened it. "I'll let you know when it's done and we can settle up then."

Jenkins clasped the big hand in his and shook it. "Thank you, Mr. Fairfax. I can't wait to find out what you do to that bastard."

Fairfax's even white teeth gleamed in a wicked smile. "When it's done, Mr. Montford. When it's done."

Jenkins pulled into his driveway moments before Sean braked at the curb. Susie hopped out of the candy-apple red, year-old Mustang almost before the car came to a complete stop. Jenkins turned to see Sean swing out his side.

"Dad!" Susie called. "Wait up. We want to talk with you." Excitement pinked her cheeks.

"Well, not out here in this heat. Both of you come inside with me." He continued into the house with the two teens on his heels and laid some papers on the entrance console table. "What do you want to talk about? Be succinct as I have an important call to make."

"I am so excited, Dad. Sean took me to Marshall High today and we went inside. He showed me all around. I'm gonna love it!"

Jenkins narrowed his eyes at his effervescent daughter. *She looks like she is going to burst.* "So, you liked the school?"

"Oh, yeah!"

"What exactly do you need to talk with me about?"

Susie looked to Sean who continued to say nothing. However, he wore a big grin.

"Sean?" Susie faced Sean and ducked her head toward her father.

"Oh, just go ahead and ask him, Susie," Sean said at last, his grin now engulfing half of his face.

Susie huffed and whirled to face her father. "I want to try out for cheerleading," she blurted.

As Jenkins raised his eyebrows in question, she continued, "And I have to have a parent sign a permission form." She flicked her eyes to Sean. "And Mom's filming on the set."

"She needs it today, Mr. Montford," Sean said, sobering at the look Jenkins leveled at him. "And it requires insurance information and other stuff that she doesn't know. She hated to ask you, figuring you'd be busy, so we're just glad we caught you now."

"I'm sorry, Dad, but I just found out while we were at the school that I could put in an application through today." Susie took his arm, her eyes begging him. "Please, Dad. See if you have time to fill it out. I want to be a cheerleader like a normal high school student."

Normal. The word struck Jenkins in the gut. His face softened. *I'll take the time to sign anything my darling girl wants. I want her to be as 'normal' as she can be for this last year of high school.* He smiled. "I shall be pleased to fill out and sign the form, Susie."

Susie thrust her fist toward the ceiling. "Yes!" She danced in a tight circle around her father then wrapped her arms around his waist and laid her head against his broad back. "Thanks so much, Dad. You're the best."

Jenkins took the form and went to his small office off his bedroom to get the information he needed. Susie watched his retreating back and took Sean's hand. "Now, I've got to make the team."

"I forgot to ask. Have you ever cheered before?"

"Nope."

Emma sat on Dr. Levy's blue sofa, relaxing in the calming room as the therapist prepared to hypnotize her. Once under, Dr. Levy asked any alter still there to come forth from Emma's body. No response. She asked again. Emma stirred in her seat as if uncomfortable. No voice issued from her mouth, however.

Letting every question settle into silence before asking the next, Dr. Levy queried, "Emmaline? Are you there? Are you still protecting Emma? We need to know."

Emma's mouth moved. "I'm here," Emmaline said.

"Hello, Emmaline. Are there any others left besides you?"

"Everything's been quiet. I don't think any of them are needed any longer."

"How about you? I'm not sure Emma needs you any longer. She seems to be doing quite well now."

"We'll see. I want to be certain I'm not needed. I'll do my job a little longer, and if Emma does well, then I'll also leave her."

"Do you anticipate any further problems? Is there something we should warn Emma about?"

"Well, Sam still worries me. But if he truly has gone, then I believe Emma will continue to be safe. She seems happy now." As was her habit, Emmaline crossed her legs and smoothed her shorts' seam, evening it so it sat directly in the middle of her thigh.

Dr. Levy thanked her and Emmaline faded. She woke Emma.

Emma put her hand to her forehead and, without speaking, leaned into her palm for a minute.

"Are you all right, Emma?"

"Just a bit of a headache." She leaned her head against the back of the sofa. "That seems to happen when a part comes or goes. Sometimes it's more intense than others." She uncrossed her legs and stood, stretching her mouth in a yawn and her arms opening wide. "So, who came today?"

"Only Emmaline." Irit Levy stood, signaling time was up, and started towards the door that led to her outer office. Her style hadn't changed much in the almost five years Emma had been her patient. She was classy in her red pencil skirt with black stripes down the sides and a classic black silk shell. "And I don't think she'll be there much longer."

Emma left the cool office and went toward the bank of elevators in the hall. Dr. Levy opened her door and called to her, "When do classes start at UCLA?"

"September twenty-fourth. I'm fired about it! Can't wait!"

I believe it's more than a hunch. I'll bet Emmaline is gone and you are no longer fragmented by then. Levy closed her office door. A satisfied smile dominated her face.

CHAPTER TWENTY-EIGHT

nita, look at this!" Jenkins waved the newspaper he held open and upright with both hands.

Anita returned the orange juice container to the refrigerator and closed the door. "What?" She turned and sat at the table. "Let's take our juice and go outside. It's such a pretty day and it's not too hot yet."

"Anita. Listen to me."

"Oh, sorry, Monty. My attention was elsewhere. What did you want to show me?"

"Fairfax did it."

She leapt from her high-backed stool, sending its seat spinning, as she rushed to bend over Jenkins' shoulder to see the newspaper article. "Really?" she gasped as she read about a forty-nine-year-old man, a native of South America, being found in an alley off Commonwealth Street with both legs shattered. His address was listed as an apartment on Commonwealth and he was currently employed as a groundskeeper.

"That's him!" She hugged Jenkins' shoulder and neck so hard that she almost dislodged him from his stool. "He got him, Monty! He got him!" She loosened the grip she had on Monty's shoulder that left half-moon nail prints in the fabric of his shirt. "Thank God," she said, a little calmer now.

Jenkins' phone buzzed. He looked at the screen and darted a glance at Anita. "It's Jack Fairfax."

He punched the green button and Fairfax, in a level voice, said, "It's done. Have you seen the morning paper?"

"Yes. We've just finished reading it. Thank you so much. I hope it hurt the bastard."

"I assure you it did."

"Are you going to be okay? I mean, I know you are a professional and the article does say that the police have no leads, but . . ."

Fairfax interrupted him. "Not to worry. It's done. And it's over. The police will not tie it to me. Or to you. Come on in today and we'll settle up." The line went dead.

Excitement bristling off her like sunrays, Anita asked, "What did he say, Monty? Tell me everything."

"He's a man of few words, Anita." He patted her bottom, as she still stood by his shoulder, transfixed by the phone call from the man Jenkins referred to as the enforcer. "He assured me it will not be traced back to him, thus not to us."

"Then it's over. We can tell the girls."

PART 3:
CHAPTER TWENTY-NINE

Susie navigated her senior year at Marshall High in her own way. Sure, she had to fit in and obey the school rules, which she did, but she also carved out a niche for herself among her friends. She was friends with most, accepted by all, and revered by the younger students. She wanted to grab the world by its tail feathers and hang on for dear life. She wanted to do it all.

In a line with the other girls trying out for cheerleading, Susie grasped the girl's left arm to her right, pulled her toward her and wrapped her fingers around the ball of her right shoulder. She repeated this with the girl on her left. Now she had the far shoulder of each girl in her hands. She felt their arms slide around her upper back and grasp the shoulder farthest from each. The girls stood with hands upon shoulders, intent upon instructions from the cheerleading coach.

The coach snapped on the CD player and spoke over the sound of the Barristers fight song. "Now watch us carefully and make every move they do." She pointed to two senior cheerleaders who were there to help show them the moves. "And watch Kenna and Maycee. They know the moves as well. Just keep time to the music. Okay, here goes."

The three stood before the girls trying out for the cheerleading spots vacated by last year's seniors.

"One," they said in unison as they raised their right knees.

"Two." They turned their knees to the left in front of their bodies.

"Three." Their legs shot straight out in perfect timing. Then they moved up together in a high kick, after which they dropped their feet to the grass. No one said anything. It happened quickly and the three stood still.

"That," said the coach, "is what I want you to do now."

Piece of cake. It looks like the Radio City Rockettes. I can do this. Susie, eager to get going, danced in place, her body bobbing up and down with the force of her high kicks.

"I'm glad to see your enthusiasm, Miss Montford. Just hold on to it a minute as I get everyone on board with these moves."

Susie grinned at the coach and stood still, almost.

The coach and her two helpers were successful in getting the girls to dance. Some were quite good with the timing, kicking in the right direction, and reaching the height of the kicks. Some were awkward, could never seem to get the rhythm in sync with the rest, and failed to get their legs high enough so they were all achieving one fluid movement. This last group the coach cut from the line amid tears of disappointment from some, resigned faces from several, and profanity from a few. In the end, eight of the twenty-four were excused.

The two senior cheerleaders showed them other dance routines and cheers. The new girls copied them all the best they could. When the try-out session was over, only six girls were needed to join the six cheerleaders from the year before who were all seniors now. The coach called out the names of the six who made the team.

When Susie heard her name issue forth from the coach's lips, she yelled, "All right!" and jumped high, pumping her right arm. She made the cheerleading team and it didn't matter to her that she was second to last at number five. Heck, she'd never attempted a cheer until the first day of practice. She'd learned that all the other girls had cheered at some point before. Her infectious personality had captivated and energized the squad during their practice sessions. Since she was fun and friendly, all but one of the girls who weren't chosen went to her as a group and congratulated her.

"I'm sorry we won't be cheering together," Susie told them. "We would've had lots of time to develop great friendships." She pursed her lips. "Tell you what, let's all pledge to be friends and talk to each other whenever we can." The girls agreed and it appeared that they left feeling much less like losers. The last girl, whose angry statements contained a number of off-color words, left with Susie's smile warming her back. Susie was unaware that in covering so many times for Emma, she'd learned quite well the art of placating with its accompanying techniques of salving and soothing.

The AP classes proved easy for Susie. She was always ready to lead discussions and ask searching questions as she delved ever deeper in her quest to learn all she could. At home she talked about the classes with Emma. They sat in the family rec room, now no longer harboring their school work stations, and Susie shared her concerns with her big sister, as she had done since a little girl.

"You know, Emma, it's not like I'm trying to show off, but so many of the kids are so smart that they sit there bored to death and never ask questions or volunteer anything. I don't mean to do all the talking." She poked out her bottom lip. "I guess they're way smarter than I am."

"Did it occur to you they may not be smarter than you? You may know a lot more than they do."

"What? How's that?"

"Well, if they aren't participating in the discussions, I would think that means they don't know enough to do so. You know, there are a lot of people who test really well, but don't have an original thought in their heads."

A grin brightened Susie's downcast expression. "Hey, maybe Zelda Bass did work our butts off for a reason. I remember enough of what she insisted we learn to at least talk about it."

"Of course she had a reason. She wanted us to shine with all the things she taught us. I was salutatorian of our graduating class, and here you are—the smartest one in your AP classes." Emma reached out impulsively and pulled Susie into her arms. She hugged Susie and patted her back. Still rubbing Susie's back, she drew away far enough to see her face. "You keep on kicking ass, and I mean it!"

Sean moved up a notch on the social scale by being Susie's boyfriend. He was good looking with his lopsided killer smile and all that hair that reminded people of the English actor, Hugh Grant, in his younger years. Naturally gregarious, he had plenty of friends. His was a popular name in the classrooms and halls of Marshall High.

Sean's position on the Barristers football team was both prestigious and rewarding as he caught an average of two balls a game for touchdowns. Some were accidents where the ball seemed to magically fall into his hands near the goal line and he was able to power his way in to score, often dragging members of the opposing team with him. Others he caught inside the goal line due to careful plays planned by the coach and executed by the quarterback and him. Oh, the Barristers were having their best season ever, and Sean was credited with a good portion of it.

Then there was Susie. Sean thought it was all due to her. She had come to Marshall hoping for a final year as a normal student. He thought she was anything but. He knew she was extraordinary. However, he had to concede that she was doing the things she thought of as normal. The things she could not do when she was being homeschooled and thought she was missing out on the fun activities offered by a regular Los Angeles county school. He thought she was really making up for lost time since she was participating in as many activities as one could possibly be involved in.

Now, Sean slung his arm around Susie's shoulders and pulled her tight against his side as they took the steps two at a time leaving the school's front door. At the bottom, he slowed them to drop a kiss atop her golden curls. "Where are you off to now? Cheerleading?"

"Yep. Coach has us learning this wild new cheer. I have to climb up and stand on Tracie's shoulders and do this summersault on the way down. It's fun, but it's also scary as hell. I about peed my pants the first time I tried it."

"Did you make it?"

"The cheer?"

"Yeah. Did you complete it?"

Susie giggled. "Sure. On my ass on the ground."

Sean laughed and hugged her again, his affection for her obvious in his beaming face. He sobered and turned her facing him.

"Susie, I miss my girl," he said, his voice soft with sincerity. "It seems we never have time together anymore."

Susie reached up and ran her fingers through his marvelous mane of thick, unruly hair.

"I'll always make time to be with you, Sean. If nothing else, you can come by at night before we go to bed and we can at least spend a few minutes saying good night."

"Your mom and dad going to be okay with that?"

"Why not? We won't have time to do anything to make them suspicious." She wrinkled her nose and produced a grin. "Besides, they were young once, too. They know the drill."

Sean's laugh rang out. Nearby students cast curious looks at them. "That's lit! I've seen your dad pat your mom's butt and then pull her tight against him and kiss her when he didn't think anyone saw them. I'll say they know the drill!"

Yes, Susie enjoyed quite a variety of activities as a smart and popular senior at Marshall. Above all, she enjoyed the public school itself. The perks it offered were glorious, to be sure. So, she was enjoying the school, her studies, her cheerleading, her clubs, all of her extra-curricular activities, and the freedom to pursue whatever she wanted that was available to her.

She tried out for chorus and found she did possess a lovely soprano voice. She became a chorus member in the second week of school, adding it to her already full schedule. A ham since age two, she auditioned for the theatre department and became a cast member. Her voice, added to that natural ability to perform in front of others without getting tongue-tied, won her the role of Christine in *The Phantom of the Opera*. Everything seemed to be going Susie's way. In her heart of hearts, she kept waiting for the fall from glory.

Sean was so happy for her he didn't resent that he could rarely spend time with her after school because she was always at cheerleading or play practice. He knew this was good for Susie in so many ways. Particularly, it provided her the opportunity to shine, for Hollywood and New York Talent scouts were always present at any play staged by the area high schools, colleges, and universities. The pool of talent was deep in the Los Angeles area theatre departments.

Sean was amazed that after being at Marshall for only six weeks, Susie was among those chosen for the Homecoming Court. She wasn't voted Queen, but then, she was practically brand new to the school. He was also proud to say she was his girl, and he loved her passionately. He looked at her lovely, vivacious face and willowy figure and longed to make her his completely.

Madonna set the buttered toast and guava jelly on the table while Susie and Emma climbed on their stools. Breakfast before they went off to classes; Emma to UCLA and Susie to Marshall High. Madonna hurried to the cabinet and returned with a box of granola and set it in front of the girls. "Milk's in the refrigerator."

Susie raised an eyebrow at Emma and mouthed, "What's up with her?"

Emma reached out and caught Madonna's sleeve as she dodged past them. "Is something wrong, Madonna?"

A mixture of anger and disappointment played across Madonna's round face and her big brown eyes flew wide before narrowing again. With indignation looming large, Madonna replied, "Yes, Miss Emma. Something *is* wrong."

"Can you tell me what has upset you so?"

"Well, Miss Emma, it's you."

"Me?" Emma recoiled in shock, dropping Madonna's sleeve as if were boiling water. "What have I done, Madonna?"

Sniffing, and drawing herself up to her full height of five feet, one inch, Madonna stated, "I know that Mr. Eric is your boyfriend. I know, too, that you are both twenty years old and are young grown-ups." She took her eyes from Emma's and gazed out the glass door at the trees gently swaying beyond the swimming pool by the tennis court.

"Go on, Madonna." Emma's expression was no longer solicitous. It was fearful.

"Your parents hired me to look after you two and I've tried my best to do that." She sighed and shook her head. "I guess I failed in so many ways. I realize I didn't know enough about what was going on with you and why you had to see that therapist. But, I thought everything was fine now."

Susie piped up, "So, what made you change your mind? Did something happen?"

Emma turned and laid her hand on her sister's arm. "Hush, Susie. Let her tell it." She turned back to look in Madonna's eyes. "Did I do something wrong, Madonna?"

Madonna began to wring her hands in the apron she wore tied around her neck and waist and took a step backward, as if distancing herself from the situation.

"Yes, you did, Miss Emma." She took her hands from the apron and waved the right one toward the stove. "I was scared I'd left the oven on, cut down real low, and

I couldn't quit thinking about it. So, I left my room and came into the kitchen to check." She looked out the door again.

Emma's face was pale as she asked, "What did you see?"

Speaking fast, as if in fear she'd lose her nerve, Madonna said, "I saw you. You were practically naked. You were wearing just this."

Madonna went to the couch in the rec room and picked up a garment and held it up for the girls to see. It was a short, sheer, diaphanous nightgown that appeared completely see-through. "You may as well have been wearing nothing." She dropped the nightie on the couch. "And then you opened the door and went out to meet your boyfriend."

"Eric?"

"I guess it was Eric. But then he spread some towels out by the pool and you two got naked and laid down together. I just couldn't watch anymore after that. I went back to my room and later I came back out and went outside and found this laying there." She motioned to the sheer nightie.

Emma slumped with her face in her hands, hidden by her fall of white gold curls. "Oh, Madonna," she whispered, "I don't remember any of it."

Susie reached over and pulled her close. "I just hope it *was* Eric," she whispered into Susie's shoulder.

"Of course it was. But, I'll find out. I'll ask him if he came by late last night by saying I thought I saw him out by the pool. He'll tell me the truth. Let's not assume the worst until we know for sure." She playfully pushed Emma upright on her stool. "Now, we need to eat something so we can both get to school."

Emma thanked her with a trembling smile.

Susie nabbed a piece of toast and slathered guava preserves on it. She took a bite and gestured with the toast to

Madonna. "Glad you told us, Madonna. We'll see what's going on. Let's hope it was a one-time thing. Oh, and don't tell Mom and Dad. We'll tell them."

Susie shot out the door to climb into Sean's red Mustang for the ride to school. Slower, and deep in thought, Emma backed her Prius out of the drive and set out for the UCLA campus.

I need to tell Mom and Dad about this after Susie checks with Eric. And I need to call Dr. Levy. I guess my sessions with her aren't over after all. Emma's thoughts were in turmoil as she found a parking spot and went to her first class. She continued worrying during her next two classes, barely hearing the instructor and learning nothing. At noon, she went to the student cafeteria and picked up a taco salad. She chose a seat in a far corner and picked at her meal, mixing the meat and cheese with the guacamole and making an unappetizing green paste. Finally, she put her fork down, withdrew her cell phone from her bag, and dialed Irit Levy's office number.

"I need to make a phone call for Emma," Susie said to Sean as they took their lunches of chicken sandwiches and fries to a table. "Be back in a minute. I can't hear in here with all this noise." She wriggled her fingers at him and with a "Tootle-oo" and a smile she left him alone at the table. He watched her disappear into the girl's bathroom located just outside the cafeteria door.

She dialed Eric's number, hoping he'd be having lunch and not be in class.

"Hello. This is Eric."

"Eric, this is Susie, and I have a question for you." She didn't wait for small talk. She wanted to know now. "I

gotta ask, were you out by our pool in the middle of the
night last night?" Again, not pausing, she continued, "I
was up and looked out and, unless I was sleepwalking, I
saw you out there."

"Um, yeah. What else did you see?"

"Not much. I actually thought I'd dreamed it. Just
wanted to check. See you later." She jabbed the off button
and heaved a huge sigh. *At least we know it was Eric and
not some stranger Emma was having sex with.*

Susie returned to Sean and wolfed down her sandwich.
She checked the time on her watch. "Yes, I still may be
able to catch Emma." She punched in Emma's number.

"Oh, Susie Darling" played and Emma answered. "Did
you find out?"

"It was Eric."

"Oh, thank God!"

CHAPTER THIRTY

Emma sat on the blue hypnosis couch in Dr. Levy's quiet room and looked at the familiar objects she had come to know well in the last couple of years. She particularly enjoyed looking at the large floral watercolor painting that hung on the wall opposite her. Its soft and subtle shades of white and lightest of blue flowers interspersed with powdery, pale green dusty miller leaves were not only pleasing to the eye but brought calmness to the viewer. It soothed Emma now as she turned her gaze from the painting to Dr. Levy.

Dr. Levy's dark brown eyes exuded compassion. She leaned toward this favored patient, her head dipped to the side in one of her classic poses. "Tell me something you *do* know about what happened, Emma. Then I want you to tell me something you *didn't* know about it."

Dejected, Emma dropped her gaze. Her shoulders slumped and her former serenity disappeared. Avoiding Levy's eyes, she looked at the objects in the room and at the ceiling as she answered, "I do know Madonna saw Eric naked by the pool with someone who looks like me." She stopped and Levy watched tears hover on her lower lids. One broke free and snaked down her ivory cheek.

Emma raised her head and threw it back on her neck as in an act of defiance. "What I *didn't* know was *all* of it."

"How so?"

"I *didn't* know Eric was there. I *didn't* know this body went out to the poolside and got naked with him. And I sure as hell *didn't* know that Angelique came back and had sex with him."

"You sound angry, Emma."

"I *am* angry. I'm mad as hell!"

"Can you tell me about it?"

Emma sniffed back her tears. "I'll be glad to." She waited for Dr. Levy to turn on the recorder and get settled for note taking.

"This is what I've been told, but I don't remember any of it." She brushed back her hair with her right hand, a habit she seemed to do obsessively in the hourly sessions with her psychiatrist but didn't do when hypnotized.

Emma told the therapist all that Madonna said and how disappointed in her she'd seemed. She told her of Susie's phone call confirming it was Eric she'd been with. Admitting to having no memory of any of it, she hissed, "I don't remember it because it wasn't *me*! It was Angelique!"

"You're sure it was Angelique?"

"It *had* to be. Eric was obviously pleased with the sex."

"How do you feel about that? Still angry?"

"Yes, I'm angry! I want to be the one making love with my boyfriend, not *her*." Emma brushed back her hair and stared down at the floor. As if she was unaware that she was doing it, her eyes traced the swirling patterns in the sky blue and seafoam green carpet between her feet. Her hair fell and she raised her hand and brushed it back again.

"I still haven't been with Eric," she said, raising her head and her eyes seeking her therapist's. "It scares me. I don't know *how* to have sex."

"I believe it comes naturally, Emma," Levy said with a slight smile.

"Yes, I guess. But I'm afraid it wouldn't be the same and Eric would know." She looked down again, this time twisting the gold filigreed ring on her finger Eric had given her.

Levy suddenly spoke sharply. "Emma, look at me."

Startled, Emma jerked her head up.

"Listen to me, Emma. We're going to tell Angelique under hypnosis that you no longer need her and it's time for her to disappear. Are you ready?"

Hope spread like sunshine across Emma's face. "Yes! Do you really think it will work?"

Levy gave her a gentle smile in contrast to the sharpness of before. "We're going to try. We can only hope it will work." She caught her bottom lip between her teeth and her face reflected her deep thoughts. "I believe it will."

Using the same hypnosis technique that had worked so well for Emma, Dr. Levy had her under in a few moments. She called for Angelique to come forth. Nothing. She implored her, stating they needed her. Again nothing. She changed tactics.

"Angelique, your time is up. You've done all you need to do. Emma can handle her boyfriend by herself now. *She* wants to have sex with Eric. She doesn't need you anymore and wants you to go."

"Well, well, well," came from Emma's mouth. "So, she's finally grown up and thinks she can handle having sex now, huh?" Angelique leaned back against the couch and spread her arms along its back. She crossed her legs and dangled one sandal from her toes. "I guess if she's going to stick with just one, that boy, Eric, would be a good choice. He's *fine*! I taught him a lot, and if Miss Goody-goody can get her act together, they'll make beautiful music together."

She stood and placed her right hand against her forehead in a military salute, "So long now. I have to say it was fun while it lasted."

Emma's body caved in upon itself and she sat, eyes closed and breathing normally. Just to be sure, the doctor called Angelique, imploring her to come back and talk. *Well, it's either of two things. She's gone or she's not answering. I hope it means she's gone.* Dr. Levy brought Emma out of the hypnotic state.

Emma opened her eyes and blurted, "Did it work? Is she gone?"

Softly, the doctor said, "Yes, she's gone."

"Forever?"

"I believe so," she said, nodding her head. "I really don't expect her to return. She seemed to know it was time for an end to her role in your life."

"Are they all gone now?"

"I think so. Of course, I thought so before. But, since no one but Angelique has returned, it's most likely that they are all integrated back into just you." She laughed and took Emma's hands in hers. "You are now you, Emma Montford! Just you. No one else."

Emma leapt up from the sofa and gathered to her the slim body of her therapist. "Thank you, thank you. Thank you so much, Dr. Levy."

Irit Levy returned the hug.

"Ummm, that smells wonderful, Madonna! What is it?" Emma swept into the kitchen, dropped her book bag on the floor and hurried to the stove. She was lifting the heavy lid on the large, red enameled cast iron pot when

Madonna said, "How did your meeting with the doctor go?"

Emma continued lifting the lid and took a deep sniff of what she determined to be lamb stew. Large chunks of lamb sat bubbling gently in a clear broth with carrots, celery, onion, and potatoes. Madonna made it just like the restaurant in Ireland did when they'd joined her mother there in Adair when she was filming a movie in the Irish setting. "Lamb stew. Yum!"

"Miss Emma?"

Emma set the pot lid back on the stew pot and turned. "Oh, Madonna, it was excellent. I can't wait 'til dinner when I can tell everyone." She took Madonna's hands from her apron where she was twisting and bunching the material. "But, I'll tell you now."

Her impish smile preceded her words as she told Madonna the therapist thought Angelique was gone for good. "She told her I didn't need her anymore and she said goodbye as if she really was gone." Emma looked down at the floor and shook her head. "God, I hope so."

"I'll pray to the Virgin Mary that it is so," Madonna vowed.

"Madonna!" Jenkins called as he leaned back in his chair in the formal dining room where he'd asked Madonna to lay their places for dinner this night. He looked for Madonna and called her again.

"Yes, Mr. Jenkins?" Madonna entered the dining room with her hands again grasping her apron.

Jenkins smiled fondly at the cook. "I do believe this is the best Irish stew I've had since I lived in Yorkshire. A job well done, Madonna."

"Thank you, Sir," Madonna said, her face turning beet red as she tried to back out the dining room door.

"I never cared for lamb before," Anita added. "It's not a dish we were used to growing up in the south. But, I'll tell you, Madonna, this is delicious."

Face now flaming, Madonna murmured, "Thank you," and hurried into the kitchen.

"Why're we eating in here, Dad? Some special occasion?" Susie put a forkful of lamb into her mouth and chewed happily as she dipped a piece of crusty bread into her stew.

"Yes, rather," Jenkins nodded. "Your mother and I wanted to tell you two that the man responsible for all Emma's problems has been taken care of."

"What?" Susie yelled.

"What? What do you mean, Dad?" Emma stammered.

Jenkins looked to Anita and raised his eyebrows.

Anita nodded, her eyes wide and bright.

Jenkins gave one sharp nod and caught Emma's eyes with his. "Okay. I'll tell you what happened." He lifted his wine glass and took a healthy swallow. Setting it down, he twirled the stem, watching the golden wine swirl inside its crystal goblet.

"I hired someone I like to think of as 'the enforcer' to find the man who did those horrible things to hurt you." He lifted the wine glass in salutation. "He found him."

"He did?" Susie asked. "What'd he do?"

Jenkins shot a glance at his youngest daughter. "Give me time, Susie. I'm getting to that."

"Emma," he said, voice calm and sure, "he found him, lured him into an alley near his home and broke both of his legs."

"Really? All right!" blurted Susie.

Jenkins gave her a steely glare and she quieted in an instant, zipping her finger across her lips.

"Wow," Emma mused. "I wondered how I'd feel when that horrendous man had something bad happen to him.

I thought of it and thought of a million different scenarios to hurt him. I *wanted* him to hurt." She implored her father with her direct look. "Are you sure he broke both legs?"

"Yes. Not only that, it was his knees he broke! He'll never be able to walk again without extensive surgery and knee replacements," Anita said, entering the conversation.

"Did he know why the guy did that to him?"

"It's certain that he knew. The enforcer told him it was payback for hurting a young girl many years ago. He told him he wanted him to hurt like he made her hurt. He knows, all right."

Emma sat quietly staring into the bowl of stew. Susie stared hard at Emma trying to read what was taking place behind her eyes. Jenkins waited silently with one questioning eyebrow raised, never taking his gaze from her hunched figure.

Anita spoke, breaking the uneasy silence. "Emma, I know you have a big heart and you're thinking of . . ." She threw her hands wide, likely searching for some title or name to give to the man responsible for all that had happened in Emma's life since she was hardly more than a toddler. ". . . this *man*. Maybe even feeling sorry for him, Right?"

Emma didn't respond to her mother, instead, she raised her head and looked at her father with shining eyes. A simple "Thanks, Dad," followed. Then she dipped her spoon into the stew and took a bite. "Yum, this is really good."

The collective breath the others held escaped into the room as if three balloons were deflating at once.

"I am so glad it's over," Anita gushed in her best theatrical voice. Everyone joined her in the laughter this produced. When the heady gaiety died down, Emma said, "I have some news, too."

Stew forgotten, they all gave Emma their immediate attention. Jenkins sat straight in his chair as if he were about to receive a commendation. Anita leaned toward her oldest daughter, her lips moving without sound, as if trying to help her to say whatever it was. Susie was alive with anticipation, her body that of a runner ready for the starting gun.

"What is it, Emma, dear?" Anita, at last, was able to make sounds and string them together into words.

"I saw Dr. Levy this afternoon." She looked at Jenkins. "And . . ." Jenkins' tone implored her to continue.

"Angelique came back." Emma directed a look at her mother.

"Oh, darling, no!" Anita cried.

Susie flung herself against the back of the chair and crossed her arms in front of her chest. "Shit!" she fired at Emma.

Emma locked eyes with Susie. "When Dr. Levy hypnotized me, Angelique came out and talked about what she'd done. But, then Dr. Levy told her all the others were gone and she wasn't needed anymore."

"It's about frigging time," Susie muttered through clinched teeth, her lips barely moving.

"Susie?" Emma cocked her head to one side.

Susie raised her eyes and her head moved from left to right as she carefully examined the crown molding running along the ceiling all around the room.

"Susie, look at me," Emma demanded.

"Why? It's never gonna be over. I was praying that all of them were gone." She sat up and raised her voice to almost shouting. "All of them! Including Angelique!"

Now Emma raised her voice. "You don't even want to hear the rest of it? You don't even care that it's *good* news?"

Susie tried to rise but entangled herself in the long tablecloth that hung from that end and puddled in her lap. She threw it aside with her plate, water glass, and silverware tumbling to the gleaming dark hardwood floor. "What *good news* can there possibly be?" A snarl marred her lovely face.

Emma gave her a look that was a combination of surprise, hurt, and anger. She turned her attention to her parents. "Mom. Dad. I think you will be interested in hearing this."

"To be sure," her dad agreed, the thundercloud on his face abating somewhat when he turned from Susie to Emma.

"Well, tell us what it is, honey," her mom encouraged, reaching over to lay her hand atop her daughter's.

"Well, Angelique said goodbye and disappeared. Dr. Levy thinks she may be gone for good." She broke into a smile as she said it. Such was her joy until it radiated around the room as her smile turned into a delighted laugh that reached every corner.

"That's wonderful, darling," Anita cooed.

"That's bloody brilliant!" Jenkins added, getting up and going to Emma where he bent to hug her.

"Yeah, well, let's see how long this lasts," Susie blurted.

Jenkins turned to glare at his youngest daughter. "Susie, that's enough. You may be excused right now!"

Susie moved with agonizing slowness from her stance at the table to the door, all the while sharing an insolent stare among the three, as with exaggerated care, she picked her way through the spilled remains of her dinner and dishes. Then she was past the mess, out the door and gone.

Bewildered, Emma exclaimed, "What bug is up her butt? I can't believe she's acting like this." She dropped her head into the palm of her right hand as she braced her elbow on the table.

Having quietly observed the outbursts, Anita said, "I don't believe Susie intends to be so unsupportive, Emma. I truly believe she is disappointed hearing about Angelique and it meaning you aren't completely integrated back to just yourself."

"I guess." Emma took a bite of the lamb stew as Madonna hustled in with a broom and dustpan. Her face lit up when she noticed Emma take a spoonful and chew it quickly before taking another. With a few swipes of the long-handled broom, the spilled stew was gone from the floor. She swabbed the residue with a wet cloth, cleared the dishes and cutlery, and hurried out.

"I suppose I'll have to talk to Susie and calm her down," Emma continued. "I feel so alone when she's upset with me." She looked from her mom to her dad and back down at her food. "I hope she knows I couldn't have done this without her."

CHAPTER THIRTY-ONE

Emma entered her Social Sciences classroom and headed to her usual spot halfway back in the middle of the rows of desks. She smiled at the classmates sitting near her and dropped her book bag to the floor beside her seat. This was a different Emma; not the girl who'd presented an unhappy, haunted face for the last class meetings. She was gratified when her smile was returned. *They like me.*

That day was a forerunner of the days to come in which she greeted her classmates and was receptive to conversation, at times even initiating it with a question, or perhaps addressing something appearing on the latest news channels. She was making friends and she liked it.

This class was Sociology 101 and she was learning where the interaction with others would lead – directly into their minds. That's what she wanted. She was following the course of action she needed to obtain the goals she spoke about with Dr. Levy. She would find out how and why alters like she'd experienced get inside one's body. That's why she chose Social Sciences, and why she planned to move on to psychiatry.

Several months ago, when the deadline for registering as an undergrad at UCLA was almost visible around the corner, the two sisters had discussed what Emma should do. Susie had laid the latest issue of *People* Magazine on the sofa cushion beside her. She'd made herself turn her eyes from the story about Jennifer Anniston and look up at her sister as Emma paced the length of the room before returning to stand looking down at her.

"So? What are you gonna do?" Susie's voice was curt.

"I know what!" Emma said, her voice rising with inspiration. "I'll call and make an appointment with a counselor. I need help making sure I get the right courses for what I want to study."

"Yeah, that's a good idea, Emma," Susie muttered. What she really wanted to say was: "Leave me alone. I want to read my magazine. I am tired of always being the one to help you through the latest crazy thing." *Hmmph, they're all crazy things, anyway!* But, she said none of it. She helped Emma find the phone number for the counselors. Together they wrote down all questions and answered any they thought might mean something to the person who answered their call.

"You could say you have special personal needs and they'll be sure to see you quicker."

"What? How do you know that?"

"If you are ever gonna beat the system, you better learn how to get on that train," Susie said. She picked up her magazine, dismissing Emma, and began to flip the pages, seeking where she'd left off when interrupted. *Emma is driving me crazy. Can't she do anything for herself?*

Today, Emma was aboard that train and reaching out to her classmates, determined to learn from them, to be like them, and to, in essence, use them to attain her goals of learning why and how a person could carry so many others within one's self. *Then I'll understand me. I just need to make friends, hang out, and find the reasons why my classmates have chosen this coursework. Maybe someone else has the same thing I've had and we can work together to learn all we can about our many parts. It would be excellent to talk with someone else who knows first-hand what I have been through.* Optimism, together with its partner Determination, seemed to have finally found lodging within Emma.

Susie ran her hands along her thighs, smoothing down the luscious golden fabric of the most beautiful gown she'd ever seen. It was halftime at the Marshall High home-coming football game and time for the queen and her court to take the field. She was part of the court and she was wearing Emma's gown from last spring's prom. Yes, they had made up after the fiasco of the Irish lamb stew meal, although Susie still carried doubt and resentment in her heart.

The queen and the four other girls comprising the Homecoming Court were each sitting along the back of cars with convertible tops that were down. Their glitzy shoes were as yet unseen as they rested firmly on the backseats, giving the girls some stability to keep them from sliding off as they adorned the backs of the cars. Each princess would be accompanied by a football player for the ride around the football field as soon as half-time started.

Sean launched himself onto the back of the white late model Mustang and slid into place beside Susie. He'd not seen Emma in the gown and now whistled at Susie in it. "Man, do you look sexy in *that*," he growled as he took her hand nearest him, her left. His hand smelled of grass, dirt, sweat, and that particular football odor found in locker rooms.

Susie had but a moment for the thought to materialize before the car's owner pulled out into the line for the procession. As the senior class representative princess, her spot was directly behind the queen and her escort who were also seniors. Their baby blue mustang led the way, with Susie's white one ahead of the cobalt blue carrying the junior class princess and the red one with the sophomore. The red and white car carrying the freshman princess fell in line at the end.

Sean leaned in as Susie waved energetically to the stands, forgetting she was to execute the more decorous royal wave, and whispered, "Having fun? I think you're making up for lost time, for sure."

Susie's shining eyes and infectious grin were all the answer he needed.

Later into the fall, after almost a full semester of study and practice had gone into learning the lines and the music to "The Phantom of the Opera," opening night arrived. Susie held tight to Emma's hand and peered at her parents in the front row from where she stood in the wings off the stage. Just seeing them brought a mixture of feelings. *Will I be good enough to please Mom? I'll never be as good as she is. Will Dad think I'm doing okay? Oh, I'm so glad they're here! I hope they'll be proud of me.*

She saw Sean saunter down the aisle, expecting him to take a seat with friends. He waved and spoke to several groups comprised of both boys and girls, but headed to the front row and took a seat near her mom. He leaned toward

Anita, exchanging a few words and smiles. He stood again to acknowledge Eric, whose height always made him easy to spot. Eric gave Sean a playful punch to the bicep, leaned down to speak to Anita, and shook her dad's hand before sitting with one seat between him and her mom. Behind her parents she saw the curls belonging to no other head than Zelda's, the teacher who had taken her to this point in her studies. *Oh, Lord. They're all out there. I've got to do good. Please don't let me screw this up.*

Susie looked, eyes sweeping the auditorium, for anyone else she knew, other than school kids. She spotted Madonna and Javier four rows behind her cheering squad on the front row. *Please don't let me forget my lines. And let me hit every note.* She just had to giggle as she added, *"That's all I ask of you,"* the words from one of the most noted songs from Andrew Lloyd Webber's lyrical play. She squeezed Emma's hand. "You better go now. Eric just got here. Along with everybody else. Wish me luck, and pray I don't pee my pants."

Emma bussed her cheek and whispered as she headed for the exit steps, "You'll knock 'em dead, Susie. Break a leg!"

Daring one last glance from her spot in the wings, Susie watched Emma take a seat between Eric and Anita. Her cheering section looked resplendent even though a Marshall High stage production didn't require the dress her mom and dad were accustomed to wearing on an opening night. Her dad had chosen a simple charcoal suit and the guys wore sports coats and jeans. Emma and her mom wore tasteful, tailored trousers and tops. Anita's was in a shimmering blue somewhere between navy and sapphire and Emma's was in a curve-hugging cranberry hue.

Soon the director was motioning for everyone to take their appointed places. The orchestra started the prelude

and played a portion of every musical piece in the reper-
toire, and then the curtains opened.

Afterward, the curtain zipped open and closed as the
cast took bow after bow in a rolling wave, each time bringing a roar of appreciation from the audience. After the
final curtain, the audience would not take their seats. Nor
were they gathering their things and preparing to leave.
Again, and again, the applause rose and fell as the actors
and musicians joined their friends and family.

Who to go to first? The thought flashed through Susie's
brain as she came down from the stage. Knots of people
were forming and congratulations were being given all
around. She need not have worried. They came to her, her
mom first with arms outstretched and pride glowing on
her beautiful face. "Oh, my darling, Susie, you were magnificent! You remind me of how new and fresh I was in my
early years."

Jenkins stood back until everyone had finished gush-
ing over Susie's spectacular performance and voice. He
gathered his daughter close and whispered, "Now aren't
you glad I insisted on you having a voice coach? You were
brilliant, my dear."

Stepping from her dad's embrace into Zelda's, Susie felt
a distinct familiarity and fondness she hadn't known until
now she had been missing. Her former teacher helped
guide her to be who she was today, and while she had
benefited from lessons learned with and from her, she
would never have had this opportunity to shine had she
stayed in the homeschool setting.

"This is a side of you I never expected to see," Javier
remarked, edging closer and speaking over Madonna's
shoulder. "But, now, I'll probably be driving you to film
sites all over the country, along with your mom." He
looked to Anita for her reaction.

Anita's trilling laugh rang out. "I think we might just have a plan, Javier."

Javier stepped aside as Madonna took Susie's right hand between her palms. "I prayed to Our Lady that you would do well, Miss Susie. And you did!"

Touched by the love and pride she felt from the people she cared for the most sobered Susie. Tears threatened as she felt her nose get that peculiar ache and she squinted her eyes and wrinkled her nose and hoped the annoying drops wouldn't materialize. She cleared her throat and quietly said, "Thanks everybody. This has been the most wonderful experience. I appreciate you sharing it with me."

Sean moved to her side and threw his arm around Susie's shoulders. "And now, it's time to ditch you old folks so we young'uns, as my grandmother would say, can celebrate 'til all hours."

Jenkins' wryly dry remark came with a raised eyebrow. "Nice try, Sean. Have her home at a reasonable time."

"Eric and I are going with them. We'll be great chaperones," Emma teased, her grin turning into giggles. The four young ones headed out, stopping every few feet to talk with school friends or members of the cast or orchestra. In another fifteen minutes they piled into Eric's SUV and were on their way to a late dinner at Barton G, the unusual restaurant where the food was good though unremarkable, but the presentation was creative and fun.

Eric held open the restaurant door and the four entered the minimally decorated space. The attention was given to the food presentation instead of to tufted banquet seats and white tablecloths. A waiter glided by with a sizzling steak with about a 4-foot-tall fork protruding from its top. "I want one of those!" Eric said, his eyes following the dish until the waiter delivered it to a table where it joined what looked to be a three- or four-foot-tall dagger piercing a large piece of fish.

"And I want whatever that big knife is served with," Emma added.

"Hey, we haven't even looked at the menu yet!" Sean said.

"I like what I see. Why mess around and try something that might be cute and clever and could taste like crap? You pretty much know what to expect with a steak."

They were seated and enthusiastically checked the menu offerings but spent more time looking around at the variety of foods the other diners were having than looking at their menus.

Seeing the macaroni and cheese in the big mouse trap at the adjacent table was enough proof to Sean that the weird dish was appealing. "That's what I want," he said, pointing at it while the man whose palate it was obviously satisfying narrowed his eyes at Sean's blatant staring. "Sorry, dude," Sean said, trying to camouflage his laugh with a cough.

The dish that caught Emma's attention, as they were led to their seats, was swordfish steak. That explained the tall sword. Emma ordered it without considering anything else. "What are you having Susie?" she asked. "It's your night to celebrate."

Susie addressed the waiter. "I'd like the lamb shank, please. That's like osso buco, right?" When the waiter assured her it was, she replied, "Do I get the butcher board cut-out with lamb written on it in big letters?"

"That you do."

"All right, then! Lamb it is!"

The four had a grand time appreciating the food presentation, tasting each other's dishes, talking about the stuff important to those of their age group, and in particular, Susie's gratifying senior year at Marshall.

"And how is it going with you, college girl?" Sean asked Emma.

"Really well. Thanks for asking, Sean." Emma sat tall and straight in her chair and took another forkful of swordfish. "Oh, this is so good!" She chewed slowly while she gathered her thoughts. With her fork tines stabbing air and keeping time with her words, she divulged, "I've finally figured out what my purpose is in my studies and I'm happy about that. I'm learning to like my classmates and I'm learning from them." She laid her fork down and reached for Eric's hand with her right and Susie's with her left. "And you two keep me grounded when I fly off in different directions." She squeezed the hands she held and looked at all three of her dinner partners. "I think that's over now and I am so lucky to have you three in my life."

Eyes bright with tears just waiting for her to blink and have them overflow, Emma unclasped their hands and with lower lip trembling, she said, "Let's eat. We can't let this crazy food go to waste."

All four chuckled, relieved, each realizing some milestone had been reached that evening. Some issues had been settled; some important things accomplished. Each would assess it alone later. For now, it was, indeed, time to eat.

CHAPTER THIRTY-TWO

Throughout Emma's first semester at UCLA, the entire Montford household paid close attention to her and were no less diligent for the second one that began after the start of the new year. Looking for any sign the DID was still lurking somewhere within her, they found none. No overt act occurred that one could definitively say was done by one of the known alters. There was no indication of a new or different alter having appeared. This further convinced Emma that she truly was one person and that person was *her*—who she was meant to be. The person she was before the sexual assaults that were the catalyst for the many personalities to develop.

One balmy Saturday afternoon in late March Emma and Susie sat together in the rec room thumbing through back issues of the entertainment industry magazines. Emma was restless and even the promised scintillating story of Brad Pitt's and Angelina Jolie's latest spat and Angelina filing for divorce couldn't hold her interest.

"Susie, let's go outside and sit by the pool. It's not cold at all today."

"Just a sec. Let me finish this paragraph."

"What's so interesting?'

"According to this reporter," Susie said, easing up from where she sat with one leg tucked under her, "Kate Winslet would like to do another movie with Leo." She stood and shook her right leg. "Darned thing almost fell asleep," she muttered. "Anyway, I think she'd like their relationship to be more than friends." She dropped the magazine on the sofa, put her weight on her numbed foot, testing it, and continued, "They'll never recreate the magic they had with "Titanic," no matter what movie they make together."

"No doubt that's true, but they could sure have fun trying!" Emma leapt to her feet and commanded, "Put on your swim suit and let's go sit by the pool. It's gorgeous weather out there."

"Okay. You're on!"

The girls sat in lounge chairs with their knees drawn up and supporting their ever-present tablets. Susie was playing an endless game of bubble blasting and Emma was attempting to stay focused on research for a class paper dealing with wants versus needs. Her mind was on something a bit different, however.

"Susie, could we talk about something personal? I really need to know the answer to this and I *need* for you to be truthful with me."

Susie turned her head to look at her sister with a frown furrowing her brow. "Well, sure. But, what are you talking about? I always tell you the truth."

Emma turned her body to face Susie, dropping her feet off the chaise. She braced her elbows on her knees, and hunched forward, placing her chin against her clasped hands. "I hope so, Susie, because this is very important to me."

Susie laid her hand on Emma's knee. "Okay. I understand. Go ahead." She closed her tablet on the bubble game and gave Emma her attention. But, simply because she was Susie, her eyes danced and a grin grew as she asked, "Should I take one of Mom's valiums first? Maybe bring you one, too?"

"Susie, be serious, please! I want you tell me how you really felt during all these years of taking care of me through all of this. You've been with me from the beginning and you undoubtedly know more of what really happened than I do. I have to know what you were thinking and how you felt about it."

Thoughts flashed behind Susie's eyes as she took her hand off Emma's knee. She clamped her lips together and stared at the sun's reflection in the pool and the water's crystal blue dance. Her breath quickened and she seemed to be battling with herself on what to divulge.

Suddenly she heaved a deep exhale and with it came a torrent of impassioned words that gushed from her mouth like boulders tumbling down a hillside.

"A lot of the time it was really shitty! I got so tired of being responsible for you and covering for you. I always had your back. Hell, I slept chained to you for months, always scared to death you would somehow hurt me — or both of us — in trying to get free. If Sam could cut your wrists, how did I know he wouldn't cut mine?" Finally, she turned her head and her curled lip conveyed her distaste as surely as her words.

Stunned, Emma sagged back into the chair. "I didn't know you felt that way."

"Of course, you didn't! It was all about you." Eyes now blazing, Susie leaned toward her sister. "Do you realize *everything* we did — Mom, Dad, and I — from the time you went bizarre on us in the eighth grade, and right on up until you started college, has been done to accommodate you and to help you get back to normal? You should. You also should have noticed I had *no* life of my own during that time!"

"Oh, Susie . . ." Emma began. She could speak no further. Tears flooded down her cheeks and her face seemed to collapse like a waterlogged washcloth.

"Well, you asked." Susie's chin was set and her lips were a pink line, surrounded by white. The blood had nowhere to flow, such was the force she exerted with her jaw and compressed lips.

Emma's sobs and sniffles were the only sound in the large backyard. It was possible that even the birds and insects had quietened due to the intense emotions that hung heavily in the air. The air was now saturated with words suppressed for far too long.

"Susie . . ." Emma began again. She couldn't get the words out. She gave Susie an agonized stare and stood up. As she started to walk away, Susie grabbed her arm, stopping her.

"Don't you dare try to walk away from me and leave like this. I have more to say!"

Though hitching breaths, Emma retorted, "You've made it perfectly clear how you feel."

"No, Emma, I *have not.*" Susie stood and faced her. She let go of Emma's arm and her own shoulders sagged under the weight of her thoughts. "I'm really all messed up about how I feel. I *do* know I love you and that I'd fight anybody trying to hurt you. I've protected you with everything I have. I've devoted my whole self to you—and there's not much left over for me."

Abruptly her legs failed her, and she sank to the concrete rimming the swimming pool. She looked up at Emma and saw the sun creating a nimbus of her fine blonde hair, haloing her head. *She looks like an angel. And I believe she—the real Emma, that is—must be. I have to remember that none of this is her fault.*

Emma sank down beside her but didn't attempt to touch her or say anything. She waited for the rest of the tirade. It came.

"Dammit, Emma, I feel used. I feel robbed. I need to scream and shout!" Her voice rose in agitation. "I am so ready to just unload all this resentment I've been carrying around."

Emma stiffened. "Against me?"

"Noooo," Susie wailed, "not really." Frustrated and aggravated, Susie said through teeth clinched so tightly it was difficult for Emma to understand her, "You need to know, Emma, I always loved you and I wanted to help you." Opening her mouth wide, she yelled "Aggghhhh! I'm obviously doing a bad job of explaining this."

Emma said nothing.

Glancing at Emma before turning her eyes skyward, Susie continued. "Okay, here's what I mean. I rejoiced when things were working out or going well. But, I never meant for it to take over my *entire* life like it did. I wanted my *own* life. Why do you think I wanted to go to public school when you started at the university?"

Deciding that Emma was not going to answer her rhetorical questions, Susie went on. "I wanted to do something *I* chose to do." She paused, expanded her lungs with a deep breath, and eased it out through her nose. "And I have. Things are good with Sean and me. I'm having a ball with all my school activities. My studies are going well. We should hear any day from USC and I feel certain I'll get in. All is fine here at home with Mom and Dad. So, why am I still feeling like this?"

Emma learned a thing or two in her therapy sessions with Dr. Levy. Now she said, "You tell me."

"Okay, here's the deal; I love you. I want everything to be perfect with you again. It makes me happy when you're happy. But, I want to be happy too, and these bad feelings I've had, which, by the way, seem perfectly normal to me, need to go bye-bye so that I can be myself without being mad at you.

"Are you mad at me now?"

"I was, but I kept it pushed down because it made me feel guilty. You're my sister for God's sake!"

"But are you mad with me now after talking it through?"

Susie considered, looking around at the place that helped define her, the pool where she spent so much time either in it or beside it; the large yard with the lovely jacarandas just now filling their branches with purple splendor; the house she'd called home for as long as she could remember; and the sister she knew loved her and whom she knew she loved.

Susie took Emma's hand and lifted it to her lips. She kissed the small knuckles and held them against her breast. "No, I don't think so. Not anymore. I completely lost myself in all this. I want to find myself again and be that person I think I would've been had I not got lost along the way."

Her eyes were again luminous with unshed tears, but her voice was strong as Emma said, "I had to know, Susie. But, now that I do, I believe we can put the bad feelings behind us and concentrate on being the best we can be at whatever we do. I'm certain I am integrated into just me. The *right* me. And I believe I'll be okay."

"Yes, you'll be fine, I'm sure." She gave a quick nod for emphasis. "And I think I've found myself again, so it's all cool. Wanta go inside and make some popcorn?"

FOUR YEARS LATER
Yorkshire, England

Jenkins dismissed with healthy stipends the servants who had lived in the manor house and had seen to its upkeep for the past many years. They adhered to the same strict guidelines Jenkins' mother had set all those years ago when he was small and an army of peasants served the three Montfords in this huge house on the hilltop overlooking the moors. Now, his plan was to place it with the National Trust who would add it to their list of manor homes available for tours. He accompanied his wife and daughters as they went from room to room exploring the imposing structure.

"Jenkins, I had no idea you grew up in such a place," Anita said, head back and eyes wide with wonder as she surveyed the high ceilings with paintings laid there by long ago artists.

"Dad, this is just so amazing. I can't even begin to describe a place like this. And to think you actually lived here." Emma walked ahead of them into the dining hall with a table long enough to seat at least two dozen, its surface gleaming with wax. "Did you really eat at this table?"

A wistful look flitted across his face as Jenkins answered, "Rarely was I allowed in the dining hall. I took my dinner in the kitchen with the cook on most occasions."

Susie flew through the high arch separating the dining hall from one of several sitting areas. Parlors, her dad called them, or libraries. *Holy cow! What did they do with all this room?*

"Didn't you love living here, Dad? I mean this place is so boss! It's crazy amazing!"

Instead of answering his exuberant daughter, Jenkins pursed his lips and said, "Follow me." He led his family upstairs to a bedroom with a single bed and a washstand with a white enameled basin sitting atop it. The rest of the room was bare, including the wide-planked wooden floor. Jenkins looked from one end of the room to the other and shook his head. A smile that was more of a grimace crossed his face,

The three women stared at him. Quietly, Emma asked, "What is it, Dad?"

His chest rose with a deep sigh that he hurriedly heaved out. "This was my room."

"What?" Anita yelped. "This room was *yours*?" She threw her hands up and then pointed to the doorway. "With all those fancy bedrooms, *this* was your room?"

"They were saved for the important guests who rarely came." He walked to the door and stood with one long arm braced against its side panel. "Let us go back down to the drawing room and take seats where we can be comfortable and I will tell you my story."

He led the way back down the winding stairs to the largest of the parlors. He chose to sit in an intricately-woven brocaded chair in tones of hunter green and deep cranberry. It had an indentation in its seat, attesting to its use.

"This was my father's chair. He always sat here and smoked his pipe. When it was family time, I was relegated to the corner yonder," he pointed to a darkened corner, "where I was to sit with my wooden toys and remain quiet."

He lifted his hand again, pointing this time to a settee in maroon velvet that sat across from his father's chair. It showed slight signs of wear on its arms and seat. "That was my mother's seat. She sat there in the evenings and listened to my father expound on some esoteric subject, giving him his master-of-the-house due attention. I would be still and silent, as requested. But, oh, how I longed to be included."

Her voice breaking, Anita moved to his side and placed her hand on his cheek, her fingers cupping his jaw, "I'm so sorry, Monty."

"Why'd they treat you like that, Dad?" Susie demanded.

Jenkins looked down at his long legs, stretched out with ankles crossed. "They were older when I was born. They were so in to each other, as you kids would say today, that they had no thought for a child they never really wanted. I was reared, and raised—there is a difference, you know—by the cook and the other servants and quite ignored by my parents. I was terribly lonely and spent hours walking on the moors. Should I come across a rabbit or some other small animal, it delighted me, as I then had another new and different living thing about me." He offered a wry smile. "It did help with the loneliness."

"No wonder you didn't want to come back when your parents died. That was really early, right after we were married, and I couldn't understand then why you were handling it all through the lawyers."

"Barristers." It was as if the mischievous Susie couldn't stop herself from correcting her mother. "Sorry, Mom. I know that because it was the high school mascot name." At her mother's frowning gaze, she added, "Okay, I'll be quiet. Go ahead, Dad."

"Girls, I must apologize to you for my distance when you were small. It's what I knew. It's how I grew up." He reached to draw Anita to his side. "But, because of the love your mother gave so freely to you girls, and to me, I learned to *loosen up* and be more demonstrative. Have no doubt, I love you three more than life itself."

Susie threw herself into her dad's lap and Emma came to his other side, opposite her mom. Jenkins stretched his arms around Emma and Anita while Susie lay against his chest. "I'm content now," he said, aiming a small smile at each of his loving family.

Emma was the first to move. She took a seat on a long low couch across from Jenkins. Emotions ending in what looked like excitement played across her face. Suddenly, sitting straight up on the sofa and with voice rising, she exclaimed, "Dad! I know what we can do. We can make this place mean something!"

"What do you mean, Emma? I'm letting it go to the National Trust."

"No. Don't do that, Dad. Instead, let's look at turning it into a place like . . . oh, like a retreat, or something similar, where people with DID who have nowhere else to go can go for help. Maybe you can even get some money from somewhere to help fund it."

"Oh, that is such a *great* idea, Emma," Susie sang out.

Anita, voice hesitating while thinking it through, said, "You might have something there, Emma. I've read that a lot of people have no one when they start showing signs of DID. Often their families think they are crazy and want nothing to do with them."

Jenkins stood and came to bend down in front of his daughter. "Emma, we went through this with you. It was tough, but we never once thought of abandoning you." He looked into her face and leaned forward to touch his lips to her cheek. "But, leave it to my brilliant daughter to think of ways to help others."

"You mean you'll consider it, Dad?" Susie asked. "Because if Emma's gonna be here running things . . ." she turned to Emma for her affirmation, and at her wide-eyed, nodding response said, ". . . then I'm gonna be here, too."

With his head wagging in wonder, Jenkins confirmed, "I'll look in to it."

"Good," Anita said. "And if that works, I can start planning that double-wedding and you girls better get Eric and Sean interested in living and working in England."

"Piece of cake." Susie laughed and flopped down on the couch by her big sister. Emma grinned and reached for Susie. The sisters sat leaning back against the velvet sofa with their heads tilted together, the fingers of Susie's right hand threaded with Emma's left.

"This is going to be a new concept in DID care," Emma mused.

"And it's gonna be awesome," Susie vowed. "Because we've got this. We know what we're doing, and we're gonna do what it takes."

A huge, happy smile stretched across Emma's face. "Precisely!"

THE END

ABOUT THE AUTHOR

LYLA FAIRCLOTH ELLZEY left Florida at age 23 and returned at age 55 after spending many years in CA and VA. She now writes in Tallahassee, FL where she lives with her husband Frank in a retirement community. An early retirement from administrative positions in the chaos that is northern Virginia and the periphery of our nation's capital has enabled Lyla time to indulge in activities she put off for way too long. A member of TWA, the Tallahassee Writers Association, and FAPA, the Florida Publishers and Authors Association, she writes almost every day and has a cache of work in various stages of getting to publication: A short story book, *Into the Unknown,* about the supernatural and paranormal; a children's chapter book, *Daniel and Elizabeth's Grand Adventures,* in which every chapter tells a different story about a lesson learned from their mother involving an animal such as a baby panther, a flying squirrel, or a big black dog. As a mother of two and a grandmother of four, she has an excess of inspiration from which to draw.

She travels extensively and a month spent in rural England in the fall of 2018 paved the way for an historical fiction novel she is writing about the known beginnings of her paternal roots in the Lancashire area of North West England eight centuries ago. The Faircloth name and its variations are quite old, having been traced back to the 1200s.

Lyla hopes you enjoy her books because she has many more waiting in the wings that just need transferring from her imagination to the page.

Now that you've enjoyed *Losing Herself,* you'll want to stay in touch with Lyla to be among the first to learn about new releases and events where you can visit with her in person.

Visit her website at https://www.lylafairclothellzey.com/ and join her on your favorite social media platform.

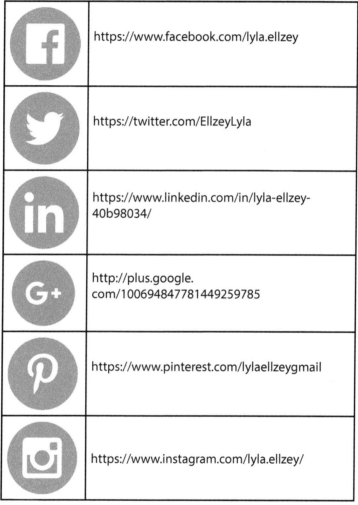

	https://www.facebook.com/lyla.ellzey
	https://twitter.com/EllzeyLyla
	https://www.linkedin.com/in/lyla-ellzey-40b98034/
	http://plus.google.com/100694847781449259785
	https://www.pinterest.com/lylaellzeygmail
	https://www.instagram.com/lyla.ellzey/

Don't forget to leave your review on
your favorite bookstore's page.

OTHER WORKS BY
LYLA FAIRCLOTH ELLZEY

Loosing the Lightning is a fiction novel whose beginnings are set in the south of the 1940s. Imagine innocence lost. Think of the horror of sexual abuse of a five-year-old child. In this book the reader meets Lily, who frequently endures this abuse until she gains the courage and strength to confront her abuser. She protects her beloved mama with her silence and carries her shameful secret throughout her life. The abuse dictates her choices and she is fearful of a relationship, but when she marries the man of her dreams, he is revealed to be a spousal sexual abuser. Betrayed by him many times, the last is the most devastating of all and Lily is left to survive on her own. Eventually, she meets a man who changes everything. Will Lily finally find the elusive happiness that has evaded her since she was a loved and carefree child of five?

ISBN: 978-1481260114 | $17.50 (includes shipping and handling)

She is Woman: Courageous, Compelling, and Captivating (And sometimes Outrageous!) is a book of 24 short stories about 24 very different women. The reader will laugh, cry, sympathize, empathize, and go through a whole range of emotions as these stories unfold. Imagine Ginger's horror as she watches snow build up on the white sugar sand outside her beachfront home on Florida's Gulf Coast. Think of Irene's fear after her lover shoots and kills her husband. Laugh with, and at, Polly as she pouts about Valentine's Day flowers. Plan with Annette the next adventure for the Pink Ladies. Travel these and the other roads with the ladies of this novel . . . but be prepared for a, sometimes, bumpy ride.

ISBN: 9781481908740 | $16.50 (includes shipping and handling)

Peregrination: The Poetry of Journeying is a slim volume of poetry about both actual travel journeys and the journeys of the heart. Walk with Lyla as she views some of the most magnificent sites and sights our world offers—from the Great Wall of China to the Great Pyramids of Giza in Egypt to the Greek mountain where the Oracle of Delphi spoke to the cave on Patmos where John, in exile, wrote the book of Revelations—and other places. Then join Lyla as she embraces the poetry of love gained, love lost, and true love that endures.

ISBN: 978-1492967361 | $10.50 (includes shipping and handling)

In *Anticipation of Evil,* when Green Bay schoolteachers, Heather and Jeff, find the body of her troubled twelfth grade student on a frozen pond at the elite Golf Club, it sets up a terrifying cat and mouse game with them the prey of the psychopathic killer. Fear consumes everyone as the horrifying events continue. Heather and Jeff wrestle with exposing the killer and with each other. The star detective duo assigned to the case, Aksel Franzen and Anja Frandsen, discover secrets about themselves better left hidden while Heather becomes unsure about everything: herself, the investigation, her relationship with Jeff, her future, and even if she will survive. Is her anticipation of evil justified? Find the answer in this dynamic suspense thriller.

ISBN: 978-1-950075-00-3 | $16.49

All titles available at https://www.lylafairclothellzey.com

CPSIA information can be obtained
at www.ICGtesting.com
Printed in the USA
FFHW021109260419
52067327-57447FF